Griffin's Revelation

Dark Patriots Bk 3

Ciara St James

Copyright

ISBN: 978-1-955751-64-3

Printed in the United States of America
Editing by Mary Kern @ Ms. K Edits
Cover background design by Tracie Douglas
Book cover by Kiwi Kreations

Blurb:

Griffin "Wraith" Voss is a man who is always up for any assignment. He and three of his closest SEAL brothers-in-arms have formed the Dark Patriots to keep others safe and continue to use some of the skills he learned as a Navy SEAL. However, he's feeling the need for a challenge, and a call from a mysterious friend within the government, Anderson, is just what he needs.

While the Dark Patriots provide security and other services to many companies and individuals, they do more work both on and off the books for their government. This is why Anderson contacts them. He has a job, and they're the only ones who will suffice to protect the US's biggest weapons and biotech contractor, Gerard Industries. There's a threat that has to be eliminated.

Griffin takes a team to handle it but only knows he'll be updated when he arrives. Imagine his surprise when he finds out the threat isn't exactly what he or his team imagines. And the danger might pale in comparison to Hadley, the woman who walks in, reveals a secret, and takes Griffin by storm.

Hadley has always had to hide who and what she is. To most, she doesn't exist. To others, Hadley is a spoiled, rich girl with nothing to do but have fun and spend money. She hates it but knows it serves a greater purpose. Being blindsided by the threat she finds out about after the Dark Patriots arrive is second to her surprise at meeting Griffin.

As they work to figure out who the threat is coming from, she and Griffin dance around each other. When a late-night caller takes them by surprise, she's whisked away to safety, and things really begin to heat up. Only in the end, they get more than a few shocks and some heartache. All it takes is one revelation, Griffin's revelation, to reveal a whole new future for both of them.

Warning

This book is intended for adult readers. It contains foul language and adult situations and discusses events such as stalkers, assault, torture, and murder that may trigger some readers. Sexual situations are graphic. If these themes aren't what you like to read or you find them upsetting, this book isn't for you. There is no cheating or cliffhangers, and it has a HEA.

Dark Patriots Members/ Ladies:

Mark O'Rourke (Undertaker) w/ Sloan
Sean Walterson w/ Cassidy
Gabe Pagett w/ Gemma
Griffin Voss w/ Hadley
Benedict Madris w/ TBD
Heath Rugger w/ TBD
Justin Becker w/ TBD
Beau Powers w/ TBD

Reading Order

For Dublin Falls Archangel's Warriors MC (DFAW), Hunters Creek Archangel's Warriors MC (HCAW), Iron Punishers MC (IPMC), Dark Patriots (DP), & Pagan Souls of Cherokee MC (PSCMC)

Terror's Temptress DFAW 1
Savage's Princess DFAW 2
Steel & Hammer's Hellcat DFAW 3
Menace's Siren DFAW 4
Ranger's Enchantress DFAW 5
Ghost's Beauty DFAW 6
Viper's Vixen DFAW 7
Devil Dog's Precious DFAW 8
Blaze's Spitfire DFAW 9
Smoke's Tigress DFAW 10
Hawk's Huntress DFAW 11
Bull's Duchess HCAW 1
Storm's Flame DFAW 12
Rebel's Firecracker HCAW 2
Ajax's Nymph HCAW 3
Razor's Wildcat DFAW 13
Capone's Wild Thing DFAW 14
Falcon's She-Devil DFAW 15
Demon's Hellion HCAW 4
Torch's Tornado DFAW 16
Voodoo's Sorceress DFAW 17
Reaper's Banshee IPMC 1
Bear's Beloved HCAW 5
Outlaw's Jewel HVAW 6

For Ares Infidels MC

Phalanx & Bullet's Entwinement AIMC 14
Torpedo's Entrancement AIMC 15
Boomer's Embroilment AIMC 16

For O'Sheerans Mafia

Darragh's Dilemma
Cian's Complication
Aidan's Ardor

Please follow Ciara on Facebook. For information on new releases & to catch up with Ciara, go to www.ciara-st-james.com or www.facebook.com/ciara.stjames.1 or www.facebook.com/groups/tenilloguardians or https://www.facebook.com/groups/1112302942958940 or https://www.facebook.com/groups/923322252903958

Griffin: Chapter 1

I was trying not to laugh at Gabe, but it was hard not to. I was waiting for Gemma to slap him or, better yet, hit him over the head with a club. He was in overprotective mode so much with her she was ready to scream or kill. You could see it, not that I could really blame him. She was pregnant with their first baby, and he was excited and scared to be a dad. He didn't want anything to happen to her or their baby.

I understood his behavior, and so did Sean and Mark. They were dads and had been through it. I hadn't, but I knew if I ever got the chance to be a dad, I'd probably be the same. Wait, make that worse. The next three and a half months until baby Pagett arrived were going to be long for them and entertaining for the rest of us.

On the other hand, Sean was doing much better with Cassidy this time. They'd announced around Christmas that they were pregnant again. They had chosen not to find out what this baby would be. They wanted to be surprised. The baby was due toward the end of August, and Noah would turn three in October. I thought it was a good age gap. He was close to being fully potty trained, so they'd only have one in diapers.

Our lives overall these days were a far cry from what they were when we all met and became friends. We were all in the Navy and battling our way through

SEAL BUD/S training when we met. All we wanted to do was survive those six months of hell. When we did, it was due to us bonding and encouraging each other that made it happen. We became friends for life. They were my brothers in every sense, except we didn't share the same blood.

I loved their wives like sisters, and their kids were my nephews. I didn't have any nieces yet. We'd see if I got any this round. I liked to tease them that if they kept it up, they might give the Archangel's Warriors MC a run for the title as a breeding farm, but there was no way. Those people breed like rabbits. Dublin Falls alone had about fifty kids. I couldn't keep track anymore. Then add in Hunters Creek, the Pagans, and the Punishers, and it was probably seventy or eighty.

I felt a tug on my pant leg to get my attention. I looked down to find Noah staring up at me. He held out his arms. I knew what that meant. I bent and got him under his arms so I could pick him up. He smiled when we were eye to eye.

"What's up, little guy?"

"Up."

"I got you up. Why did you want up?"

"Fly," he shouted.

I chuckled because I knew that's what he wanted even before he said it. He loved for me to hold him out and pretend he was a plane and fly him around the room. I swear, if the kid didn't become a pilot one day, I'd be shocked.

Making sure I had a tight grip on him, I held him out and began to weave him through the air and around the room. He was making engine sounds and laughing loudly. I knew it wouldn't be long before Caleb, Mark and Sloan's fifteen-month-old son, would want his turn. Whatever Noah did, Caleb had to copy. I had a feeling those two would cause hell when they were older. God help us all.

I spent over a half hour with those two until their parents told them it was enough and rescued me, as they called it. I told them I didn't mind, but they still made the boys stop. Sean shook his head.

"Man, you don't have to do that just because Noah or Caleb ask, you know?"

"I do know, but I don't mind it unless I'm in the middle of something. Speaking of kids, I have a question. Did you talk to Gabe and give him advice on how to handle this pregnancy so Gemma doesn't murder him?"

He laughed. "I tried, but you know Midas. Cassidy and Sloan are talking to Gemma to try and explain why he's that way and how she can keep him from losing his mind or her resorting to murder."

"I hope they can help."

Each of us had our nicknames from our time in the Navy. They didn't get used often anymore, but occasionally, one of us or someone who knew us back then would slip up and use them. Midas was Gabe's. Sean was Fiend, Mark was Undertaker, and I was Wraith. Reaper, the president of the Iron Punishers MC, used them sometimes. He was a SEAL with us. Actually, Mark was called Undertaker most of the time. His years undercover in an MC had left their mark on him. He'd always been a man to be wary of, but now, he was on a different level of scary.

"Before Noah and then Caleb got a hold of you, you seemed to be thinking awfully hard over here. Mind if I ask what you were thinking about and can I help? It appeared to be heavy thoughts," Sean inquired.

"I wouldn't say they were heavy. I was thinking of pregnancies and how everyone is acting, and then I was thinking about kids. I was trying to imagine us like the Warriors. That's all," I assured him.

"You find it boring?"

"No, actually I don't. If anything, I find myself a bit envious, but in a good way. I don't begrudge any of you what you have. I'm happy as hell about it, but I do wonder sometimes if it's for me."

"What do you mean, if it's for you?" he asked with a frown.

"Not everyone is meant to have a family, to be married. Some are destined to go through life single. I've wondered if I want those things because I've been conditioned to want them or because I truly desire them. All of you and even our friends in the clubs knew immediately when you met your women that they were the ones for you. Yeah, you denied it and fucked around for a long time, but it wasn't because you didn't want Cassidy. You were afraid of what Mark would say or do since she's his little sister, and you had baggage. I've never felt an inkling for a woman like that. It makes me think my destiny is different."

"Grif, I wouldn't discount it just yet. Sure, I lusted after women before Cassidy, but when I saw her after she was older, it was nothing as tame as what I felt for those women. It was like a damn Mack truck ran me over. Some of us find it sooner than others. Hell, look at Bull down in Hunters Creek. He wasn't expecting to find a second chance at love at his age, and you can see how he is with Jocelyn and his younger kids. You've got time."

He was right about Bull, and then there was Bear. Hell yeah, he might be right. Or he could be wrong. I guess only time will tell. Until it happened, I'd keep enjoying my work and life. Which reminded me I had somewhere to be.

❦❦❦

Thank God it was finally Friday. This week had gone by excruciatingly slowly. I was ready for the weekend. A few beers, watch a game on the television, maybe a nice steak dinner somewhere, and if they had time, hang out with my best friends. Who knows, I might go out and see if I could find some company for at least a night or two. It had been a while. Maybe if I had a good session of fucking, it would relieve this tension that had been building for what felt like weeks.

If we were out in the field, like when we were in the Navy, I'd say our mission was about to go FUBAR, fucked up beyond all repair, and we needed to get the hell out of there. Only we weren't on a mission, and none of our people at Dark Patriots were doing anything remotely dangerous like that. Not that we didn't accept missions with risks. We did. When you did off-the-books work for your government, you could find yourself up to your neck in shit really fast, with no one to help you or even acknowledge your existence. However, we weren't running any of those types of missions at the moment.

I glanced at the clock on my office wall. It was three o'clock. Only two hours to go. Of course, as one of the bosses, if I wanted to leave now, I could, but I didn't do that. If I expected our people to work, then I would have to do so as well. Looking back at my computer, I tried to read the field report Beau had completed on his last assignment. I'd barely been reading for a minute when there was a knock at the door. I gladly stopped and called out, "Come in."

The door opened, and in came Abigail. She was one of our two indispensable receptionists, slash assistants, slash researchers, slash whatever else they got their hands on. Abigail had been with us for two and a half years. She was the younger of the two. Margie was an older woman who technically should be retired, but she claimed if she did that, then her husband, Chuck, who was our armorer, would retire, and she'd go insane, stuck at home with him all day. She loved him, but that wasn't in her marriage vows, according to her.

"Hey, Abigail, whatcha need?"

"Sean wanted me to tell you to meet him and the others in the conference room in ten minutes. You have a conference call. It's a code black call."

Code black meant no cell phones or other electronics were to be taken into the room. It would be turned into a SCIF, a sensitive compartmented information facility, which would ensure there were no listening devices and cameras that weren't ours prior to the call and that the room was sealed so no one could see or hear anything. We usually did this for top-secret meetings or ones involving national security. This news made me perk up with interest.

"Oh yeah, do you know who the call is with?"

She gave me a look that screamed, *Is this my first day, and are you kidding me? I know everything.* I snorted, which made her lips twitch, but she refused to smile.

"Yes, I know."

"Do I have to ask you to tell me?"

"I think you should."

"Fine. Please tell me who the call is with." I was fighting not to grin.

"It's with Anderson."

Oh, that meant it had to be important. Anderson was a shadowy figure who worked for the government. No one knew exactly in what capacity or which agency he was attached to. He seemed to cross all lines and agencies. My interest was piqued, and I grinned at her. "Thank you, Abby."

She gave me a death glare and then walked out. It wasn't that we didn't like each other. In fact, we did, and she was like a sister to us, but when we wanted to tweak her, we called her Abby. She hated it. I knew I'd have to wait for her retaliation for doing it. It would be worth it. I didn't waste time getting up to head to the conference room after I locked my computer. When I walked in, Sean and Gabe were already there. Gabe grinned at me.

"What?" I asked.

"You called her Abby."

"Did she come tattle?"

"Nope, I could tell by her face. I wouldn't accept any coffee or other drinks or food from her for a while.

It might be poisoned."

I groaned. I hadn't thought of that. Shit, I'd have to bring in my own food and drink and keep it locked up. "Damn," I muttered. They both laughed. That's when Mark chose to saunter in.

Looking at him, you had no trouble imagining him as a biker. We were all fit and had tattoos. He went beyond that. Mark gave off the enforcer vibe he earned. He took his seat. "What're you assholes laughing about?"

"Assholes! Who're you calling an asshole? It takes one to know one, shithead," Gabe told him.

"I swear someone just farted. Did you hear it?" Mark asked with a deadpan look.

"Don't go there. We don't have time for an insult fest. Anderson will be calling any minute. Hold on to them until we get done, then go wild," Sean told them. Even though we were all equal partners, Sean was often the one taking a slightly bossier role. That wasn't to say we shirked work—we didn't. He seemed to like the role more than we did.

"Did you speak to him?" Mark asked Sean.

"I did, but no, he didn't give me a hint about what he wanted to talk to us about. All he said was it was extremely important, and it couldn't wait."

"How many years have we known him?" Gabe asked.

Thinking back, I was the one to answer him first. "I think it's been ten or twelve years. Why?"

"You'd think after knowing us that long and

following us from the Navy to here, he'd loosen up and let more stuff out. You know, give us a hint or something," Gabe suggested.

"I don't think Anderson will ever do that. Hell, his great-niece is married to a Warrior, and he doesn't let him or his club know more. Zara can't even tell you which agency he works for. If we ever found out, he'd have to kill us. He's a shadowy and scary bastard. Thank God he's on our side and such a patriot that we never have to worry about him betraying his country. If he did, we'd be fucked six ways to Sunday," Sean added.

I couldn't disagree with that. Before we could debate more, there was a buzz on the phone at the conference table. We knew what it meant. Immediately, Sean pushed the hidden button on the panel on the table, which locked down the room. Once it was done, he pushed another button, and the screen on the wall came alive. Anderson was staring back at us.

Now, he rarely showed much emotion, but I could tell by how tense his mouth and eyes were that he wasn't happy, and this was not going to be a fun assignment. "Gentlemen," he said gruffly. We all greeted him. Once we had the pleasantries out of the way, it was down to business.

"I know it's Friday and almost the end of your business day, so thank you for arranging this so fast. It couldn't wait until Monday. If you take this assignment and let me say you're the only ones I want on it, then by Monday, you'll have to be deployed, so it means weekend work. I have no idea how long it'll last."

"Anderson, we don't just work Monday through Friday, eight to five. We're used to weekends and nights.

Tell us what we can do for you. Is it an official request situation or an off-the-books one?" Sean asked.

"I know you guys work anytime. I merely wanted you to know what you're looking at. It's coming from the top, guys, and while it's not being touted as an official request and is being treated as off-the-books to a degree, believe me, it's a damn priority. There'll be so many goddamn eyes and fingers in it, you won't be able to fart and them not know. We can't fuck this up."

Excitement surged through me. It sounded like my kind of mission. Hell, who was I kidding? It was all our kind of job. I saw the eagerness on Gabe, Sean, and even Mark's faces. "Don't keep us in suspense. Tell us," I said a tad impatiently.

Sean gave me a *shut-up* look, but I ignored him. While I was usually the quiet one in our group, or at least when around others, it didn't mean I wasn't impatient. I just hid it better, usually.

"Alright, Wraith, I'll get to it. Do you all know who Travis Gerard is?"

This got our attention. Travis Gerard was known to many people all over the world. His company, Gerard Industries, was the biggest provider of weapons and biotech to the US government. The man was a billionaire, and unlike a lot of men who dealt in that kind of work, he was an extreme patriot and a good man by all accounts. He gave millions away every year for research to help the underprivileged, abused, and severely ill in our country and others. If he was involved, then it was extremely important and probably dangerous.

"Hell yeah, we know who he is. We don't live

under a rock. What's this have to do with him?" Mark asked.

"What I'm about to tell you is beyond top secret. His company is in the process of developing a new weapon for our military. He's under a time crunch to get it done, tested, and viable. Several threats have been made that could derail the whole thing."

"Against his developers, researchers, the company, or personal threats?" Sean asked.

"At first, it was the standard protests against them developing anything—you know, the ones who protest everything as the end of the world and that we're being bullies and murderers for developing weapons for defense in the first place. Those were ignored. Later came the actual vague threats against some of his more well-known researchers and developers. However, now the threat has been made personal, and he's scared."

"Doesn't he have his own security people? I mean, a man like him would have a large detail for him, his home, offices, and his family if he has one," Mark pointed out.

Anderson nodded. "Yes, he does, and he pays well for some of the best. He wants more, and it so happens that our government agrees. When they were going through the list of possibilities, your name came up, and not just from my recommendation. Mr. Gerard has heard of the Dark Patriots, and he likes what he hears. He knew enough to assure everyone he'd had you guys researched. Although several others in the discussion wanted other groups, he insisted it was you guys. They gave him what he wanted. You don't piss off a billionaire who keeps our country safe," he said with a slight smirk.

We chuckled. I could imagine how nervous they'd been. It made me feel proud that our reputation was growing, not only in the private sector but also in the government sector.

"What exactly have the threats been, and how many people do they want us to give them?" Gabe asked.

"The kind where people are taken, body parts removed, and they're sent back in pieces. Mr. Gerard is freaked out. He wants at least four of you, if not more. At first, he wanted all four of you, but I was able to convince him that your people are highly qualified and it wasn't possible to take all of you away from the company. I know, I know, you'd do it, and I appreciate it, but Beau, Benedict, and the others I've met are all more than capable of handling it. If you find you need more and want to send in all the Alpha team, then so be it. As long as one of you goes with them to start, we should be good."

"When and where?" Sean asked next.

"On Monday at eight a.m., you'll need to be at his home in Fairfax, Virginia. I'll send you the address. His security team will still be involved."

We groaned. This was gonna be a pain in our asses. In our experience, when you brought in outsiders, the regulars got pissy and tried to exert their authority over stupid stuff.

"Don't do that. I know what you're thinking, but that won't be the case. Mr. Gerard said his people would be under the direction of the Dark Patriots. What you say goes, and anyone giving you too much grief will be fired. He's not playing around." That answer made me happier.

Fairfax was a nice area that wasn't far from Washington, DC, proper. It wasn't the most affluent area of DC, which surprised me. I would expect a bazillionaire to live in one of those places. Fairfax was a more suburban area and considered a college town, but the small-town feel and the diversity of its community made it great for families. There were over two hundred acres of parks and recreational space. If you didn't want to drive and deal with DC traffic, you could catch the Metro. It served as a gateway to central and southern Virginia. It was less than three hours from there to us here in Hampton.

"We can do that. What kind of weapons should we bring?" Mark asked.

"Anything you personally prefer to use. Otherwise, he has you covered. Call it a perk of being the developer of so many weapons. Mr. Gerard is not all talk or full of hot air. He walks the walk, meaning he knows how to handle guns, and he's a hunter, too. You'll be given quarters on his estate. If you find anything needed for his security there, just tell him, and it'll be done. In fact, he's eager to have you thoroughly go over his security measures and people to see if there's any need to make changes."

The more he talked, the more I started to like Gerard. I'd seen him on television and in papers and magazines. He was an older gentleman, probably in his mid-sixties. He was distinguished and oozed money and power. I admit I thought he was your typical rich person who was out of touch with reality, but Anderson made it sound like he wasn't. If he weren't, then this might be an even better assignment.

We talked for a few more minutes, and then Anderson said goodbye after promising he'd send over the information we needed to get to the estate and onto the property. He said Gerard wanted to brief us personally about the exact nature of the threats and his concerns. It was a little unusual, but if that's the way he wanted it, so be it. When Anderson hung up, we got down to discussing who would go. I jumped on it right away.

"I think I should go. I can take Beau, Justin, Heath, and Benedict. I think they're all available right now."

"Is there a reason you want to go versus one of us?" Sean asked.

"Yes, a few. One, you all have wives and kids. We have no idea how long this assignment will take. You don't want to be away from them for days or weeks on end."

"They'll understand," Gabe objected.

"They would, but why do it when I have no family other than my parents? You know them. They're used to not seeing me until they see me. Two, I've got an itch. I need something to occupy my time. This is perfect. Those four I named are in the same boat as me. They're single and always looking for something to do. It'll give me a chance to see more of how Justin handles himself."

Justin was a recent recruit. He was related to two members of the Warriors in Dublin Falls. He was Voodoo's older brother and Blade's cousin. He'd recently gotten out of the DEA and came to work for us. All the reports on him were excellent, but this would allow one of us to see him in action. Although Justin didn't say it, we knew he'd gotten tired of being used by the DEA, like he was expendable. We did dangerous work, but we didn't treat any of our people that way. We'd gotten enough of that ourselves while in the military.

"I like the idea of seeing how Justin does, and the other three are good, really good, so I have no objections to them," Sean said.

"Agreed. As for you going instead of us, we don't want you to think we expect it or begrudge going. We're all here to do the jobs, no matter what. Yes, we have families, but Cassidy and Sloan know the business. Gemma is learning, and she's adapting fast," Gabe added.

"I don't think you expect me to go, and I don't begrudge it. I wouldn't offer to do it if I didn't want to go. So, is that a yes? Can we call those four in here and tell them what we need and shit? We have plans to make before they get caught up in their weekends," I reminded them.

"I'm fine with you going, but if you find you need more help, don't fucking not tell us. I'll come if you happen to need more help," Mark said with a determined look. I knew that expression. No one would talk him out of it. I nodded in agreement.

Sean and Gabe quickly agreed. We took the room off SCIF mode and called Margie to get her and Abigail to track down our four operatives. Hopefully, they hadn't left the building for the weekend. A few minutes later, we found out we were in luck. They were all still here.

It was about ten minutes longer before they came

filing into the room. They had inquisitive looks on their faces as we directed them to take a seat. Beau was the one to ask what they were all thinking. "So, bosses, what's about to blow up or go to shit? It has to be big if you call us in here like this."

We chuckled as Sean said, "Damn right it is. We need you to listen up. We can't fuck this up. Understand?"

"Understand. Lay it on us," Benedict added.

It took us less than an hour to lay it out and for me to organize them and plan our trip. Once it was done, they were released to enjoy as much of the weekend as they could. I planned to go home and have those beers and watch a game. It might be the last bit of rest I get for the foreseeable future. I was looking forward to Monday morning.

Griffin: Chapter 2

The weekend passed quickly. In some ways, I was grateful. I was bored and this would definitely give me something to do. On the other hand, I didn't do much to alleviate my dissatisfaction. The idea of going out and seeing if I could find someone to enjoy some time with never happened.

To make sure we got there on time, we left home at four in the morning. That gave us four hours for a trip that should take less than three. If we got there ahead of time, it would give us a little time to scout the area before we met with Mr. Gerard.

The guys and I joked and swapped stories about our time in the military, as well as the assignments we'd been on. Justin had the least of those since he'd only been with us for four months, and a chunk of that had been putting him through our training, although he had been trained by the DEA. Benedict had been with us eight months and his buddy, Heath, ten. Beau was the veteran with two and a half years under his belt. The talk made the time fly, and it served another purpose. It relaxed us one last time before we had to go into work mode.

I drove, so we got there in only two and a half hours. Yeah, I broke the speed limit, but only when it was safe, and there was a low chance of a cop catching us. I'd never hear the end of it from Sean, Mark, and

Gabe if I got a damn speeding ticket from the po-po.

We entered Gerard's neighborhood if you could call it that. It was really a community of a few homes spread out on huge tracts of land, and the homes weren't small farmhouses either. They were mansions in some cases, or at least high-end expensive homes. The properties were all fenced in with gates. You needed to ring a buzzer to get through them.

We slowly drove around the area. I did that for two reasons. One was to familiarize ourselves with the area and what we had to work with. The other was to see if we attracted anyone's attention. Were they as alert as they should be? If they were, what would they do about the strange car slowly and obviously casing them?

At Gerard's place, I saw guards at the gate. I hoped there would be more patrolling of the grounds. The estate appeared to be extensive, and it would be easy to penetrate anywhere along the fence line unless they had cameras covering and alerting them.

I was disappointed when it was close to fifteen minutes before a cop car pulled up behind us with its lights on. We pulled over and waited for the officer to approach. There were two who got out of the patrol car. One was a woman. They cautiously approached our vehicle. We made sure to have our hands in view and not to move suddenly. The male officer came to the driver's window. I had it rolled down already.

He eyed us suspiciously. I could see why. Five men in a Suburban, dressed mainly all in black with tattoos showing, gave off a vibe that would make him uneasy. When I worked at the office or attended meetings, I wore suits when appropriate, and my tats were covered. It made me more approachable.

"Good morning, Officer. How may we help you?" I asked calmly.

"License and registration. And keep your hands where we can see them," he said gruffly.

"Of course, Officers. May I ask why you pulled us over? We weren't speeding or breaking any other laws that I'm aware of," I said politely as I handed him my license and registration. I couldn't wait for him to run it. The Suburban was registered to our company. He probably didn't know who we were, but it would raise questions. The name Dark Patriots always did.

"Just stay here and don't move," he snapped before he walked off. His poor partner was left watching us from the passenger side. Heath rolled down his window and smiled at her. "Hello, how did you get stuck with Mr. Happy as a partner?"

There was a flicker of surprise and a twitch of her lips, which made me think she was trying not to smile or laugh. She got it under control quickly, though. "Sir, please stay still and keep your hands where I can see them."

"Sure thing, but we'd still like to know what we did wrong. Is it illegal in this area to drive down the road and enjoy the views? We didn't disturb anyone," he told her.

"Just relax, and we'll be done soon," was all she would say.

My patience was starting to run thin. We had work to do. I raised my voice so she could hear me. "Tell your partner to call Mr. Gerard and tell him the Dark Patriots are here. That should clear it up since you have no cause to detain us."

"Why would Mr. Gerard know who you are?" she asked suspiciously.

"You'll have to ask him that," I said, then shut up.

She looked torn for a couple of seconds. Then she hurried back to her partner. I saw him in the mirror arguing with her. She argued back. We waited.

"Great way to start our day," Beau said.

"Yeah. I want to know, if there's a credible threat to Gerard and the local cops know about it, why did it take fifteen minutes for any of them to get their asses here? At least one patrol car should be assigned to him. We're not talking about some rich guy who thinks he's all that and demands special treatment. He's responsible for most of the defense of our goddamn country." I scowled.

"I get it, I do, but we don't know if he's involved with the locals or not. Where are his guards? Do they only patrol the grounds? You'd think he'd have some military personnel involved. That doesn't make sense to me, Wraith," Beau added with a frown.

He was right. Where were they? His calling me Wraith had evolved since he heard my brothers use it, especially on assignments. It was a habit. I didn't mind if others did it. In fact, I noticed Heath and Ben had started to do it, too. Justin was still new to me.

"He's right. Where are they?" Ben muttered.

"Shh, here they come," Heath said.

I watched them approach the same way they did last time, only now with more caution. The male officer handed me back my stuff. "You're to go to Mr. Gerard's estate. We'll follow you. Just a piece of advice—don't creep around people's houses if you don't want to be pulled over."

"But it accomplished what I wanted and gave me invaluable information, so I think I'll keep doing it when I feel it's necessary. Thanks for the advice, Officer, but I know what I'm doing. Lead on. We have a schedule to keep." I let the edge of my bite come through. He stiffened, and the looks he'd been giving me when he came back told me he resented us. I wondered what he'd been told about us.

As they walked off, Heath chuckled. "Making friends already, Wraith. I bet the cops and Gerard's security people will throw us a welcome party."

The rest of us chuckled. "Yeah, and maybe you'll even get a kiss outta his partner," Ben teased his buddy.

"Hey, she was cute. I wouldn't say no, but I don't think her partner would appreciate it. Wonder what crawled up his ass?"

"It's hard to tell. Forget them, and let's remember why we're here," I reminded them.

It was a quick ride the last half mile to Gerard's place. The squad car followed us right up to the gate. An armed man came to my window. He was studying us and had a frown on his face. "ID," he barked. I handed him mine.

"All of you," he said as he eyed my guys. I was starting to get tired of the attitude—first from the cop and now from this guard.

"That's enough for you to check. Mr. Gerard is expecting us, and we've had enough delays. Either call him and open the gate, or we'll leave. Your choice."

This guy would be under our command if what Anderson said was true. I didn't want anyone who was resentful working with us. It could get in the way of the job. Resentment was coming off him in waves. I got it. They weren't happy to have outsiders helping, and it stung to have those outsiders be in charge, but it was their boss's call.

"I need all of your IDs, or you're not passing through these gates," he said forcefully.

"Call him first and ask if he needs you to see them all," I pushed back.

It wasn't that I was being a bastard. I wanted to see if he could be made to ignore security protocols and let us in without seeing all our IDs. He was right to insist on seeing them. Would he bow to pressure and let it slide? If he did, that would be unacceptable. He didn't realize it, but he was being evaluated. As soon as we hit this neighborhood, my assessment and that of my men had started. I might be taking the lead, but they were working on it just as I was.

He hesitated, then walked off. I saw him on the phone. I assumed he was talking to someone at the house. I sighed. He'd just failed the first part. Not only did he let me back him down, but he also left us unattended. Where was his backup? Someone should be guarding us while he was on the phone. I could take out my gun and shoot him dead.

"This is already shaping up to be a lot of work, Wraith," Ben muttered.

"Yes, it is. We'll be earning our money this time," I told them.

"Hoorah," Beau said, giving us the Marine cry.

Not to be outdone, I made the Navy's hooyah call while Ben and Heath uttered the Army's equivalent, hooah. We all grinned.

It took a minute or so before the guard came back. He was scowling. He handed me my ID and muttered resentfully, "You're cleared to go in. Head up the drive. When it branches right, go that way. It'll take you to the house. They're expecting you."

"What's your name?" I asked as I put away my ID.

"It's Reynolds. Why?"

"I just wanted to know what to call you. I'm Voss. This is Madris," I pointed to Ben. "And this is Rugger, Powers, and Becker." I pointed to Heath, Beau, and Justin. We stuck to last names on most jobs.

All he did was grunt and walk off. He must've pressed something because the gate began to open. I waited until I could get through it, and then I took off. We left Reynolds and the police behind as we drove up the hill and then to the right. When we got to the top, I could see the house. It was a mansion like I expected, although not as big as some. I'd call it more of a mini mansion. There were several cars in the circular drive in front of it. We found a spot and parked.

I looked at my guys. "Here we go."

"We've got this. Let's go find out the details and

then show them how it's done," Beau said confidently.

Giving him a chin lift, I opened my door. We all climbed out and scanned the area. I was noting the locations of the cameras I could see, what kind of cover there was close to the house, and looking for more guards. In the distance, I saw two walking, but they didn't come toward us. A swift walk up to the double doors, then I rang the doorbell.

Moments later, it opened, but it wasn't a guard who opened it. It was an older gentleman dressed in a suit. I knew from photos it wasn't Gerard. He greeted us. "Hello, gentlemen, Mr. Gerard is expecting you. If you'll come with me, I'll show you to his study. I'm Porter, Mr. Gerard's butler. Welcome."

"It's nice to meet you, Porter," I said as we came inside, and then he closed the door. I examined the huge foyer. There wasn't a guard here, either. I exchanged speaking glances with my men. None of us liked what we saw so far.

We followed Porter out of the foyer and down a long hallway. Off to each side were doors for various rooms. Thc whole place screamed wealth and privilege, not that I thought Gerard would be living simply. He was as rich as Croesus. I did like the gleaming, rich wood throughout. There were what had to be priceless paintings and pieces of art all over.

Finally, Porter paused before a closed door. He knocked twice, waited a couple of seconds, then opened it. He waved us inside. I went first. As I entered, I saw Gerard moving from behind his desk. There were other men in the room with him. Some I tagged as guards. The others were in suits, and I had no idea who they were.

He had a welcoming smile on his face as he reached us.

"Thank you, Porter. Please see that breakfast is ready to be served in thirty minutes. I know you gentlemen got on the road early to get here. You must be starved. I know I am. Oh, how rude of me. I'm Travis Gerard. Welcome. Please have a seat and make yourselves comfortable. Can we get you anything?"

I was rather taken aback by how nice and unpretentious he was. I expected the typical attitude we got from the rich and mighty, which was disdain at times or just indifference. He was even holding out his hand. We all shook it.

"Mr. Gerard, thank you, we're fine. I'm Griffin Voss. This is Beau Powers, Benedict Madris, Heath Rugger, and Justin Becker."

"Yes, yes, I recognize you from your photos. I'm honored to have the Dark Patriots helping with this. Having one of the founding members is unexpected. Thank you for agreeing to do this. And please, call me Travis. Mr. Gerard sounds so stuffy," he said with a bigger smile.

I heard a throat clearing, and it sounded disapproving without the words that came out next. It belonged to one of the men in suits. He had a frown on his face as he studied us. "Travis, they're here to provide added help, although I don't see why you need them. They're not here to be your friends. Subordinates should be respectful," he said snottily.

Gerard frowned at him. "Ansel, don't. The Dark Patriots are a very welcome addition, and I look forward to seeing what they can do for us. As for first names, I don't have a stick up my ass about that like you do. You should loosen up."

I had to fight not to laugh at the look on Ansel's face. He wasn't happy. Gerard addressed us again. "Sorry for that. This is Ansel Dewitt. He's on my board of directors for Gerard Industries and has been my friend for many years. He can be somewhat rude, as you have heard, but he's a decent guy underneath. Please, take a seat and let me introduce you to the others."

The other men in the room had remained quiet. We took a seat, placing ourselves close to Gerard. He quickly ran through the other names. The men in suits were more of his board members. The guards I took care to study so I could recall their names. There were three of them. They appeared stoic.

"Okay, I know you must be anxious to hear all the details of what's been happening. I'll gladly tell you, but after breakfast. Just understand, I expect there to be some resistance to you being here and to the added security."

One of the men, I didn't catch which one, snorted. Gerard nodded. "I know, I know, but she'll just have to deal with it."

She? Who the hell was he worried about? He was our package. Why would some woman he was involved with care? I thought he didn't have a wife. I read something that said she had died years ago.

"She's gonna lose her mind?" one of the guards, Fletcher, muttered. The other two guards, Ellis and Royce, nodded.

"We'll handle it, Fletcher. Now, why don't we all head to the dining room for breakfast? We'll eat and then talk on a full stomach. We have a lot to cover," Gerard said, his tone abiding no arguments.

As much as I wanted to get started, I was hungry, and my days in the Navy taught me that you eat and sleep whenever you can because you never know when you might get to again. We followed him out of his study and down yet another hallway to a large dining room. There were silver chafing dishes, I think they were called, set out on a long buffet counter along one wall. The table was set for over a dozen people. Gerard pointed to the food.

"Please, help yourselves. If there's something you want and it's not here, just let me know. Our chef is excellent. I'm convinced there's nothing he can't make. Don't be shy."

The others all seemed to hesitate. Gerard didn't appear to be upset, and he was waiting for us. He was being a good host rather than an entitled asshole. Deciding to take the lead or we'd never get anywhere, I went to the buffet and picked up a plate. My guys came with me. This unfroze the others, and they moved our way. Soon, there was a low hum of chatter over the selection, which was impressive as hell. I couldn't think of a single thing missing.

Once we were all seated and eating, I decided to ask the question I'd been thinking since we left the study. "Who were you referring to as being upset?" I asked the man across from me. His name was Maynard. He was a board member. He grimaced when I asked and shifted his gaze to Gerard. It was our host who answered.

"He meant that—." He was cut off by the door

opening and a woman walking in—or, I should say, a woman storming in. She wasn't happy. That all registered at the same time she did. She was stunning, even with the scowl on her face. Then she knocked all thoughts of her looks right out of my head and stopped any fantasies I might want to have about her.

"Daddy, what in the hell is going on around here? There are guards, the board, and whoever these men are. Here at eight in the morning. What's wrong?" she asked as she stopped to stare at him with her hand on her hip.

Daddy? I didn't recall anything I read saying Gerard had any kids. That's when I noticed another man had entered the room behind her. He had the bodyguard vibe, and he watched her every move.

"Sweetheart, we're eating. I'll talk to you about this after we're done. If you'd like to join us, please do, but we won't be discussing this over the breakfast table," Gerard told her. The tone of his voice and the way he was looking at her told me he was serious. I wondered if the spoiled princess would listen.

Yeah, there was no way someone as rich as her father hadn't made her into a spoiled rotten, useless piece of fluff. You know, the kind only good for decoration and as a way to get in good with her father. I'd dealt with many spoiled brats in this business, and if I never had to again, it would be too soon. *God, I should've let one of the others come*. Was it too late to call and ask them to send Mark? He'd scare the shit out of her. I grinned, thinking about it. She saw it.

"What's so funny?" she asked.

"Just thinking of one of my partners. He'd love to

be here."

"Why?"

"To scare the shit outta people."

"Who needs the shit scared out of them?"

"I'm still making the list."

She glared at me. I didn't say another word. She rolled her eyes and faced her dad again. "I'll expect a conversation after this. I need to know what's going on."

"You will. Now, sit. I'd like you to meet our guests. Get your food, and then I'll make introductions."

I was surprised she didn't argue with him again. As she passed him, she dropped a kiss on his head, and he patted her back. As she got her food, I couldn't help but catalog her. She was in her mid-to-late twenties, by my calculation. She was of average height, maybe five six. She had a pale ivory complexion with honey-blond hair in a ponytail that hung to the bottom of her shoulder blades. She had a body that would grab anyone's attention. She was curvy, which I loved. As beautiful as she was, what really snared my attention were her eyes. They were an electric blue color. They jumped out and didn't look real. Made me wonder if she wore colored contacts.

As she filled her plate, I noticed her bodyguard moved to hover next to her. She said something to him, but I couldn't hear what it was. He was frowning and shaking his head. She said something again, more forcefully, and he finally moved away to stand by the wall.

"Rockwell, you'd better grab some food. She's not going anywhere. Sit, eat, and relax. You don't know when you'll get a chance with her," Gerard told the guard. I saw Rockwell relax a smidge.

"Thank you, sir."

"You've been with us long enough to know to call me Travis. For God's sake, you're in my home more than anyone. You practically live here."

"I'll try s—, uh Travis." He caught himself.

As Rockwell got his food, I watched her. She took a seat close to her dad. She was waiting for him to speak. He waited until Rockwell was seated before he did.

"Gentleman, this is my daughter, Hadley. Sweetheart, the men you don't recognize are from the Dark Patriots. I've asked them to come here and help us with a situation. They'll be working with our men. These are Benedict Madris, Beau Powers, Heath Rugger, Justin Becker, and last but not least, Griffin Voss. Mr. Voss is one of the Patriots' owners."

She gave each of us a nod, but when she got to me, she lingered. She was studying me with a slight frown on her face. "Gentlemen, welcome to our home. Daddy, may I ask what situation they're here to help us with? I can't think of one that would require you to call the Dark Patriots."

"Does that mean you know who we are, Ms. Gerard?" I asked. Her tone made it seem like she did, but I didn't know why she would.

"Actually, I do, Mr. Voss. My father has spoken of your group several times. He's a great admirer. I'm just at a loss as to why he thinks we need you here. And, like my father, I prefer being called by my first name. Please call me Hadley."

"Thank you, you can call me Griffin. None of my team stands on formality. My closest brothers and I were surprised to learn your father knew of and requested us."

"Brothers?"

"Yes, my brothers-in-arms. There are four of us, and we created Dark Patriots together. You might hear me refer to them as Sean, Mark, and Gabe."

"And pray tell what are you helping Daddy with?" she batted her lashes as she sweetly slipped that into our conversation.

"Stop trying to charm it out of him. It won't work. I'll tell you. There's been another threat. I'm not prepared to overlook it this time, hence the Dark Patriots involvement," he dad stated.

She stiffened. "When? Why didn't you tell me? What did this one say they were going to do and why?"

"It was last week. It took a bit of time to get Griffin and his men here. I need to brief them on the situation before I tell you or anyone else more. They'll be working with our guys and directing this whole operation until we catch whoever made the threats."

"You think it's a credible one?" she asked at the same time the guards reacted. They all sent glances our way. They didn't necessarily look happy, but I think they were trying to stay neutral, all except for Rockwell. He was outright scowling and glaring at me as he met my gaze. He looked back at Gerard.

"Sir, I mean Travis, why bring in outsiders? We have more men we can enlist. And even if we do need them, it doesn't make sense to put them in charge. They don't know you, your daughter, or the intricacies of your life like we do."

"One of the reasons I want them is because they're outsiders, as you call them. They'll look at everything we do with fresh, unbiased eyes. I want them to identify our weak spots and fortify them, as well as point out what or who we need to replace. We've become lax, and I want it to stop.

"Secondly, they're in charge because these men are experts in security and defense. Most of them are former military men or have served in key agencies in the field. They're hands-on kind of men. That's invaluable. Third, I've followed them and their work for a while, and they have impeccable reputations. They get results."

"Some of us have served as well. I was in the Marines. Do you mind if I ask what makes you so qualified to be in charge?" Rockwell asked me. I could tell it was hard for him not to sneer. I wasn't sure if Gerard knew it, but his daughter did. She was giving Rockwell a censoring look.

"You can ask. Ben and Heath were part of the Army's 10th Special Forces Group- Airborne. Justin was in the DEA for many years, and Beau was part of the Marine Raiders. I know you're familiar with them if you were a Marine," I told him with satisfaction.

His mouth tightened before he spoke again. "And what was your training? Did you serve, or are you just an owner of the company?"

I gave him a smirk. "I was in the Navy." I paused. As he gave me a condescending smirk, I continued, "You know, the Navy that the Marines work for. I spent the majority of my years as a Navy SEAL. In fact, all four owners of Dark Patriots were SEALs. It's how we met and became lifelong friends."

This news raised murmurs from all around the table. I guess the board and the guards had no idea who or what our company was. Hadley was scrutinizing us more closely. There was a glimmer of respect in her eyes now. I was surprised when she turned to Rockwell and called him out.

"I guess he told you. Navy SEALs, DEA agents, Army Special Forces, and Marine Raiders make them very qualified to lead and assess threats. Don't be mad. You can't always be the best every time, Wayne."

He flushed but didn't say anything. I caught the smirks on the other guards' faces. They seemed happy he'd been put in his place. Hmm, that needed exploring. It should've all made me happy, but I wasn't. Hadley had called her bodyguard by his first name. That needed to be explored, too. A relationship between the protected and the protector almost always ended badly. I'd have to watch and see. If I found it to be true, I'd have to have him reassigned.

Hadley: Chapter 3

I couldn't believe Daddy brought in more men and men like the Dark Patriots without telling me. He was always open with me and told me everything, or I thought he did. For him to go to this extreme, the threat, whatever it was, had to be big, or he was overreacting.

I would've never accused him of the latter in the past, but recently, he'd become even more anxious about me and my safety. He was constantly asking me where I was going and who I'd be with. He'd ask when I expected to be home, and he insisted Rockwell was with me at a minimum all the time outside the house. I asked him more than once what was wrong, but he kept denying there was anything he was concerned about. Well, after today, he wouldn't be putting me off again.

I'd heard him and a few of his cronies talk about the Dark Patriots around the dinner table before. It was clear from their comments that they respected them immensely. One of his friends, Anderson, seemed to be the most vocal. I'd known Anderson forever, but I couldn't tell you much about him. He was a mystery, and when I asked my dad, he'd smile and say Anderson was a guardian, and that was it. I knew he worked for the US government, but not what his job was. He gave off a dangerous vibe, but not one that made me fear I was the one in danger.

The five men at our breakfast table emitted this same vibe. They looked tough, capable, and menacing. However, one of them did more than make me think they were dangerous men to mess with. Griffin Voss made me think of long, hot nights wrapped around each other, which was a shock.

I didn't have an immediate response to men like this. I might note one was attractive but that was it. It took me letting them in and getting to know them. If we click, then it might lead to hot nights in bed. It had been a long time since that had happened. Nowadays, my life consists mainly of work and charity. It didn't leave me much time for a relationship. Plus, those never worked out.

It was hard to know if a man was interested in me as a person or me as Travis Gerard's daughter if they even discovered that. If not, they only knew I was wealthy, and that was what attracted them. I didn't go around bragging about it, but my clothes and the fact I had a guard with me most of the time gave it away. The guys in the past had all turned out to have ulterior motives. If a man didn't want me for myself, then I'd spend my life alone. It would be a lonely existence, but I had work, a couple of good friends, and my charities to keep me company and busy.

As Griffin was talking, I took in his many attributes. Was it shallow to focus on the physical so much? Yeah, but God, who wouldn't? He was a fine specimen. He was older than my twenty-seven, maybe as much as ten years older. He was taller than me by at least half a foot or so. He was tan from spending so much time outdoors, I had no doubt.

His dark blond hair was long on top, and he wore it slicked back. The sides were shaved down to almost nothing. There was gray on those sides, but they added to his looks, not detracted. His face was strong with a square, defined jawline. He had a goatee, but he kept it shaved to barely there. I could see a few gray hairs in it, too. And those eyes… he had deep forest-green eyes. His lips were full and a distraction since they made me think of kissing them.

His body was all lean muscle. I knew this by the way his clothes clung to his body. He wasn't as bulky as several of the men with him, but I knew he was tough. His short sleeves, even though it was the middle of winter, revealed his tattoos. All five of them were in short sleeves, which showed they had tats, but it was him who grabbed and kept my attention. Maybe I was just sex-starved. That had to be why I was sizing him up as my next sexual partner. It had been four years since my last disastrous relationship.

Not to say I was gonna have a relationship with Griffin. For one thing, he was here to do a job. That alone put him in the no-touch zone. I didn't sleep with our employees. Two, even if he wasn't in category one, I didn't see him as someone who was looking to settle down. Although maybe he was already settled. It was hard to tell sometimes. The lack of a ring didn't mean anything.

The thought of him having a wife and family depressed me. *Stop it! You're acting like a crazy fool. Griffin Voss isn't for you. Snap out of it!* My inner voice told me. That voice tried to keep me from making mistakes, and I usually listened to it. But God, if I thought there was a chance with him, I'd ignore the depressing bitch and jump his bones.

I tuned back into the conversation in time to catch Griffin telling Rockwell he'd been a Navy SEAL. Rockwell was being an asshole, and I didn't like it. He could be condescending and superior at times. I hated when he did that. It was my only excuse for what I said next.

"I guess he told you. Navy SEALs, DEA agents, Army Special Forces, and Marine Raiders make them very qualified to lead and assess threats. Don't be mad. You can't always be the best every time, Wayne."

I knew I scored a hit when he flushed and his face tightened. I only called him Wayne when he was being annoying or an asshole, and he knew it. He and I knew each other pretty well after four years of him being my main bodyguard. The man followed me everywhere except my bedroom and bathroom. I originally had been free of him in the house, but lately, he kept popping up when I was home to make sure I was okay. It was annoying, and I needed to talk to my dad about it. Having a guard in the house with me was unnecessary. Yes, we had a few roving the grounds, and occasionally, they might come inside, like when we had company, but those reasons weren't the case with Rockwell.

"Just because someone was a SEAL or those other things doesn't mean they know everything. These guys probably have been out for a while. If you don't use those skills, you lose them," Rockwell said as his comeback once he stopped smarting from mine.

I was about to defend the Patriots, more specifically Griffin, but my dad beat me to it. "I can assure you, Rockwell, that Griffin, his whole team, and everyone who works for them are more than fit for this work, and they keep up their skills. They can't tell us about many of their assignments. It's for those reasons and others that I asked for them. Now, enough of this. Eat. Your food is getting cold. We'll resume this discussion afterward in my study."

I knew that tone. He wouldn't allow anyone to argue. Silence descended as we got back to our meal. As we did, I couldn't help but sneak peeks at the Patriots, especially Griffin. I found him fascinating. Eventually, we finished, and we all got up and followed Dad to his study. When we got to the door, he stopped.

"I'd only like Hadley and the Patriots inside. The rest of you can relax. Porter will show you to the living room. If you need anything, just let him know."

Porter had popped up out of nowhere. He was good at that. He always seemed to know what Dad wanted before he said it or called him. Porter haunted the halls, and you never knew when he might appear.

The guards exchanged uneasy glances, but they didn't say anything. I saw Rockwell about to burst as he tried to hold back whatever he wanted to say. The board members, which consisted of Dewitt, Maynard, and Monroe, protested. The only ones missing were Truman and Fleming. I knew they'd be doing the same if they were here. It was odd they weren't.

"Travis, this involves Gerard Industries. We're the Board. We should be there for this talk. We have to know what the threat is so we can help you protect yourself and the company," Dewitt argued.

Dewitt had been Daddy's best friend for ages.

Usually, Dad listened to him, which was why I was shocked when he shook his head no. "No, I don't need you in there. The exact details need to be kept to the fewest number of people possible. It's for everyone's protection. It doesn't directly involve the company, so you have nothing to worry about."

"Even if it doesn't, we might have insight that could help," Monroe added.

"He's right," Maynard chimed in.

Out of those two, Monroe was the one to speak up, and Maynard followed him. Maynard never seemed to have an original thought, but I knew he was brilliant at his work. That was why he was on the board. All five of the members were brilliant in their own ways, and that made them ideal for our board of directors. The company excelled even more with their insights.

"Sir, maybe one of us should be with you," Ellis suggested. He was Dad's main bodyguard, and he oversaw the other guards.

"Ellis, I appreciate that, but I'm in no danger from the Patriots or my daughter. Stay and relax. Hopefully, this won't take long, and then we'll fill you in on what you need to know. Come, we're wasting time. Hadley, here, hold my arm," he said as he held it out to me. I walked over and took it. I swear, for a second, it trembled, but when I looked at his face, I saw that he seemed to be in control. We led the Patriots inside, and then Porter closed the door behind us.

"Please be seated wherever is most comfortable," Dad told them as we took a seat together on the loveseat.

His study was huge. Not only did he have a big desk and loads of bookcases, but he also had a large seating area like a living room. It had a loveseat, two couches, and a large chair with a coffee table in the center of the rectangle they created. I saw there was coffee and ice water in the middle of the table along with the necessary cups, glasses, and sugar and cream to doctor the coffee. I doubted these men took it any way other than black. This setup was thanks to Porter.

Remembering my manners, I made the offer. "Gentleman, may I get you some water or coffee? Just let me know how you take your coffee. I know this one contains French vanilla creamer, but the other will be half and half. If you want something else, we can get Porter to get it." I knew my dad liked his coffee, and he hadn't had nearly enough at breakfast, so I was busy fixing one for him. I was taken aback by the scowl Griffin gave me. What had I said?

"We're more than capable of making our own coffee, Ms. Gerard. There's no need to wait on us," he said rather gruffly.

"I know you're capable. I'm just offering. I do this often, you know. I'm right here with my hands on the pot. And please, call me Hadley."

"You go ahead and get yours. If we want some, we'll get it," he said.

Deciding not to get into a spat over something so simple, I let it go. I finished preparing Dad's and then made a cup for myself. It wasn't until I relaxed back in my seat that they got coffee or water. I was right. Those who had coffee all took it black.

"Now that we're all settled, I want to say thank

you again for coming to help with this. It means more to me than you know," Dad said, breaking the silence.

"We're happy to help, although it would be more helpful to us so we can make our plans if we knew exactly what the threat is. All we were told was there was one, and it involved severe consequences," Griffin told him.

All of this was news to me, so I jumped in. "Daddy, what in the world is going on?"

He reached over and took my free hand. He gave me a loving smile—one I'd been receiving my whole life. "Sweetheart, I'm sorry. I didn't want to say anything until I had everything in place. I told you we received a threat last week."

I nodded. "Yes, but why not tell me then? You always do. Let me guess, they plan to destroy your evil company. That's the typical one."

He shook his head, so I made my second guess. "Then they plan to take you and ask for ransom. Kidnapping is always a close second. Have they demanded money to leave you alone?"

He shook his head again. He looked so somber. "What then?" I asked.

"Let me catch these guys up, and then I'll answer that. Gentlemen, as you can imagine, with the work I do and the wealth I've accumulated, I'm often a target. I usually get two types of threats. Either they see the research and development we do as evil and want to destroy my company to prevent more needless killings. Mainly radical groups or activists fall into this category."

As he paused, Griffin spoke. "We've seen that often. They want to end death and war but are prepared to kill to do it, so what makes them any different? They don't understand righteous kill versus murder."

"Exactly. The other group is those who want to profit by kidnapping me and holding me for ransom. There are the typical death threats with it if I don't comply. You need to know that I've kept my daughter out of the limelight of my life for this very reason. Did you know before you met her that I even had a child?" They shook their heads no. It was true. Most people had no idea. It was for a reason.

"That's because I'll do anything to protect her. I lost her mother, and I won't lose her," he said through gritted teeth. Any mention of my mom made him this way. Not because he disliked her memory but due to the pain of it. I squeezed his hand, and he gave me a faint smile.

"Sir, Travis, I read somewhere that your wife died in a car accident," Griffin said.

"That's what we told everyone, but it was a lie. We didn't want to sensationalize it more than it already was. My wife and I always kept her and Hadley out of the media. My company was rapidly growing, and the more money you make, the bigger the target you are. Of course, there were those who knew about my wife, but they didn't know we had a child.

"My wife was several years younger than me. I married later in life. I know some of those who knew about us thought it was a case of a young gold digger going after an older man's money, but that wasn't true. We loved each other very much. She was my everything.

When Hadley was nine, my wife Hailey was kidnapped coming from the doctor's office. She had her bodyguard with her, but he was overpowered and killed."

He paused to swallow and take a drink of his coffee. Wanting to spare him, I took over. "My father was informed when my mom didn't come home, and a search was conducted. It was while they were doing the search that he got a call from the kidnappers. They were demanding a hundred million dollars in the next twelve hours, or they'd kill my mom."

"Christ," Beau hissed. The others looked equally pissed off.

"Dad agreed to pay them, but he said he might need longer to get that amount in cash. They didn't believe him and said he either did it or she would be sent back to him in pieces, so Dad scrambled to get the money. He called in all the favors he had to get the money. He promised to pay his friends and business acquaintances back. He had the money but not in available cash, as you can imagine. He didn't tell his friends and business acquaintances what he needed the money for. He got the ransom together and had an hour before they were to call and tell him where to drop the money when there was a box delivered by courier to the gate. He opened the box to find my mom's finger inside. He knew it was hers because it had her wedding rings on it." I had to stop and take a deep breath. I knew this all secondhand. Dad explained it when I was older. At the time, I was kept in the dark.

"Do you need to stop?" Griffin asked in gruff concern.

"No. You need to know this. Daddy was frantic

as he waited for them to call. When they did, he told them he had the money and not to hurt her anymore. He asked for proof of life. They put her on the phone. After she spoke to him, they told him where to leave the money. Of course, they'd all along told him not to involve the police. He didn't. He had one of his men make the drop, and there was a note there, as agreed, telling him where to find my mom. When he and his men got to the location, it was too late. The bastards had killed her anyway."

Tears ran down my face and Dad's. Griffin swore, then got up to pace. His guys were scowling darkly. "Did you ever find the men who did it?" Griffin snarled.

"Yes, I did. I hired some people who were good at finding unscrupulous people. You understand that they were not my usual colleagues, but they got the job done. When those animals were found, I had them rounded up," Dad told him.

"You had them killed," Benedict said flatly.

Dad didn't answer. Smart. He'd already told them too much. I didn't want to see my dad in prison if they decided to speak of it.

"Travis, we'll never speak of this to anyone. Your secret's safe with us. I can tell you, if that had been my wife, I would've done the exact same thing. So after that terrible tragedy, you worked even harder to keep your daughter out of the spotlight, I presume," Griffin guessed.

"I did. I never took her out in public with me. She used a different last name when she attended school. It's been hell not to acknowledge her. The day my wife was killed, they didn't just take her from me. They took

Hadley's mother and our second child. She'd been to the doctor that morning to confirm her pregnancy. We'd been trying for a long time to have another baby."

All of them swore this time. Tension was high. I needed to divert it. "Dad, what does this have to do with the threat you received last week?"

He stared deeply into my eyes. I knew before he said it what he was about to say. My heart jumped. "It's important because the threat isn't against the company or me. It's against you. The person or persons who made it said if I don't speed up production on our latest project, you'll pay the price. I was assured they could get to you, and you'd suffer a fate worse than death before they killed you. You'll be sent back to me in pieces." His voice broke.

"Like hell, they will! We won't let that happen," Griffin snapped.

"Wraith is right. We won't let that happen," Beau said adamantly.

"Wraith?" I asked in curiosity.

"Sorry, Wraith is his nickname from the military. Some of us call him that," Beau explained.

I liked it for some reason. I could see him moving in and out of enemy territory without them knowing it. How, I didn't know. I just did.

"That's why I asked for you. Anderson has told me about you and your company. He trusts you, which means I trust you. I want you to seal this place down so no one and nothing can get to my daughter. She has to be protected at all costs."

"Daddy, I understand why you'd react like this,

but you can't keep me as a prisoner in the house. I have things I have to do," I reminded him.

"Ms. Gerard, going shopping or to the salon aren't things you need to be doing when there's a threat to you. Those can wait," Griffin said bitingly.

His assumption that I wanted to go out for frivolous things pissed me off. I wasn't an empty-headed socialite. It also disappointed me. I expected more from him than to make assumptions. I now knew what category to put him in. I squeezed my dad's hand when I saw him about to speak in my defense. I shook my head slightly. Griffin was looking away, so he didn't see it. Neither did his men since they had their eyes on him. I almost bit my tongue in half, keeping my snarky comments to myself.

When I didn't respond, he faced us. "First thing, we have control of everything. That means who comes and goes, which won't be many or often. Your board, for example. They don't need to meet here. Your men will report to us. We'll give them their assignments. Anyone who doesn't pass muster will be replaced. We'll need to see your security system and walk your grounds. I can assure you more security measures will need to be added. I already spotted a few issues on our way here."

He walked around the study as he fired off his orders. I tried not to be affected by them. On the one hand, I found his confidence sexy. On the other hand, it made me want to hit him over the head and tell him to stop being bossy.

"If at any time we determine the current security measures aren't enough, it will be my decision to move her elsewhere."

"Wait, I don't want to leave my dad. I have things here I can't leave for an extended period of time."

"Your safety is the only thing we care about. You can leave your friends and boyfriend behind to save your life, surely?" he asked with a slight sneer.

This time, Dad squeezed my hand. "We're in your capable hands. Just tell us what to do."

"Good. Now, we can't assume they're only going after her. We have to assume you could be a target as well. I know you have to work, but we'll make sure to beef up the security there. What I'd like to know is, how did this person or persons find out you had a daughter? There's a chance it's someone who knows you. I noticed the board knows of her. The guards and the servants obviously do. Any of them could've mentioned her to someone that they shouldn't have."

"I can't see any of our people doing that. They've worked for us for years and have never told anyone that we know of," I protested.

"Like I said, it could've been a slip. Or they thought whoever they told was trustworthy. I'm not saying they're behind this, but we will be investigating all of them to be sure. Is there anything else you can tell us?" He directed this to Dad.

"No, that's it for now."

"Okay, I'd like to see the note they sent and get it to our people. My guys will start the perimeter walk, so we need to warn your men. I suggest you keep this between us. The guards can know there's a security issue, and so can the Board, but I wouldn't tell them the details. The less they know, the less they can tell."

Dad sat there for a minute in silence before he answered him. "Agreed. I'll have all the men brought in so you can speak to them. Do you want them all together or in groups?"

"Groups. I don't want the grounds left totally unmonitored. Also, do you have guard dogs here?"

"No, we don't. Why?" I asked.

"It would be beneficial to have one or two. I'll get to work on that. After we talk to everyone and do the checks, I'd like to know where you'd like me and my men to stay."

I figured Dad would put them in the guesthouse or the small apartments where some of the staff lived. Some staff took advantage and lived here rather than somewhere else. I was surprised when he offered neither.

"I want the five of you to stay here, in the house with us. We have plenty of rooms, and I'd feel safer with you here."

"Are you sure? I know it might feel safer, but we could also invade your privacy," Griffin said.

"Our privacy isn't important. My daughter's life is. Bring as many dogs as you want, hire as many men as you need, and add whatever security you think we need. No cost is too much."

Tears filled my eyes as I saw the way Dad was staring at me. All the love and fear he was feeling was there plain to see. I leaned toward him, and he wrapped me in his arms. I felt him kiss the top of my head.

"I love you, Daddy," I whispered.

“And I love you too, sweetheart. More than my own life,” he whispered back.

As we held each other, the men in the room faded away. All I could think about was how this would kill my dad if anything happened to me. He barely survived losing my mom and the baby. I vowed he wouldn’t suffer something like that again. I’d have to fight my tendency to push back and be my own boss with the Patriots. It wasn’t going to be easy.

Griffin: Chapter 4

It was late Monday night. We'd been at the Gerard house for over twelve hours. My head was spinning for a variety of reasons. The one I was concentrating on at the moment was because of the results of our security checks. My men and I were gathered in the sitting room of my suite. Yeah, this damn house had suites. We weren't given a broom closet in the back of the house or in the attic. They gave us great rooms which you could tell were for important guests. We tried to tell Travis we didn't need anything this fancy, but he refused to hear it.

It took us hours to complete our evaluation. Now, we were gathered in front of my laptop, having our debriefing call with Mark, Gabe, and Sean. They'd all just gotten on the call.

"How did it go?" Mark asked.

"What details did you get out of them?" Sean asked right after him.

"Any problems?" Gabe asked.

I chuckled. "Well, who do I answer first? Hmm."

They laughed, and the guys with me chuckled, too. We were tired, but this needed to be done tonight so everyone could get started first thing in the morning.

"Whichever order you wanna go in," Sean said.

I quickly filled them in on the secret history of Gerard's wife and the fact he had a daughter most people had no idea existed. They were just as stunned as we were to find both out. We were determined to make sure he didn't lose his daughter after the tragedy he already suffered. Once they had the background, I began to tell them about our evaluation.

"The local cops are too damn slow to respond to anything suspicious in this vicinity. Took them fifteen minutes to get to us when we were obviously casing the place. We didn't see them patrolling anywhere either, so no one has been dedicated to the area. I asked Travis if he had told them about the threat, and he said he had spoken to the chief of police. I doubt they'll be of any help."

"Well shit, that sucks but not necessarily unexpected," Gabe muttered.

"True. Then we got to the gate, and the guard there asked to see our IDs. I gave him mine but told him he didn't need to see the rest because we were expected. He let me pressure him into not insisting on it and left us to make a call without having someone to guard us. Two more strikes."

"Damn, okay, keep going," Sean said.

"There were several bodyguards inside the house and three of the five board of director members when we got here. We met with just Gerard and his daughter. He hadn't told her or them about the threat. She wasn't happy about being locked down here, but I'm not letting her flitter around hell and back while someone could be gunning for her. Her socializing, shopping, and fun will have to wait," I growled.

"She's a party girl, is she? I wonder how she does that and hasn't been outed as his daughter?" Mark asked.

"Come on, you know she is. Women like her, who don't have to work and are handed anything they want, only socialize, party, and shop. They wouldn't know what to do if they had to work for real. I have no clue how everyone doesn't know who she is," I muttered.

"Whoa, what did she do to tick you off?" Gabe asked.

"I don't know what you mean. She didn't tick me off," I protested.

"You're being kinda harsh, aren't you? Do you know for sure all she does are those things? Even if she does, it doesn't matter to our job other than we might have to curtail her extracurricular activities. Does she have a man we have to be concerned will be in the picture?" Sean asked.

"We don't know, but if she doesn't, I don't know how it's possible," Heath told him.

"Ahh, she's good-looking, I take it. Don't get any ideas," Mark warned him.

"I won't, but damn, she's gorgeous. There's no way in hell she doesn't have a man," Heath added.

For some reason, his talking about Hadley raised my hackles. I wasn't sure why, and I had to bite my tongue so I wouldn't say anything. I thought I had it under control by the time Gabe chimed in.

"What about you other guys? Is she as gorgeous as Heath says?"

"Yep, she's damn hot," Beau said.

"She's a ten in my book," Ben added.

"I wouldn't kick her out of my bed," Justin chimed in.

They all turned to stare at me when I didn't say anything. Trying to play it cool, I shrugged. "She's alright, but I've seen better." I felt like I'd burn in hell for that lie. The truth was she was an eleven in my book, and if she weren't a rich spoiled girl and not our client's daughter, I'd be all over her.

"Bullshit, don't tell us that! She's totally hot, sexy, and gorgeous," Heath protested.

"Can we get back to what's important? We're here to save her and Gerard's lives, not talk about how hot she is or isn't," I reminded them. They all sobered up, and that line of talk was abandoned.

"Wraith is right. What did you find on your rounds of the estate and house?" Sean asked.

"They have cameras close to the house, and there are roving guards. They don't have enough of either. There are so many gaps in them, it would be easy for someone who's determined and who studied the guards' duty and patrol patterns to get inside. They all follow the same route at a predictable time, and they don't have dogs either. I think we definitely need to get one or two dogs here. They need more cameras and motion-detecting equipment and more guards," I told them.

"Shit, we were hoping it was better than that, but we've had this before. How's the house?" Mark asked.

I gestured to Beau to take over. While I'd been

involved in most of the assessments, they needed to feel comfortable reporting on things, too. I was the leader, but we were all equally involved.

"The house is better. They have a pretty decent security system, but it could be made even better. Ours would make it great. There are guards in the house, but I got the impression that it wasn't normal all the time. Gerard has a few who seem to be his regulars. His daughter, so far, we've only seen one who follows her like a hound. None of them are happy to see us or to be put under our command, as you can imagine. It remains to be seen if they'll push back on us. I thought we might have to set one straight when he puffed up about our qualifications." Beau chuckled.

"Oh yeah, which one, and what didn't he like?" Gabe asked with a smirk.

"It was Hadley's guard, Rockwell. She kind of pushed it. He was being snide about our qualifications, and when Wraith told him what they were, she basically told Rockwell we were way more qualified than him."

"He doesn't like anyone stepping on his toes. He thinks he's a badass. Mark my words. We'll have trouble getting him to fall into line," Ben said.

"If we do, then he's got to go. At least until this is resolved, we can't have rebels and resistance within the ranks. If we do, whoever is making the threat will use it against us," I pointed out, even though they knew it.

"Is Gerard okay with us replacing people if we deem it necessary?" Mark asked.

"He is. He's actually very accommodating and not

what you'd expect from a billionaire. He insists we call him Travis. He gave us suites in the house rather than out where the other staff and guards stay. Or at least the ones who live on the grounds versus elsewhere. I can tell you this. If we're here long eating their chef's cooking, I'll need twice-a-day workouts," Heath said.

We all had to nod at that one. Lunch and dinner had been as great as breakfast. Thankfully, we did a lot of walking and climbing around, checking everything out, so we did get some exercise today. That was another thing. This huge house had a fully equipped gym and indoor as well as outdoor pools. Since it was winter, the indoor one would be great. We'd been told to use them anytime we wanted and to let Gerard know if there was some equipment they didn't have. I checked it out, and nothing was missing.

"Well, it sounds like you're settling in nicely. We'll work on getting someone out there to beef up the cameras and security system. As for the dogs, let me see what we can get and how soon. I assume you have the names of everyone who works for them, who was at the house, and those who will be there but weren't today?" Sean asked, tapping away on his tablet.

"I do, and I'll send those now. I included the board members' names as well. Until we say otherwise, everyone needs to be vetted. As we meet new people, we'll send their names and any info we get to you. I know this is our thing, but if it gets crazy because of the other assignments we have going, you know we can always reach out to the Warriors or the others and get help from their computer people," I reminded them, not that I needed to.

"Already ahead of ya. I've got Outlaw, Smoke, and Everly on standby. If we need more, then I'll ask," Gabe told us.

"Anderson called today and basically told us whoever and whatever we had to do to keep Gerard safe was authorized. He didn't come out and say it bluntly, but we read between the lines. If we need to kill people and make their bodies disappear, no one will say a word. We can't let anything happen to Travis Gerard or his daughter. Do you need us to send more people now?" Mark asked.

I thought about it for a minute, then shook my head. "Nah, not right now. Maybe later. Let's beef up the security to our standards, and then we'll see. Now, it's late, and I know you have to be tired and want to go to bed. Tell the ladies hello, and we'll let you get to sleep so we can, too. Morning will be here before we know it. Goodnight."

There was a flurry of goodnights, and then the call ended. I faced the four in the room with me. "Go get some rest. How about we hit the gym at five? We can get in a workout before the household is awake and then get to work. This is going to be stressful, so a good workout may keep us from choking some people," I said with a grin.

They all chuckled and agreed. Once they left my room, I shut down my laptop and took a shower. I was tired, and I needed to rest not only my body but also my brain. There was so much running through it that I couldn't sort it all out.

The hot shower, with its endless hot water, relaxed me a bit, and I fell asleep rather quickly.

Tomorrow would be soon enough to sort things out better.

ᔕᔕᔕ

As we all walked into the gym at five a.m., on the dot, we got a surprise. We weren't the only ones there. Imagine our shock to see Hadley. She was on an elliptical machine. I tried not to stare but seeing her in her workout clothes only emphasized her body, and it was something to look at.

She wasn't dressed in skimpy shorts and a tank top like so many women who went to the gym wore. You knew the ones who were more interested in being seen than working out. She had on a pair of yoga pants and a tank. They molded her curves, but she was covered. Her hair was up in a ponytail, and there wasn't a bit of makeup on her face, unlike yesterday. I found I preferred her without it. Her skin was sweaty. She looked surprised to see us and slowed her movements.

"Hi, good morning. Come on in. There's room for all of us. I see we're all morning workout fans," she said with a smile.

"We'll work out anytime, but mornings are my preference. Do you do this often?" Heath asked.

"I try to do it several times a week. I don't always get to do it in the morning, which I prefer. Please, don't let me stop you. There are towels in that cabinet and water in the fridge over there. Help yourself. I've got a bit to go if you need this machine."

"It's alright. We have plenty we can do. You're lucky to have this in your home," Beau told her.

"I am. Sometimes, Dad joins me, but he hasn't

been lately. As you can imagine, it was impossible for him or me to really join a gym, so he made sure we had one here. I hope you'll take advantage of it as well as the pool. It's heavenly to get into it after a hard workout, and the spa with its hot water is divine," she said with a happy sigh.

"We should get to work. We won't bother you," I told her gruffly before walking over to the weights. I felt like lifting first. She gave me a tentative smile and nodded. The guys followed me.

"Hey, what was that all about?" Beau whispered to me.

"What was what about?"

"The curt shit. She was only being nice," he hissed.

"We're not here to be her friends. We're here to keep her safe, find out who's threatening them, and eliminate them. Getting all friendly is not the way to go. Just remember, she's our job, nothing more. Now, let's get to work."

They gave me puzzled looks, but they didn't say anything. I tried like hell to focus on my workout and ignore her, but it was impossible. Even if I closed my eyes, I could still see her in my mind. When she was done with the elliptical, she went over to the rowing machine. Seeing her back flex as she rowed made me want to trace her musculature. I'd never been this fascinated by a woman's physique, but hers grabbed my attention.

I was trying to be sneaky about watching her so none of them would see it. I was about to get up and go over to her when the door opened, and Rockwell walked in. The smile he had on his face melted away into a scowl when he saw all of us. He marched over to her.

He leaned over and whispered something to her. She frowned at him and shook her head no. He whispered something else, and I could tell he was upset. Whatever he said had her shaking her head more emphatically. She turned her face away from him when she was done. That's when he grabbed her arm. I was up and moving across the room without giving it a thought. No way was he manhandling her. I heard my guys coming behind me. I didn't make it to her before she was up off the machine and in Rockwell's face.

"Wayne, I don't know what crawled up your ass this morning, but it doesn't give you the right to try and boss me around or to grab me. Don't ever grab me like that again. I said I wasn't done working out yet," she snapped at him.

I came to a stop right behind her. I put a hand on her shoulder. She glanced back at me. I gently but insistently shifted her over and back so she was behind me. She made a protesting sound, but I ignored it. I knew my men would be surrounding her as I faced Rockwell. He was scowling even more than before.

"I suggest if you want to keep your face intact, you don't ever grab her again. She's working out. Why don't you leave her alone and come back once you've calmed the hell down?"

"Don't tell me what to do. This is between me and Hadley. She needs to come with me. She can finish her workout later," he snapped.

"And I told you, I'm halfway done, and I'm not

stopping. What's gotten into you? I always work out at this time."

"Yeah, but you shouldn't be in here with them," he hissed softly.

"And why shouldn't she be in here with us?" I asked, barely holding back my growl.

"Wayne, don't say a word," she snapped at him.

"I wanna hear what he has to say," I told her.

"He's being silly."

"I'm waiting," I told him. I crossed my arms and waited to see if he'd be brave enough to answer me. Did he have the guts to say what I knew he was thinking?

"You're five strange men, and she's one lone woman," he said. I heard her groan.

"So, do you not want her alone with us because you're afraid we'll force ourselves on her or because you're afraid she'll like what one of us offers and take us up on it?" I asked with a smirk.

"She wouldn't give you the time of day! Just because you were special forces doesn't mean shit. There's no way in hell she'd ever want one of you," he said hotly.

"So that means you think we're rapists." I stepped closer until we were almost nose to nose. I saw fear dilate his pupils. I dropped my voice lower. "Let me tell you something, boy. Not a single one of us would ever hurt a woman, and we certainly wouldn't rape one. Would we flirt and see if she was interested? Hell yeah, but no means no, or didn't they teach you that where you come from? From what I just saw, you don't know what no means."

"You son of a bitch!" he snarled right before he threw a punch. I was waiting for it. I easily avoided it and twisted around until I was behind him and had my arm around his neck. I placed him in a chokehold he couldn't break. He was flailing and trying to get away, but he wouldn't. I was gonna put him out and hope he learned a lesson from it.

"Stop! Let him go. This isn't necessary. Griffin, let him go," she shouted as she tried to get away from Beau and the others.

"He needs to learn to mind his p's and q's and not run his mouth."

"Maybe he does but choking him out won't do it. Let him go, Wraith!" she yelled again. It was her calling me Wraith that made me loosen my hold, and I let him drop to the floor. He gasped and gagged for air. I figured she'd run to him and make over him, but she surprised me.

She looked disgusted. "You're all a bunch of idiotic Alpha Neanderthals," she said before she stormed out of the gym. A part of me wanted to go after her and make her see why I did what I did, but the rest of me wanted to stay and make myself crystal clear to Rockwell. She must've been too mad at us to care that we might hurt him after she left.

I leaned down to his coughing body on the floor. His face showed fear and anger. "Don't ever, and I mean ever, accuse me or any of my men of such a despicable, cowardly thing again. Hadley is perfectly safe with us. In fact, she's safer with us. If you keep up the attitude, you'll be off her security detail so fast, your goddamn head will spin. Get the fuck out. Be ready at seven with the others. We have a full day planned," I barked. He wanted to say something, I could see it, but he didn't. Instead, he staggered to his feet and hauled ass out of there. Once he was gone, the guys started.

Beau whistled. "Damn, you sure know how to make friends, Wraith. I'd watch my back with that one. He doesn't like any of us, but he hates you."

"Yep, that's an accurate assessment, Beau. Maybe we should make Wraith wear a Kevlar vest even in the house. You know, in case Rockwell takes a potshot at him," Heath added.

"Fuck that. He needs one of us to sleep in his room to keep guard. I'm not doing it, so one of you assholes gets that job," Ben snickered.

"Don't say it's me just because I'm the new guy. I'm too young to die," Justin pretended to whine.

Their antics made me laugh and helped to dispel my dark mood. "Shut up, you fuckers. I can handle Rockwell. Let's get our workouts done so we can shower and meet the others at seven. I think we need to test their physical readiness with some running, push-ups, burpees, and such. See what their stamina is like," I told them with a grin.

They snickered before we got back to our workouts. I'd be lying if I said I didn't do mine with my mind half on the workout and half on Rockwell and Hadley. Just what was their relationship? Was he just overprotective of her, unsure of himself and his skills, or was there a secret relationship between them? If it was the latter, that wasn't good. I'd have to keep an eye on him and see if I could figure it out.

By the time we finished up and showered, we made it downstairs to the dining room with two minutes to spare. We'd arranged for all the usual bodyguards who patrolled the grounds, were on personal details, and stood duty in the home to come to breakfast so we could talk to them. We couldn't take everyone off duty at once, so we were doing it in groups.

First would be the personal detail guards. Next would be the ones who worked the grounds and gate. Lastly would be the rest. Later, we'd talk with the staff in the house, like Porter, the chef, and anyone else who helped to keep this place going. I knew they had to have cleaning staff. We had to investigate all of them. For anyone not seen as essential, we'd recommend they not come back until this was over. I explained this to Gerard yesterday in a private meeting. He said whatever we thought was best, he'd do. He was decent enough to pay them even if they weren't working.

When we entered, I saw there were eight guards. Rockwell was among them. What surprised me was Gerard and Hadley were there, too. It didn't matter if they were or not, but they weren't necessary. I went to them first. Hadley was still pissed at me. I could tell. Oh well, she'd get over it, or she wouldn't. I was prepared for her dad to say something about it. No doubt she ran to him and whined about me hurting Rockwell and not listening to her.

"Travis, Hadley, good morning. I'm surprised to see you here. There's no need for you to sit through these meetings this morning. We're just going to get to know everyone a bit, let them know what we expect, and that sort of stuff. After we're done, we plan to take them to do some physical training and assessments. It'll be boring. I'm sure you have plenty of important things to do."

"We want to be here. If I need to leave for any reason, then I'll do so. We're just here to observe. We're curious about how you do what you do. Hadley, honey, you said there was something you wanted to tell Griffin," he said to her.

Fuck, here it came. I waited for her to rip into me for putting Rockwell in his place. Imagine my shock when she didn't say anything about that. What she did say took me aback.

"Yes, Daddy, I'd like to go out and see what the physical part they plan to put the guys through is like. I'm interested in seeing it."

"It's a lot of running, sit-ups, chin-ups, and burpees. Those are—," she cut me off before I could explain.

"I know what those are, and I'd really like to be there."

If she thought by being there, she'd protect her pet, she'd soon find out she was mistaken. I shrugged. "It's your time and home. Sure, you can watch. How about we get started with this bunch, and then we can get the others in and out? We want to make this as efficient as possible."

They nodded, and we moved off to get our plates. We might as well eat while we talk. Gerard seemed to be in a slightly less happy mood today. Maybe this was wearing on him more. I wish we could give him an exact date of when this threat would be over, but we couldn't.

We'd all have to learn to get along and live together.

Hadley: Chapter 5

The past several hours watching Griffin and his team talk to all of our guards had been enlightening in many ways. One was the way they went about it. They didn't do much more than ask about their past experience and if any was spent in the military. They asked them about how long they'd been working for my dad. Then they switched to asking them if they were in control of making the security decisions here and at the office, what would they add or eliminate. When it came to that question, they all looked at Dad first, then me. Dad was quick to assure them they were allowed to speak freely. I was impressed by what some of them said.

Others, I thought, were giving the Dark Patriots vague answers. Maybe they were worried they'd lose their jobs if they were truthful. Maybe they really didn't have the capacity to come up with ideas. Or maybe they were resistant to outsiders coming in and telling them what to do. I could understand it, but this wasn't a game.

People might think I only say that because I was the target, but that wasn't it. I wasn't as concerned for myself as I was for my dad because I didn't believe I was the target. There were very few people who knew of my existence. Why do this now? If they wanted me dead, they could've just kidnapped or killed me and been done with it. No, they wanted my dad to take the focus off his security and put it on me, making him easier to get to. I planned to talk to him and the Patriots later about this, but first, I had some physical training to be a part of.

It was chilly outside, but they insisted we had to do it outdoors. I made sure to be bundled up. The first group up was the ones who guarded the grounds, the gate, and the corporate office. I watched as they put them through their paces. It became clear early on who was in top shape and who wasn't. Some were panting like they were about to die after running and doing the other things.

Griffin and his guys kept telling them they were lucky they didn't have their obstacle course here, or they'd be given a real workout. Some did alright, though, which was good to see. I wasn't sure if the Patriots wanted to instill resentment in them or force them to work harder. By the time they walked off, I wondered how the others would do.

I was surprised Dad stayed for part of it, but then he got called away to take business calls in his home office. When our personal guards came, I noticed that Justin and Heath had left. All of Dad's guards —Fletcher, Ellis, Royce, Holloway, and Kellogg, were there. And all of mine were, too—Rockwell, Ortiz, and Sanders. Rockwell was my main one, but the others filled in when he needed downtime or time off. Since most people didn't know who I was, I didn't need people around the clock like Dad. Wait, if they were all here, who was guarding my dad?

I whipped around to run for the house, but Griffin caught my arm. "Let go. I need to check on my dad."

"He's fine. I'd never leave him unguarded. Justin and Heath are on him. I need you to stay here so we have eyes on you. Come on, don't you want to see how your guy, Rockwell, does?" I heard the faint taunt in his voice.

"Sure, let's see how he does. He might just surprise you, you know. He's not a bad guy. I know you're pissed at him about this morning, but he was just worried about me. He would never hurt me. I admit, he should've never insinuated what he did. He was upset and worried. I'll talk to him about it."

"No, you won't. If I have anything I need him to know, I'll tell him. No matter how upset he was, he shouldn't have grabbed you like that."

"You just grabbed my arm. Why is it okay for you and not for him?"

"I caught your arm, and I didn't grip you hard enough to leave bruises. He did," he muttered, then before I could stop him, he shoved up my sleeve. Dark fingerprints were visible on my skin. I jerked it down, and then I walked off to stand by Beau. Ben was talking to the guards and telling them what they wanted them to do.

"We don't like to see women hurt, no matter the reason. Protecting innocent people is what we do. Rockwell's anger with you bothered us. You can't blame us for being worried," Beau said softly.

"No, I can't, but you also don't know him. He's been with me for four years. He's never hurt me, and he's had ample opportunity if that was his goal. We're alone together all the time."

I swore I heard a faint growl coming from Griffin's

direction, but when I glanced over, he was watching Ben and the others. When I faced Beau again, he shrugged. "Then I guess we'll just have to wait and see. I gotta earn my paycheck," he told me with a wink.

I grinned. I did like them even though I didn't know much about them. Well, I liked four of them. Griffin, I was still trying to figure out what I felt. Like was too silly of a word. I found him attractive but also infuriating. One second, I wanted to argue with him. The next, to punch him, then I flipped to wanting to kiss him. Wow, I'd obviously been without sex for too long. I needed to get laid. An image of me and Griffin in bed popped into my head. I shoved it away. *Nope. Not happening, forget it, Hadley*, I lectured myself.

I moved closer so I could hear and see everything. Like the first group, they put them through their paces. Most of them could at least do it for a while, and they didn't give up, but only Rockwell, Ellis, and Royce made it through all of it.

Griffin nodded. "That's enough. Nice job, you three. The rest of you didn't do too badly. We'll work on improving everyone's stamina. That's it for—," he started but was interrupted by Rockwell.

"Improve our stamina! Why the three of us? We did it. It's those guys who need it, not us."

"Yes, you did, but you can get even better," Griffin told him.

"How the hell do we know you big shot SEALs, or whatever you were, have what it takes? I didn't see any of you out here doing it with us," Rockwell snapped.

I'd seen how they had been working out in the

gym before Rockwell interrupted us. I knew they could do it. I tried to divert his attention. "I'm tired. Why don't we go in and get something to drink? I want to talk to you about a few things we need to plan for," I said as I walked over to Rockwell. I put a smile on my face and placed my hand on his arm.

I was taken aback when he shook it off and glared at me. "Did you tell your dad what that bastard did to me this morning?"

"No, I didn't."

"Why the hell not? I don't trust them. We know nothing about these men. Just because someone recommended them, your dad brings them in and gives them control? That doesn't make sense, Hadley. He has qualified men here who can do what they're doing. He has never allowed unknown men near you without thoroughly vetting them. Hell, I worked for him a year before I was given your main security detail. There's no way I'm leaving you alone with any of them."

"Dad has his reasons. I trust my dad, and you should, too. These guys are the real deal. They don't have anything to prove. Stand down."

"No, I won't, and I don't take orders from women," he said with a sneer.

Fury filled me. There had been times in the past when I suspected he was a chauvinist, but he was careful never to say anything too incriminating near me. However, it was that suspicion that made me not work out fully with him. Sure, he saw me on the treadmill, lifting small weights and using the elliptical, things like that, but he didn't know about the other stuff I did. At night, when I was at home for the night, and he went back to his apartment on the grounds, I did my real workout.

I saw Griffin charging toward us. He looked furious. I held up my hand, and he stopped. I shifted my gaze back to Rockwell. "I'll tell you what. I'll go up against you, and I'll match you in push-ups, sit-ups, chin-ups, burpees, and the run. If you beat me, I'll go to my dad and have him send them away." I paused as he began to grin. "But if I can keep up or I beat you, then Griffin and his guys don't have to prove anything to you. You'll back off and let them do their job, and you do yours."

He laughed, the cocky asshole. "You actually think you can beat me? Come on, Hadley. Those cute little girly push-ups I've seen you try to do, running on the treadmill and lifting three-pound weights won't match me, let alone beat me. I'll give you a chance to take it back before you humiliate yourself. You're a woman, and women aren't as strong as men."

"You're on. I just need a minute," I said with a smile.

His smile remained as I unzipped my jacket. I tossed it to the ground and took off my gloves and hat. Underneath were my workout clothes. I'd hoped I might get a chance to do this, and here it was. I shoved my heavy sweats to the ground and stepped out of them. I was left in my tennis shoes, yoga pants, and a tight, long-sleeved workout shirt—the kind that wicks moisture away when you sweat. My hair was still in a ponytail.

"Hadley, you don't need to do this. I have no problem showing him what I can do, and neither will my guys," Griffin said urgently as he came over to me. Beau, Ben, and the others had gotten very quiet.

"I'm not doing this for you. I'm doing it for me and every woman out there who has had to listen to a man belittle and downgrade them just because we're women. I might not have the muscle mass of a man, but I'm not weak, and I'm not afraid. So, are you still wanting to do this, Wayne? I'll give you this chance to take it back before you humiliate yourself."

His face flushed dark before he answered. "Bring it on. Same rules as before. A mile run, followed by a hundred sit-ups, fifty push-ups, and they have to be the man ones, not the sissy ones, fifty chin-ups, and twenty-five burpees. I win if you tap out, or I finish first. You have to swear in front of these guys you won't renege on your promise to talk to your dad. Deal?"

"I agree to it all. Deal. I believe we line up here, and it's to that marker and back for the run. Who wants to start it?"

Griffin wasn't happy, but I had to do it. It now had less to do with him and his men and more to prove a point, mainly to Rockwell but also to the others. I wasn't nearly as weak and fragile as they thought. Dad should've remembered that.

Seeing I wasn't backing down, Beau came to stand next to us. "On the count of three, go. You go to the marker and back to this marker. Understand?" We both nodded. "One, two, three."

We took off. Rockwell pulled ahead, but I knew he would. I'd seen him train hundreds of times. I knew his technique. He'd come out of the gate like a bull and run as fast as he could until he had to slow down, then he'd bring it home at a much more leisurely pace. It was his thing. I let him do it.

He threw a grin over his shoulder as he edged further ahead of me. I didn't let it bother me. I knew I'd have him soon. He made it to the marker ahead of me. As he passed me on the way back, he blew me a kiss. That's when I hit my high gear. See, I was the opposite of him. I started out steady and running at about seventy percent of my capacity. It left me with plenty to kick it up with when I needed to. By the time I did that and hit my stride, my competitor was losing strength and speed and becoming winded.

I vaguely noticed Dad, Justin, and Heath had joined the ones at the finish line. This spurred me on even more. I was catching up to Rockwell at that point, but seeing them gave me a burst of speed. I came charging up and then passed him. I heard Rockwell swear, but I kept going until I passed the finish line. I saw the Patriots smiling, well, all but Griffin. He wasn't smiling, but I swear I saw his mouth twitch. I'd take it... for now. Dad rushed over and gave me a hug.

"Honey, you did great. I heard what was going on and why. I'm not sending them away, no matter what. You don't need to finish this," he whispered in my ear.

I gave him a squeeze and whispered back, "Oh yes, I do. It's not about the Patriots anymore. It's about me as a woman and him as a chauvinistic asshole. He's gotten too big for his pants lately. I need to correct that. I can do this."

He stepped back. "Then go finish it. I'll be here until you're done, and then we'll go inside and have a glass of champagne to celebrate."

I gave him a quick peck on the cheek and then went over to Griffin. Rockwell wasn't far away. He didn't look happy as he studied me. I could tell that even though my win grated on him, he still thought he had this in the bag.

"Next?" I asked Griffin.

"A hundred sit-ups. They have to be full ones where the whole back comes off the ground. Each of you can have someone hold your feet," he said.

"I don't need it, but she can have someone. I won't call it cheating," Rockwell said with a smirk.

"I don't need anyone either. Let's go." I challenged back.

We lay on the ground and waited. This time, it was Ben who counted us down. Again, Rockwell came out of the gate in a rush. He was pounding out the sit-ups. It wasn't until he was at thirty and I was at twenty that he began to flag. I took off my brakes and began to fly with them. I had killer core strength. Sure, he had a six-pack, but so did I, and as a woman, I had to work harder to get and keep mine. I did two hundred sit-ups on abdominal days. In the end, we finished together. He flopped back on the ground to stretch out his cramping stomach. I did the same. He wasn't smirking now.

After a five-minute rest, we went to the next one. This time, it was the chin-ups. I personally hated them. As a woman, I didn't have the upper body strength of a man, so I had to learn to use not just my arms but my entire body strength to do them. After many years of battling them, I had perfected my technique. It was time to see if I could beat him or at least finish in a tie.

The other guards and Dad were cheering now. Justin offered to do the countdown this time. We went to the erected bars in the yard where the training had been happening. Large spikes held the metal legs into the hard ground.

Rockwell was taller, so it was easier for him to reach the bar. I saw Griffin coming toward me, and I knew he was planning to lift me up to it. I wouldn't let him do that. I took off in a run, then jumped up using my strong thigh muscles and grabbed the bar with both hands. I was five foot seven. The bar was close to seven feet off the ground. I heard a few whistles.

When Justin said three, I zoned everything and everyone out. I had to in order to do this one. All that existed was me, the bar, and the count. I counted them off in my head and never glanced at my competitor once. When I hit fifty, I dropped to the ground. I was breathing hard, and my arms ached like hell. I shook them out as I looked over at Rockwell. He was on the ground, grinning. Shit!

"He beat you by one second. Don't let him see you sweat," Griffin muttered as he passed me. I kept my expression bland.

"Ready to admit defeat?" Rockwell asked.

"I can keep going as long as you can. Even longer," I taunted him before walking off. We took another five-minute break. I kept moving and drank water. I couldn't afford to let my muscles cramp due to dehydration and lactic acid accumulation.

Round four was push-ups. Rockwell had seen me do the sissy ones when I was around him. He had no idea those were for show. In my real workouts with my trainers, I did the same ones as a man. This was where my arm strength wasn't more important than my core strength. You needed both to do them.

Heath happily came to do the honors. "Hadley, when you beat his ass, I owe you a drink. What's your favorite?"

I grinned at him. "I love top-shelf tequila. You can have the groceries."

He laughed. "Got it, no salt or lime." Then he got to the countdown.

This time, I could see Rockwell out of the corner of my eye. I didn't bother to track his count. Mine was the only one that was important. I did a hundred of these each time I did the real ones. Sometimes, I did more than one set of them. Fifty didn't seem to take long at all. When I stopped and looked over, we were both stopped. He wasn't smiling or smirking. I glanced at Heath. He winked, so I knew we were tied.

For the final bout, we took ten minutes to rest. Burpees were intense, and we'd been working the hell out of our arm, leg, back, and stomach muscles. They were all important for these. As we waited, Griffin came over to me. "These burpees are no joke. Have you ever done them?"

"It's kind of too late to worry about that, isn't it? Don't worry. I know what I got myself into, and yes, I've done them. Just sit back and watch."

As I walked off, I heard him say, "You've got this. Give him hell."

His words filled me with pride. Griffin came to stand in front of us. "You know the drill and what a burpee is supposed to be. The count is twenty-five. You're tied going into this. One win each and two ties each, and whoever gets done first or can do more than the other wins. On your mark, one, two, three."

We started in a squat position with our backs straight, knees bent, and our feet shoulder-width apart. From there, the next moves flowed one right after the other. I lowered my hands to the ground in front of me so they were just inside shoulder-width. I shifted my weight to my hands and kicked my feet back until I was on my hands and toes in a push-up position. I kept my body straight and did a push-up, then went right into a frog kick, which was just a jump back to my feet.

As I stood, I put my arms over my head and then jumped in the air, landing back where I had started in a squat. That was the start of another one. I completely ignored everyone and everything. I pushed my limit to do it as fast as I could. When I finally landed on my feet and knew I couldn't do another one, I stole a glance at Rockwell. He was on the ground with his arm over his eyes. That's when the cheering registered.

I was swarmed by the Patriots and Dad. The other guards congratulated me, but I wasn't sure if it was sincere. As Dad hugged me, he told me what I had missed. "You did thirty-five to his twenty-eight. He couldn't keep up, and his legs gave out."

"Really?"

"Really," Griffin said as he joined us. I was taken aback when he gave me a quick hug after Dad let go of me. As soon as he let go, the other Patriots each gave me one. By the time they were done, I saw Rockwell walking off. The other guards came over to me.

"That was amazing, Hadley. I had no idea you were that strong," Holloway admitted.

"Neither did I," Sanders said.

The rest pretty much agreed. "You didn't just do that without a lot of time and practice. I've seen you in the gym. You don't do those," Ortiz stated.

"You're right. The times you all have seen me working out, I haven't. Your misunderstanding was that those were the only times I worked out, and I only did the girly stuff. My mom was kidnapped and murdered. There was no way my protection would ever only reside in others, no offense. I've learned many things over the years. In order to do those things, I had to be strong and fast. I hope there are no hard feelings."

They shook their heads. "We're not the ones you have to worry about having hard feelings. You showed up Rockwell," Ellis stated.

"No, he did that on his own by assuming because I have a vagina, I'm weaker and less than him. Hopefully, this defeat will make him rethink his attitude."

Ellis sighed, but he did nod. They didn't stay long. After they left, Dad came back over to me. "I think this calls for a drink, and then you can tell me what happened this morning in the gym to start all this. I know you were out here and challenged him, and the winner determined whether the Patriots stayed, but I didn't hear why."

I glared at Griffin. He shrugged and raised his brow. Knowing I had no choice, I settled for glaring at him for a few seconds, then took Dad's arm and walked back to the house. Our five silent elite guards followed us.

We ended up in Dad's study. I told him to save the champagne, so we opened the bar he kept in there. He had a variety of alcohol. Heath did the honor of pouring him and me a shot of tequila. Griffin and Dad both had Dad's favorite scotch, a Macallan 25. Justin, Ben, and Beau went for the whiskey. Once we all had a glass, Dad raised his and made a toast.

"To my beautiful, strong, and amazing daughter, you made me proud, but then again, you always do. *Slàinte Mhath*."

I should've known he'd say cheers in Scottish. It was where our ancestors were from. We all said it back then drank. Instead of slamming them back, we took our time. Macallan and the whiskey, in particular, deserved to be sipped, not used as a shooter. We sat down and enjoyed them. Once our glasses were empty, Dad leaned toward me.

"Hadley, tell me what happened this morning in the gym."

"Why did you tell him?" I asked Griffin.

"He didn't tell me anything. Porter overheard Heath and Justin talking about what was going on outside. They had no idea he was around. You know he likes to ghost around to be sure everything is in order. He came to tell me, and that's why I went outside. He didn't hear what exactly happened."

Heath and Justin groaned. Griffin frowned at them. I hoped they wouldn't get into trouble for it. "Fine, I'll tell you." As quickly as possible, I filled him in on what happened. By the time I was done, he didn't look happy at all. I didn't want to get Rockwell fired. He'd always looked out for me. I only wanted him to learn a lesson.

"Even if he'd won, there's no way I would've sent the Dark Patriots away! Your life is at stake. Is he stupid to think he and the others can protect you better than they can? I know you spent the day evaluating them. Who should I keep, and who should I let go? I can't have men unable to protect my daughter. I'll make sure they have a generous severance package, but they can't stay," he told Griffin. Crap, things were about to get serious.

Griffin: Chapter 6

"Mr. Gerard," I started to say until he raised his brow, then I changed it. "Travis, I don't think all your men are unsalvageable. They have the foundation of skills we need. We just need to build upon them. There are security measures going into place as early as tomorrow. We'll add as many as we need. We'd like to begin tomorrow, working with the guards and security personnel to get their skills up to par."

"What about Rockwell? I don't think he's one you want to stay."

I heard Hadley make a slight protesting sound when her dad said that, but she didn't say anything. As much as I personally disliked Rockwell, he was one of the best we had, although his attitude had to go if this was to work.

"Not necessarily. If he can get rid of his attitude toward us and focus on the job he's paid to do, I want him to stay. He, Ellis, and Fletcher are the best. We can work with the others who function as your personal guards. Some of the ground and gate guards have to go. They're not gonna cut it."

"Okay, if you're sure, but I'll make it clear to him if he doesn't straighten up, he's gone. Hadley, do you have any objections to that?"

"No, Daddy, I don't," she responded quietly. I tried

to determine whether she was lying, but I couldn't tell.

"Fine, I'll tell the ones we need to let go tomorrow. I have to get their severance packages together, and the payroll manager has to cut their final checks. How do we fill their spots? There's no way I can get more guards from the staffing agencies I use in a day or even two. They have to be vetted and the whole nine yards."

"True, and you can work on doing that for when we're no longer here. For now, we can take care of it for you. We have men and women we can use. If we need more and we don't personally have them working for us, we have others. How do you feel about bikers?"

Hadley gasped, and her mouth fell open. Gerard didn't even blink. "I assume you mean the ones like Anderson's niece is married to?"

I slowly nodded. I didn't know Anderson had told anyone about Zara and the Warriors. "Yes, that club and others like them. They're our friends, and we've worked together in the past several times. Sean, Mark, Gabe, and I stake our lives and reputations on them."

Justin told them, "My brother and my cousin are members of the club in Dublin Falls, Tennessee."

"My sister is married to one there too, and they rescued her after she was taken and raped and was to be sold. That's how I met the Dark Patriots and decided to join them when I got out of the service. They helped with her rescue," Beau said through gritted teeth. He still hadn't fully forgiven himself or his brothers for all being away when it happened. Hadley gasped.

"One of my sisters is married to Blade in Dublin Falls, who is Justin's cousin. They saved her from the crazy cult we grew up in. Heath and I served together. That's how we came to be part of the Patriots. We can all vouch for them unconditionally. Many of them served as well," Ben told them.

"Wow, Anderson never told me all that. Okay, I say I don't have an issue with bikers as long as they're part of the clubs you trust. How soon can we have replacements here for the men I have to let go?" Travis asked.

"I'll have the first few here by noon tomorrow. We'll go from there. Until we have the current guards better trained, I need you and your daughter to remain here at the house. We can't risk you out in public."

"Dad, we can't—" Hadley started to protest, but he cut her off.

"Hadley, we'll make it work. You can postpone your trip, and we'll figure out the rest."

She didn't appear happy, but she didn't argue. Whatever useless or insignificant things she had planned could wait. "Good. I suggest if we're gonna make this happen, we need to get to work. I'm leaving Heath with you, Travis. Ben will watch over Hadley. Until you talk to your men, I don't want them guarding you. I especially don't want Rockwell guarding Hadley while he's pissed."

"He won't hurt me," she argued.

I flicked my eyes to her arm, then her face. She hadn't told her dad he left bruises. If she resisted, I would. She received my message loud and clear. She gave me an upset look, but I didn't care. I was here to keep her safe, not be her friend.

After the details, we got up to go our separate ways. Hadley said goodbye to her dad and then walked out. Ben followed her. Heath took up his position outside the closed study door. Beau and Justin came with me.

"She's not happy with you," Beau observed unnecessarily.

"I don't give a damn if she is or not. We're here to keep them safe. I'm not looking to make friends."

"What about looking for something else?" Justin asked.

"I'm here to do a job, and so are you. Don't forget it," I warned them. They both nodded.

As I went to call the rest back at headquarters, I tried not to think of Justin's something else comment. It wasn't in the cards, and I wouldn't waste my time thinking about it. The sooner we found whoever was behind this and eliminated them, the better. I could go back to Hampton and forget Hadley Gerard, and she'd go on to live in her ivory castle like the princess she was.

It wasn't until the next morning that Travis was able to talk to the guards we'd determined could stay if they agreed to do as we said and would work to bring their skills up to par with what we expected. He spoke to them after he discussed the severance packages with those who we believed wouldn't be able to keep them safe no matter what we taught them. I offered to be present when he told them the news, but he refused. He said it was ultimately his decision, and he'd do it. I was a little surprised when Hadley sat in on all of them.

I'd just finished explaining to the ones we wanted to keep how the process would go. I scanned all their faces intently as I explained. I knew my guys were doing the same. We were trying to see who was merely agreeing to keep their job but wouldn't do what was needed. Most looked a bit apprehensive, which wasn't unusual.

Rockwell was the one I watched closest. He'd come in and sat down, not saying a word to anyone, not even the other guards. I noticed they sat away from him. He was trying to hide his hostility after the explanation of who went and who stayed. I didn't want him here, but he was one of the best. I couldn't let my personal dislike of him dictate our decision. If he stayed in line, then we had to keep him.

After we finished, Travis addressed them. "I know some of you may be upset about the decisions made. It wasn't personal, and the people I let go weren't left adrift without a generous severance. However, this situation has illustrated to me how lax our security is in some ways. We haven't stayed current, and this threat, I believe, is real. With that said, I've given the Dark Patriots the authority to act in my name when it comes to anything dealing with security on the estate and every place in between, including my offices. If you won't abide by that, give them respect, or follow their training program to hone your skills even more, then please see me afterward. I'll arrange for your severance as well."

No one said a word. He let the silence stretch for a good minute or two before he nodded at me. "Griffin, would you like to fill them in on what they can expect today and in the coming few days? We're gaining several new people, correct?"

"New? How? It takes weeks, sometimes months, to hire a qualified bodyguard. I wasn't aware of any candidates being vetted," Ellis asked, sounding mystified and slightly miffed.

"We haven't done that. We want you to work on those hires so that when we leave, you have properly trained guards to fill the gaps. We'll be happy to help you with the process. Since you're the guy in charge of all the guards, I understand. We'll work on that together. However, in the interim, we are bringing in our people who are vetted and qualified. We'll start with more operatives from Dark Patriots. If we find they're not enough, we have another bunch we can ask to help," I explained.

"What makes these people qualified? All we have is your word," Rockwell popped off. I knew the little bastard wouldn't be able to remain quiet. I narrowed my eyes on him. I was about to put him in his place when Travis did.

"I say they are based on what the Patriots shared with me. Make no mistake. You work for me. If you want to continue to do so, you'll stop challenging every decision Griffin or his men make. Or would you like my daughter to beat you again in a physical challenge and find herself a new bodyguard? Straighten up, or it will be arranged. I hate to see you lose five years of great employment over an attitude problem."

Everyone stared in shock. You could tell Travis was about at the end of his patience with Rockwell's behavior. I fought not to grin and clap. I heard a faint snicker from somewhere, but I couldn't tell who had made it. I knew it wasn't one of my guys because they were next to me, and it came from across the room.

The thunderous expression on Rockwell's face was getting worse. Suddenly, the door opened, and Hadley walked in. I didn't know she would be attending this meeting. She gave us an apologetic smile. "I'm sorry I'm late. I had an important call that I had to take. Please, don't mind me," she said as she slipped onto a chair next to her dad.

As I watched her move to that seat, I saw I wasn't the only one. Everyone gave her a short glance, and some had a smile or nod for her. Only Rockwell stared at her the whole way. Even after she sat down, he kept looking back at her. The hairs on the back of my neck stood up. My trust level with him when it came to her was almost zero. I'd see about having him reassigned. Ortiz or Sanders could take over full time. They'd both let me know that when they came today. They're full-time jobs had been reduced to part time or more like as needed.

Neither was where I wanted them to be skills-wise, but they took directions and tried hard to do everything we asked for yesterday. If we assigned both of them to her and found someone else to help, she'd be fine.

I cleared my throat. "We're through the explanations, and they know we have people coming from our teams. The first ones should actually be here any moment. They texted to let me know before we started this meeting that they were close. We'll introduce you to them, and then your assignments will be given out. Every day, we'll hold a variety of skills training sessions. There will be different instructors based on the skill being taught. You're expected to attend the ones you're assigned. You'll be given a deadline by which to have them completed. We don't have time to do this leisurely. The faster, the better. It's vital you do it and put your all into it."

Fletcher raised his hand. I nodded at him. "What if we can't work our eight hours and then work even more on top of it? Don't get me wrong, I want to do it, but I take care of my mother at night while my wife works. She has dementia, and she can't be left alone, not even to sleep."

I felt for the man. Dementia is a horrible disease. I wasn't sure what to tell him. I was more than okay with working with him, but if he had to be home every night and he was doing guard duty full time to get paid, I wasn't sure how to circumvent it.

"Fletcher, you and I will work on this. I'll get someone who can stay with your mother at night when Ana works on the days you need to do your classes. This is an added work requirement, and I won't penalize you for it. I know your circumstances, and I've already reached out to a couple of staffing agencies. Don't worry, I'll cover the cost as well since it's work-related." Travis informed him.

The relief on Fletcher's face was obvious. I thought I saw his eyes get glassy. "Mr. Gerard, I don't know what to say. Thank you so much. I swear I'll get through the training as fast as I can, so you don't need to pay for someone long. Ana doesn't work every night, so she'll help cover some of it."

"We'll do it as long as we need to. Alright, anything else we need to know?" Travis asked the rest of them. They all shook their heads. We were interrupted by a knock at the door. Travis called out, "Enter." I wasn't surprised to see Porter walk in.

"Excuse me, sirs, but Mr. Griffin has several people here to see him. I was told earlier that they were expected. Do you want them brought in here, or should I take them to the study for refreshments until you're done?"

"Bring them in here, please. Thank you, Porter," I told him.

He gave me a slight bow. I thought it was odd but dignified for him to do it. It reminded me of times past, like in those old movies, when having servants was much more common. He walked out, and a minute later, he was back with our team. There were four of them, and I was glad to see them.

As they entered, everyone stared at them. I watched to see what their reactions would be to Mark in particular. He came in, looking like a biker with his tattooed arms straining the seams of his shirt. His jeans and black riding boots completed the look, along with the black leather jacket he had slung over one shoulder. His sunglasses were pushed up on his head, and his steely eyes scanned the room. He wasn't smiling. These days, it was Sloan and Caleb who made him smile and laugh, although we were getting more of them. The Mark we knew years ago had been irrevocably changed into Undertaker.

I motioned for them to join us at the front. They made their way over. Once they claimed a spot, I made introductions. I pointed to Mark first. “This is Mark. He’s one of the other co-founders of the Dark Patriots. We served together in the Navy. He was a SEAL as well. This is Aryan, Giovanni, and Jae-Joon, but he goes by Jae. They’re all experienced security specialists with our company. They’ll be helping not only with patrols, guard duty, and training, but Jae will also be adding more cameras where we think they’re needed and upgrading the alarm system.”

The guards murmured. I saw some apprehension when they looked at Mark. Wait until they discovered his nickname. It would inadvertently come out. We all called him that a lot. He didn’t mind. He said it was hard for him to remember to respond to Mark unless it was Sloan using it after living as Undertaker every day for five years.

With nothing left to say at the moment, I turned it back over to Travis. He didn’t waste time dismissing the others after telling them to go about their usual duties until we came to find them. After the last one left, which, no surprise, was Rockwell, who was eyeing us and Hadley, Travis came up to the new additions with his hand out and a smile on his face.

“It’s so good to meet all of you. I’m Travis Gerard. Please call me Travis. Welcome to our home and thank you for coming to help us. I thought it best to get them out of here so we could relax and talk freely. This is my daughter, Hadley. Please sit. Can we get you anything to drink?”

They shook their heads. I knew they were taken aback by his friendliness even though I’d warned my brothers. Hadley was smiling at them. I saw Aryan and

Giovanni eyeing her appreciatively, even though they knew better than to do anything about it. I'd have to remind them of that fact just in case it slipped their minds.

"Hello and welcome. Thank you so much for coming to help us. I'd like to talk about something before we get into whatever we need to discuss. I planned to talk to you about it yesterday, but then things got busy and tense." She directed this at me.

"Sure, go ahead, what is it?" I asked as we all sat down.

"It's about the threat against me. I don't think we should be taking it so seriously."

I sat forward abruptly as I spoke in a low voice, the one I used when I was trying to intimidate someone. It wasn't intentional. It just slipped out before I could stop it. "What the hell are you talking about? They specifically said they'd make you experience a fate worse than death before they killed you and sent you back to your dad in pieces, Hadley! What's not serious about that? Have you lost your mind?"

"Don't get all snarly with me, Griffin Voss! Just let me explain. Yeesh! There aren't many people outside of this house and a few at the office who know I even exist. After all these years, it's suspicious that suddenly, my identity would be exposed and me targeted. Dad is the face and backbone of the company. If they want to mess with the completion of the latest project, they'll get more of a response by taking Dad and holding him for ransom or, God forbid, killing him. Doing that to me won't destroy Gerard Industries with Dad there. The board will be able to continue it. I think it's a diversion.

The focus is being shifted to me, leaving him more vulnerable. I want him to have more protection on him rather than on me. Two guards should be more than enough for my detail."

You could've heard a pin drop when she was done. The frowns on everyone's faces told me what they thought. It was the same as me. There was no way in hell we'd have less protection for her. Both of them were our priority. Before I could tell her that in no uncertain terms, Mark surprised me by speaking up. Usually, he kept his own counsel until it was needed.

"Hadley, I'd hoped you'd learned enough over the past couple of days to know there's no way we're pulling protection off you to put on your dad."

She opened her mouth, but he stopped her. "Hold on, let me finish. We plan to provide extra protection for your dad as well. You're right. This could all be a diversion tactic, but we won't take the chance we're wrong. Our mission is to always protect our country, the innocent, and those unable to protect themselves. What your dad's company does for our country earns him our protection on its own. Add to it you're innocent and less able to protect yourselves than we are. You're not getting rid of us until this is over. My wife would kick my ass if I went home and said we didn't do our job."

I snickered. I couldn't help it. He was a monster of a man, but he wasn't lying about Sloan. She was a badass. All you had to do was hear how she went undercover with him into an outlaw MC and freed more than one club from their poison. Plus, she was a Marine before she joined us.

"What's so funny?" Hadley asked.

"I was picturing Sloan doing it. She's a mean thing. She has to be to live with Undertaker and put up with him. He's not lying about her, though. So you see, you have to let us do both and not give us grief about it in order to protect him."

She glanced at him, and I saw her mouth twitching. She finally got it under control. "Should I ask how you got the name Undertaker?" she asked Mark.

"One day, when we know each other better, I'll tell you. Just know I come by it honestly."

"Is this look of yours for fun, or do you actually ride?" she unexpectedly asked.

"I ride. In fact, I rode here."

"Cool. I'd love to see your bike and go for a ride sometime."

"Whoa, that's not happening. Only his old lady, his wife, I mean, rides with him," I jumped in to warn her.

She rolled her eyes at me. "I wasn't suggesting I ride with him. I have my own bike. It's just been a few months with the weather since I went out, and I'm antsy. If we have a nice day and you think we can do it safely, then I'd love to go. Do any of the rest of you ride? We have more than one motorcycle in the garage you can use."

I was stunned by the news she rode. I couldn't imagine her doing it as a passenger, let alone by herself. Then again, I hadn't imagined her capable of what she did yesterday in the contest against Rockwell. For a spoiled rich girl, she had a few good qualities, I guess.

"I do, and so does Griffin. Sean and Gabe want to learn," Beau told her.

"Well, you're both welcome to use them if we get to go. Now that I know you'll keep Dad well covered, I feel much better. What do you need from me to help you with the training? Since I can't go anywhere right now, you have extra hands to use."

Giovani smiled at her. "Well, what is it exactly you can do that you think will help train your guards? It sounds kinda backward for the person being protected to be training her protectors."

"Well, I could put them through the physical assessment gauntlet you had them do yesterday. I assume you'll do it a few more times to help you gauge their improvement. Firearms training is a must, I assume. And don't forget hand-to-hand combat. I can help with that, too."

I didn't know who was more stunned—our newest arrivals or us, specifically me. I glanced over at Travis to see if he would tell me she was messing with us. He was smiling. When he saw me looking at him, he shrugged.

"What can I say? She's been taught since I lost her mother to protect herself in as many ways as possible. Even though she's more than good at all those things, I've never left her totally unprotected at all times. I can't take that chance." I could hear the sorrow in his voice. He genuinely loved his wife. I couldn't imagine losing someone you loved that much and in such a horrible way. Add to it, he lost a child, too. It was inconceivable.

"I understand. I'm not sure if Hadley's help will be a benefit or not if her skills are as good as you say. Some might feel threatened or stifled by her being there," I pointed out.

"On the other hand, she could motivate them, especially if she's better than them. I say let's have her come and observe, and then we can decide. If nothing else, we could privately evaluate her skills and give her pointers on improvement if needed," Mark suggested.

I was mulling the idea over when Beau added something. "You're worried Rockwell will lose his shit and give us more attitude, aren't you?"

I nodded. Travis interjected his own comments. "If he does and you deem him too much trouble to deal with, he's gone. Hadley, I know he's been with you a long time, and you two get along well, but I can't have that. Do you know what's up with him? I've never seen him act this way. Have you and you've never told me?"

She shook her head. "No, he's never been close to this bad. Sure, I suspected he was a chauvinist, but he kept that tendency under tight wraps around me. His arrogance was always there, just not so blatant. He's skilled, and he likes to show it, but then again, who doesn't? I don't have a clue why he's acting like an ass. His loss to me yesterday didn't help, but I couldn't let him go unchallenged. He feels threatened by Griffin and the others. If he gets to be too much, you're right. He has to go."

I was surprised she was okay with it. Maybe I was wrong about them having a relationship, although it brought up a couple of topics we needed to discuss. Before I could bring them up, Aryan popped in.

"What loss are you talking about?"

Heath was more than happy to explain. The whole time he did, she merely sat there looking calm. There were the expected exclamations and congrats when he was done. I jumped back in before we got derailed again.

"There are a couple of things we need to discuss. First, it involves Rockwell. While he remains here, however long that may be, I don't believe he should remain as Hadley's main bodyguard. In fact, I don't think he should guard her at all. His attitude, the way he acted in the gym yesterday, and then the challenge, he's pissed, and I don't want a man like that watching her or you," I told Travis.

He frowned and nodded. Hadley looked somewhat worried. "If we do that, won't it make him worse rather than better? He'll see it as a punishment. What can you have him do if he's not being a bodyguard?"

"It might make him worse and if it does, he makes the decision for us. It might have the opposite effect, and he'll straighten up because he realizes what he's risking. He'll know we're not fooling around. He could be put on gate duty or roving patrols. Or we could have him as part of the team who provides security when your dad goes to the office or to anything outside the house that can't be postponed. In a group, I'd be fine with him. He's skilled, one of the best you've got, but he needs to be brought to heel."

"Who would take his place?" Travis asked.

"Both Sanders and Ortiz mentioned to me this morning that they're available to work full time. Their other jobs recently went to per diem. I know they need to improve, but both of them, together with help from one of us, would be more than adequate. They can more than keep an eye on her here. If she needs to leave the house, then for sure, we'd have one of us added to her team."

I saw my guys eagerly perk up—well, all but Jae and Mark. They'd do it, but as married guys, they didn't have other reasons to be guarding a beautiful woman other than it was a job. Instantly, I decided none of them would be chosen.

"Who would we add from our team, or have you decided yet?" Mark asked. His voice had an odd tone, which I couldn't place. He was staring intently at me.

"All things considered, I think it's best if I'm the one. If I can't go for some reason, then it'll be you or Jae. How does that sound?"

I didn't want to dictate to Mark. He had as much right to decide as me. He shrugged. "I'm fine with it. You've been here longer, so I'll defer to you on this."

"You and Undertaker will be so busy with so many things. Why don't you let one of us take this off your plate?" Giovanni asked.

"Yeah, we can do this," Ben added. I saw the others all nod.

"It's not a problem. We'll keep it that way." I told them.

There were disappointed looks but no more protests. I looked at Hadley. "Any comments?"

"Nope."

"Good. Now, this next one is kinda personal and I

don't mean to pry but we need to know everything."

"Okay, what do you need to know?" she asked.

"In order to manage your protection, we have to know everyone who's a part of your life, regardless of their capacity. You gave us the names of your close friends so they can be vetted. We need the same for any men you have in your life. Who should we expect to want to come calling? You realize we can't allow them contact with you while this is going on. If you'd rather tell me in private, I understand. I'm sorry if I'm embarrassing you."

"If you cared about embarrassing me, you wouldn't have asked it in the first place in front of everyone and my dad. Lucky for you, he knows everything about me. As for the names of the men in my life, I assume you want to know who I'm fucking."

"Hadley! There's no need to be so crude," Travis hissed.

"Why not? That's what he wants to know. I guess him asking about men rather than a man tells me what he thinks of me. Well, Mr. Voss, here are the names of my current lovers, fuck buddies, and booty calls. None. I have no boyfriend or anything else. However, if I happen to pick up someone for a one-night stand, I'll try to get his name before I screw him. Now, if you'll excuse me, I have work to do."

She stood up and marched to the door. "Hadley, come back here," Travis called after her. She didn't acknowledge him.

I felt conflicted as I watched her go. A part of me wanted to go after her and bring her back and apologize. Another was happy to know she didn't have a man, although the one-night stand remark I didn't like. Lastly, I was conflicted by the fact I cared if she had one or a million lovers. It didn't matter other than for our protection detail. I wasn't looking to get involved with her. She was a client and even if she wasn't, rich women with their entitlements didn't interest me. She had to have them. I just hadn't discovered them yet.

"Way to go," Mark muttered in my ear as the others all murmured. Travis looked upset. Shit, I'd have to apologize to him. Damn, why couldn't shit be simple?

Hadley: Chapter 7

The past two days had been decidedly frosty at home. Well, only when it came to me and Griffin. Anytime we met, I made sure to keep our conversations brief, to the point, and strictly business. Yeah, I was still pissed over how he'd asked what he did in front of Dad and the others, but more so that he obviously thought I was a slut. The knowledge hurt, and I didn't know why. Who was he that I should care what he thought of me? No one.

He attempted to apologize, but I waved him away. Our interactions were stilted at best. Thankfully, I could relax with the others. It was them I spent time with as they put the guards through their various training sessions. So far, I'd only watched, but I was itching to join them. It was obvious the Patriots were extremely skilled.

I had really good instructors over the years, but I knew I could learn even more from these guys. Dad saw how upset I was. He tried to talk to me about it, but I just couldn't do it. Instead, I assured him I was fine. I knew he didn't believe me, but he let it go.

Another thing that sucked was Rockwell. As expected, when he found out he was no longer my main personal bodyguard, he'd been super upset. He ranted about it and demanded to know why. I wasn't there when they told him. They thought it was best if I wasn't.

I got the story secondhand from Beau and Heath.

Those two became the ones I spent the most time with, and I found them to be friendly and good company. Sure, Heath liked to flirt a bit, but I didn't take it seriously, and he didn't go too far. It was kinda nice to feel attractive, if I was honest. Beau was like having an older brother. All the guys were attractive and to see any of them was a treat for the eyes. I had to admire their looks and physiques, but much to my chagrin, only one captivated me, and it was Griffin, the asshole.

Anytime I caught him working with the men, I had to stop and watch, although I made sure he didn't see me. In order to avoid more discomfort over my infatuation with him, I stopped going to the gym in the mornings. I was working out late at night. Lucky for me, Sanders and Ortiz didn't seem to mind, and they would join me sometimes.

Today, I had to talk with Dad and then the Patriots. I needed him to back what I was going to tell them. There was no way I could get out of this. It was too vital. I knocked on his study door. If he wasn't in his bedroom or the dining room for a meal, he could be found here, hard at work. He worked too hard. I needed a way to get him to take more breaks. An idea began to form. One that would still keep him safe but would be fun for us.

"Come in," he answered.

Opening the door, I walked in and came to a halt. Griffin and Mark, or Undertaker, as I'd come to think of and call him, were sitting there with him. I got an expectant look from all three of them.

"Oh, sorry, I didn't know you were busy. I'll come

back later." I tried to back out of the room, but Dad stopped me.

"No, don't go. We were just finishing up. Come, sit, and then we can talk. Give us five more minutes," Dad said as he gestured to an open chair. Knowing I'd look churlish if I left, I closed the door and went to take a seat. Thankfully, it was next to Undertaker. He gave me a lip twitch. I knew that was his version of a smile. I smiled back. I ignored Griffin completely, but I could feel his gaze on me.

"I think today's schedule sounds good. Is there anything you need that I can provide? Do you need more equipment or anything?" Dad asked them.

"No, we've got everything we need. I do want to ask Hadley when she's planning to join in on the training sessions. She said she wanted to, but my understanding is she's only been observing them," Griffin said, bringing attention to me.

Damn him, I knew he was doing it to get me to acknowledge him. Steeling myself, I gave him a calm, blank look. "I decided it's best if I don't. I don't want to make them self-conscious. Beau and Heath have been great at doing things one-on-one with me. I'm more than comfortable with whatever they want to teach me." I didn't mean to make it sound sexual, but the way his mouth tightened, I knew it had. Dad was frowning at me, but he didn't say anything.

"I'd prefer you not to stick to only a couple of us. We all excel in different things, and the more people who evaluate you, the better," he added.

"Undertaker, would you be willing to evaluate me? I'd be fine with that, too."

He gave me a slightly amused look. "I wouldn't mind at all, but I need to discuss it with Wraith. Why don't we put this on hold? We can talk about it later. We need to get started, and you have something you need to talk to your dad about."

"You're right, I do. I'll catch you later."

Dad cleared his throat to break the tension. "Well, I think that's all. Thank you for the briefing. I'll see you later."

They got up, knowing they'd been dismissed. They bid him goodbye and me as well. I threw out a casual one. I met Undertaker's gaze but looked off to the side of Griffin's face as I said goodbye to him. Once the door closed behind them, Dad called me out.

"Hadley, you need to get over this attitude you have with Griffin! He's here to help us, and you being a brat toward him isn't helping anyone. Everyone feels it. Ignoring his offer to help improve your skills is childish. I understand he embarrassed you by asking if there was anyone in your life, but it wasn't that horrible."

"It's not the fact he asked in front of everyone and you! It's the fact he insinuated there were several men in my life, in whatever capacity, which makes it clear he thinks I'm a slut! I haven't been in a relationship in four years. I don't go out having one-night stands or shit. You know what my life revolves around. I felt dirty after he said it. And who is he to think that? So, I decided to avoid any unnecessary interactions. It's for the best. I'm learning plenty from the others. Can we not talk about it? We have something more important to talk about."

He studied me for several moments, then sighed. "Fine, we'll table it for now, but I'm not letting this go.

What is it that's so urgent?"

"I need to go to the office and do a hands-on day. I can't do any more remotely. It's crucial I do it, and I have to do it soon."

He winced. "I was afraid of that. You know they're not going to like it. They want us here, and I don't disagree. Out there, there are too many variables they can't control."

"Variables to control? You sound more like them every day." I chuckled.

He grinned at me. "I know. Okay, so we have to convince them you need to go, so we have to tell them why."

"No, we don't. There's no reason for them to know. They have to be like almost everyone else. What I do there isn't their business. You know it's better that way," I warned him.

"Hadley, they can be trusted."

"Maybe they can, but why tell them? There are only a handful of people who know. If more do, we might not be able to keep it under wraps. It's best that it continues to be this way, especially now."

He winced again, then sighed as he nodded. "You're right. I don't like it, but we'll continue as we have. How can we convince them to let you go then?"

"Can you tell them there's something you have to do there that you can't do remotely and then say you want to take me along to get me out of the house? Maybe tell them I'm getting stir-crazy. When we get there, we can both go together to where I need to be. They can stay outside. There's no need for them to stand inside. Tell them it's top secret or something."

"I could do that. Ansel and the other board members have been clamoring for a meeting and an update. I could combine that with the work I have to do. I'll tell them I have to be there to supervise and even be hands-on for a critical part of the project or it won't progress."

"Sounds good to me. Can we get them to take us in the next hour or so? I need several hours."

"I'll make it happen. You go get ready and let me handle them. I'll let you know when we're leaving."

Jumping to my feet, I rounded his desk and kissed him on the cheek. "Thanks, Daddy! I love you."

He smiled at me. "I love you, too. Now, try to forgive Griffin. I don't think he meant it the way you took it."

I rolled my eyes but nodded. It was all I could do not to skip out of his office. I was about to be free for a few hours and do something I wanted to do. I rushed to my room to get ready. I had to be dressed for the part.

❧❧❧

An hour and a half later, we were in the car, on our way to Gerard Industries' office and research complex. I could barely contain my excitement. The Patriots seemed less thrilled. They all wore grim expressions on their faces, at least the ones who came with us. We not only had half of them, but we had some of our regular guards.

We had Griffin, Undertaker, Beau, Ben, Ortiz, Sanders, Ellis, and Royce with us. I thought it was a bit much, considering there was security at the office. No one could just drive up to the building. They had to stop at a gate with armed guards and be allowed inside. Once visitors got to the building, there were more guards who would check them out and run them through the metal detectors.

When we left our estate, we went out the back way. It wasn't well known we had a rear exit, which the Patriots liked. They hoped to get us in and out without anyone being wiser. For this reason, we went in their regular vehicles, not ours. I was fine with it, although I thought that having three big SUVs would still attract attention. As we rode along the roads into town, I couldn't help but be envious of Undertaker. He was riding alongside us on his motorcycle, what I wouldn't give to be on one of mine.

Dad had hated the idea of me getting on one, let alone learning to ride a motorcycle, but I'd insisted. After several lengthy arguments, he gave in. The only thing I had to do was wait until I was eighteen. I tried to get him to agree when I was sixteen, but he refused. In order to make me as safe as possible, he paid for several different riding instructors, and one had been all about defensive riding. There were never any guarantees when you rode but I felt better knowing what I did.

I was in one SUV with Dad, Ortiz, and Griffin. I would've preferred to have Ben or Beau, but I wasn't that lucky. In car two were Beau, Ellis, and Sanders. They were riding ahead of us. The other car had Ben and Royce and they were behind us. I noticed Griffin and Ortiz were constantly scanning around us and ahead. I caught Griffin looking in the rearview mirror over and over. When he did, he always made sure to hold my gaze if I happened to be looking. I tried to stop glancing at it, but I couldn't.

I could tell he wasn't happy with us leaving but, so far, he hadn't said anything. I knew Dad had to become insistent to get them to take him, and Griffin balked at taking me at all. I didn't understand why. They had to take men anyway. Besides, I still wasn't convinced I was the real target.

When they approached the gate, the guards came to attention as they saw three cars and a motorcycle. There were three of them there. I saw them speaking to Beau. They took what I thought were IDs from him. When the main guard walked off, the other two remained alert. They didn't have their guns drawn, but they seemed tense. I'd never seen them this way before. Sure, they checked people and stuff, but they never acted this way.

I wasn't sure why they were being so anal. They'd all met the Patriots and knew the other guards. Why the hold-up? "Why're they holding us up? They know all of us."

"They were told to check everyone regardless of whether they recognized them or not. It's good to stay in the habit," Griffin explained. I guess I could understand that, so I didn't say anything else.

"Why so impatient? You're just here to hang out and do whatever since you're bored at home. I promise we'll get you to your diversion as soon as possible." There was a slight bite to his voice. I wanted to tell him the real reason we were here—to make him eat those words—but I didn't. I pretended I didn't hear him. Dad gave my hand on the seat between us a squeeze.

I squeezed back. My mind was occupied with more important stuff than sparring with Griffin Voss. I had to keep my head clear today.

Eventually, Beau's car entered, and we were up next. They did greet Dad and me, but we still had to give them our IDs. It was a good five to seven minutes before we were all through and headed to our private parking. There was a private elevator, which we could take directly to our offices rather than going through the main lobby. They were all for us doing that.

Dad entered the code at the elevator and we all got in. Thank goodness it was a spacious one. Ten of us were still a squeeze. Just my luck, I was pressed up against Griffin. I tried not to let my body react. His smell was teasing my nose. I think it was his bodywash, but it was this woodsy scent that I found very appealing. His hard body wasn't doing me any favors either. At one point, I swore his hand caressed my back, but I had to be wrong.

When the door opened, I practically shoved the others out of the way and headed toward the lab. As we went, I made sure to speak so the others would hear us. "Dad, I know you want to go to the lab and work first. I'll come with you. It's been a while since I've seen what's happening down there."

He went with it without missing a beat. "I sure do. Guys, this part is top secret. I can't allow anyone in there who hasn't been read into the project. I'm sorry."

We'd reached the secure door to the lab. Griffin stopped us, of course. "Travis, I can't let you go in there alone. I have to ensure there's no risk to you or your daughter. Either one of us needs to be read into the project, or you can't go in. All my guys have greater than top-secret clearance. I'm sorry. I wish you'd told us this at the house."

I wanted to growl in frustration. Dad had the authority to determine who to allow access, just as I did, but I didn't want them, well, him, in there. However, it didn't look like I had a choice. I sighed. "Let him, Beau, Ben, and Undertaker in. It's fine," I told Dad.

"Are you sure?"

I nodded.

"What the hell is going on? Why are you asking her? In fact, if it's so top secret, why is she allowed in?" Griffin asked suspiciously.

I turned to look at him. "You'll see," was all I told him. Turning back, I punched in the code, then pressed my eye to the retinal scanner as I put my finger on the biometric pad. There was a ding, and the light turned green as the door unlocked. Dad pulled the door open and waved for us to go inside. Not surprisingly, Griffin and Ben entered first, with Beau and Undertaker bringing up the rear.

Inside, they were met by a few startled engineers and scientists. They gave us wide-eyed looks. Dad was quick to greet them and explain who our entourage was. As Dad spoke, Undertaker leaned down to whisper in my ear.

"You have a lot to explain, little missy. You're not what you want people to think, are you? Why hide it?"

"I don't exist, do I? It's for a reason. Although it looks like you guys are about to be let in on the secret," I whispered back. He gave me an assessing look and then nodded.

The engineers and scientists moved over to say hello to me. They always greeted Dad first, which was only right. It was his company, after all, well, partially. That was something else not for public knowledge.

"It's good to see you, Hadley. We've missed you. We have so much to show you, and we can't wait to see what you do today," Grace said excitedly. She was one of the scientists, along with Claire and Levi. The engineers were Nora, Henry, John, and Silas.

"I'm excited to see what you've done, too. Let me get changed, and then we'll get to it. I'll be right back. I just need to go to the ladies' locker room," I informed the guys.

"We need to check it first," Griffin said sternly.

"Then check it so we can get this show on the road. Dad, I'll be back."

I would've preferred one of the others to check it out, but it was Griffin. He made me stand outside until he came back. He gave me a puzzled look as I passed him to enter after he said it was clear. I had no doubt he'd stand outside the door and not allow anyone inside until I was done. Inside, I got into my locker and changed into my white antistatic gear. I even had coverings on my shoes and over my hair. Walking out, I saw Griffin's eyebrows shoot up. I admit, it gave me satisfaction to surprise him. He was in for a lot of those today.

Passing him, I went to Dad, who had gone to change too. We faced the guys. "We have to move into the actual assembly area. It's kept clean, and you have to wear suits like us. There can't be unwanted electrical charges or dirt. John, would you take them into the men's locker room and get them some suits, please?" I asked.

"Sure thing. Come with me, gentlemen."

"We'll have to go in pairs. Mr. and Ms. Gerard aren't to be left unattended," Griffin informed him. I saw how taken back John was, but he didn't say anything. As we waited for Beau and Undertaker to come back, I chatted with Claire, Grace, and Silas. It took about ten minutes to get everyone else suited up so we could enter. I was anxious to get the show on the road.

At the next door, we had to scan our prints. Opening the door, once again, two of them went first. It was Undertaker and Ben this time. The rest of us slowly followed them, with Griffin and Beau bringing up the rear. This room was my favorite. It was huge, with lots of space to work on more than one project at a time. The one that was the focus, and we were scrambling to get done, was in the back. When we got to it, I saw the guys' shock.

The Navy had been working on different guns and new ballistic options. The rail gun was one of those for many years. Our company was currently perfecting long-range, high-velocity, and hypervelocity projectile (HVP) gun-launched options that could be used in a variety of guns and weapons the Navy currently already had on their ships. When this was done, the missile defense and force protection it would give them would be wonderful. That was why the government was so anxious about us completing it.

I didn't waste time talking to anyone. I climbed

up on the raised platform, and Henry handed me my toolbox. I had my own, which no one touched. I opened it and went to work. The seven of them gathered around me to excitedly tell me everything they'd been doing even though we'd had contact every day over FaceTime. I got so lost in the work and what they were telling me that when I raised my head, it was to find three hours had gone by.

Dad had joined in the conversation, but I was the one to do the work. He was now talking to Silas. I groaned as I straightened my back. It cracked as I flexed it. I put my hands back there to try and rub it. I was startled when my hands were pushed out of the way, and big, strong ones took over. I moaned at how good it felt. I glanced back to find Beau rubbing my back.

"Woman, you sure know how to shock the shit outta someone. Why didn't you tell us you're a genius inventor or whatever, like your dad?"

"Why did everyone assume I was a useless spoiled snob? God, if you keep rubbing like that, I'll marry you. What do you say?" I teased him.

He grinned at me. He opened his mouth to smart off, but he was interrupted by a gruff voice. "Beau, I need you to go do a perimeter walk. It's your turn."

Beau snapped to attention, and his hands fell away. I wanted to cry. "Sure thing, Wraith. I'll see you later, Had," he told me before he walked off.

Ignoring Griffin, I started to get back to my work. His hand on my arm stopped me. Knowing I had no choice, I faced him. As I suspected, he was frowning.

"Why the hell didn't you or your dad tell us that

you actually work here? And what's going on between you and Beau? There's a no-fraternizing policy at the Patriots."

"You didn't need to know about me. As for Beau and me, we're friends; however, since we're both adults, I don't see what difference it would make if we were more than that."

"It makes a difference because we can't afford to have anyone's attention divided. You can't guard someone if you are involved with them. Period. If that's the case, I'll have him changed out to someone else. He can't be on this assignment."

I didn't want Beau to be sent away. I liked him but only as a friend. No way Griffin was doing that. "We're just friends. We're not fucking. Despite what you think, I don't sleep with every guy I see. I can be friends with a man without screwing him. Now, if you'll excuse me, I have more work to do. I'm at a critical point."

"Hadley, I never said I thought you slept with every guy you see."

"Maybe not in those words, but what you said made it clear. I'm not after any of your men, so you can stop threatening to make them leave. If I need sex, I'll be sure to go outside of your team," I hissed at him.

"Goddamnit, I—" he didn't get to finish because I walked off. I heard him say *"fuck"* and then he walked away.

It took some time to clear my head enough to get back to work. Finally, I got caught up in it and didn't come up for air for hours. I was like Dad when he got started. It made us focus well, but it could be tiring.

I'd inherited his love of things mechanical and even chemical, hence my degrees.

It was Ben who I found watching me this time. He came over to me and whistled. "Man, you sure get lost in that shit, don't you?"

I nodded. "I do. I always have."

"I gotta ask. What did you do to piss the bossman off so badly? He's walking around, looking like he's ready to kill someone." He shifted his eyes to the left. I did the same and saw a scowling Griffin watching us.

"He seems to think I'm sleeping or trying to sleep with all of you. He told me that wasn't allowed, and if it became an issue, he'd reassign you guys. Well, he was talking about Beau at the time, but still, he meant all of you. I assured him I wasn't trying to get any of you in bed, and if I needed sex, I'd be sure to seek a man outside the Patriots."

He let out a loud bark of a laugh, then quieted down when we became the center of attention. He lowered his voice. "Jesus Christ, no wonder he's looking ready to kill. Now, don't take this wrong, but if you were interested, I wouldn't say no, but I know that's not happening. You know why he's acting this way, don't you?"

"Because you can't guard your client effectively if you're in a relationship with them."

"It could affect it, but that's not why. Honey, Griffin has a thing for you, and he's fighting it like crazy."

I snorted. "Yeah, right. He thinks I'm a slutty, airheaded, spoiled brat."

"He might've thought some of those, but he can't ignore what we've seen today. Even before that, the real you was showing through. Despite himself, he was still attracted to you even though he thought you were a spoiled rich girl."

"You're crazy, Ben, there's no way..." I shut up when I saw Griffin stalking toward us.

Ben saw where I was staring, and he shut up after a quick, "We'll talk later."

"Is everything alright?" Grif asked.

"Everything's fine. Ben was just asking me about my work. If you'll excuse me, I think it's time to take a break. I need to use the ladies' room. No need to check it. No one has entered since we came in. They won't, by the way. Who you see are the only ones allowed in here," I told him quickly, then hurried off to the bathroom.

I did have to go, but not desperately. I needed some air. What Ben told me, along with how Griffin had been acting, had me confused. I needed to settle my mind before I could get back to work. Whatever was going on with him had to wait until later.

Griffin: Chapter 8

After we got back from Gerard Industries on Friday, I spent the whole weekend trying to understand what I'd learned that day and how I was feeling. Thank God I had work to distract me. It was now Monday, and I was still confused, but I knew something had to change soon. It was all Hadley Gerard's fault.

The woman was driving me insane. I didn't know how to feel or how to deal with it all. First, there was the fact I found out she wasn't the frivolous, lazy spoiled rich girl I assumed she was. After seeing her at work, I had to ask Travis about her. Recalling all he revealed still shook me.

"Travis, I have to ask. Why didn't you tell us Hadley had an actual role in your company? Why hide it?"

"We hide it because we're used to doing it. Remember, most people have no idea she exists. The staff do, but they were all carefully selected and signed ironclad non-disclosure agreements. Believe me, if they talked, they'd be ruined."

"Okay, I get why you don't tell the general public, but surely she's been seen or had to attend different work functions. We know about her, so why not tell us?"

"The rare times she's been exposed to the public, I introduce her as another engineer, which she is, and use her mother's maiden name, Mansell, which is how she's listed

in payroll and in her employee file. I hate hiding the fact I have a daughter, and once this whole nightmare is over, I'm done. It didn't keep her safe, so I'll deal with it. She's the future of Gerard Industries. In fact, all the paperwork is drawn up and signed. As soon as something happens to me or if I choose to execute it, she'll be named the CEO and Director of the company. All voting and stock rights will be hers. When it is executed or I die, she'll inherit everything. You asked why we didn't tell you. Why did you assume she was some kind of useless ornament who did nothing but shop and spend money?"

I felt foolish and embarrassed to answer him, but I did. "I've had some past experiences in our company as well as personal experience over the years. I've been around rich women, and they've always been the kind of women you described. You're right. I assumed she didn't have to work for anything she had, and she took rather than gave."

"And now you know that's far from my daughter. We're not selfish people. We give to others. We have concerns and causes. We try to use our wealth to make things better for those less fortunate than us. My daughter had to grow up fast and without a mother for the most part. I did what I knew, which was to immerse her in what I did. She has mechanical and science aptitudes like me. She's also a genius, literally. She graduated from college with her first doctorate in chemical engineering at sixteen and her second in mechanical engineering, specializing in mechatronics at nineteen. She has been the one mainly responsible for many of the developments the company has made over the past eight years or at least played a part in them.

"She sits in on the board of directors' meetings and provides input. Like the others, they've signed non-

disclosures too. When she's not working, she's involved in charity work, which gets identified merely as Gerard Industries, not as the work of Hadley Gerard. My daughter is a responsible, hardworking, and loving person."

I'd left that meeting feeling like the lowest asshole. He hadn't yelled at me or even threatened to have the Dark Patriots or just me removed from their security detail. He merely gave me disappointed looks and told me more about the things she'd done over the last several years. She was nothing like I thought.

You'd think that would help me, but it made things worse. All those things made her more desirable in my mind. I didn't like women who I couldn't hold a conversation with, even the ones I just fucked and was done with. I wanted to at least be able to talk some before doing the deed.

Take her intelligence, caring nature, beauty, and sexiness, and she was an irresistible package that I was barely resisting. And I couldn't stop resisting, not after making such a big deal about not getting involved with our clients and threatening to send all my guys home except Jae and Undertaker.

At night, when I went to bed, it was the worst. I dreamed of her. They were hot, sultry, and frustrating dreams. I imagined what she'd look like naked in my bed. I dreamed of the things I'd do to her and let her do to me. I'd kissed, licked, and touched every inch of her in my dreams. My mouth had been on hers, and my cock had been inside of her in every possible way. I woke up hard and could do nothing but jerk off to get some relief, as unsatisfying as it was. Once was never enough.

It was those dreams, the work, and everything

else that had me dragging all day. I attended all my training lessons, and I took my turns patrolling and monitoring the cameras for anything unusual, even though there were people who did that as their job. What I didn't get to do was lay eyes on Hadley. She was holed up in her room working was all I was told. She even took her meals there. I was assured by her dad that she was fine, and she did this from time to time.

By the time evening rolled around, I knew I had to take a break. I needed to ask one of my guys to take my last patrol so I could get some real rest. I was going to take a sleeping pill. I hated using them, and I rarely did, and never on an assignment, but I needed it. I called the guys to my suite. As they filed in and found a place to take a load off, they gave me puzzled and concerned looks.

"Hey, you look beat, Wraith. Are you alright?" Heath asked.

"Yeah, you look dog tired, man," Jae added.

"I am, and that's why I asked you all here. I hate to do this, but if I don't get some real sleep tonight, I'm gonna be useless. Will one of you take my last patrol and be on-call for anything coming up so I can take a sleeping pill? I hate to ask, and I usually never take them, but I can't take much more of this no-sleep shit," I grumbled tiredly. I hated to appear weak or struggling in front of our people, but it was happening.

"Hell yeah, I can do it. You get some sleep. You look like hell," Beau offered. Right after him, the rest were all offering to do it.

After profusely thanking them, I chose to let Beau do my patrol with Undertaker as the on-call person.

After they assured me they had it covered, they left to let me rest. Well, they all did except Undertaker. As the door closed behind the others, I laid my head back and closed my eyes. I was sitting on the sofa in the living area of my suite.

"What's up, Mark?"

"Wanna tell me why you're so frazzled and tired? It's not like you to get like this, especially on an assignment. You're used to going hours without sleep and for more than a day or two. Are you coming down with something?"

"Nah, I just can't get any sleep even when I have downtime. My mind won't shut off."

"You know what I'm thinking?"

"What?" I asked warily as I pried my eyes open to look at him.

"I think you've come down with Hadleyitis." He smirked.

"I don't know what the hell that is?" I lied.

"Like fuck, you don't. You want her, and you're fighting it for some stupid reason."

"I don't want her," I lied again.

"Okay, well, that's a good thing then. It'll prevent a fight anyway. I'll see you in the morning. Don't worry, I've got this tonight," he said as he headed for the door. I was up and across the room. I slapped my hand on the door to keep him from opening it.

"What fight? Who would I fight with?"

"Come on, just because you don't find her attractive doesn't mean the rest of the men here don't, and I don't just mean ours. I know more than one of our guys would give his left nut to have her in his bed. As long as it doesn't interfere with guarding her or her dad, it's all good. I'll let them know."

"Who the fuck wants her? Tell me," I snapped. All sleepiness was gone. Anger pumped through my veins. I wanted to call them back and find out who dared to want her. If they were having dreams like mine, I'd kill them.

He threw back his head and let out a loud bark of laughter. "I knew it. You're fucking gone on her."

I let go of the door and moved away. "No, I'm not. It's just not professional. Tell them that. Anyone touching her will find their asses off the case and maybe fired."

"I'll let them know, but I don't think it'll deter a determined man. See you in the morning. Sleep tight," he said as he opened the door and walked out. As it closed, I fought not to go after him.

It took me a couple of hours to settle down, even with the aid of the pill. Finally, I found myself getting drowsy. My eyelids fluttered until eventually they closed, and that's all I remembered.

❧❧❧

A persistent pounding slowly dragged me from a deep sleep. I didn't want to go, but something nagged at the back of my mind. It was telling me to wake up. Finally, hearing Undertaker yelling my name made me surface. I stumbled out of bed and to the door in the other room.

"Goddamnit, Wraith, open the fucking door, or

I'm coming in," he bellowed.

I jerked the door open to find he wasn't alone. Giovanni was with him. They pushed their way inside. "What the hell is going on?" I grumbled, my head still blurry.

"We have a situation. Are you awake enough to hear this?" Undertaker asked.

"Yeah, no, give me a minute. Jesus, I hate these damn pills. Okay, tell me," I said as I sat down. They found seats.

"Jae got an alert."

"Alert? What kind of alert?"

"The secret one we told no one about. The one he put on the doors of Travis and Hadley's bedrooms. That kind."

This woke me the hell up. "Whose door, and did we catch who it was? Or did Travis or Hadley set it off?"

"No, it wasn't them. They were both asleep. As for catching who it was, no, we didn't, because whoever it was knew about the cameras in the hallways, and they avoided every one of them or turned them away without being seen. It wasn't until the alarm went off when her door was opened that he or she knew anything was wrong. They beat their ass out of there before any of us could get to them. We've got the others out looking. Shit, we need those fucking dogs," Mark swore.

"Is she alright? Who do we have searching?" I was up and running to the bedroom to get dressed as I asked. I was in my damn underwear, and I couldn't go roaming the house or grounds like this.

"Just our guys. I didn't know who to trust out of the others. She's upset, and so is Travis. We have them secluded in his study, with Ben and Jae guarding the door. We wanted to let you know, and then we'll get out there," Mark answered from the doorway as I jerked on my jeans.

"Give me five minutes, and I'll be out there too."

"I think you'd better go talk to them. I don't like this. How the fuck could someone make it inside the grounds, let alone the house?" he snarled.

"It has to be someone with access or who lives here. It's the only answer."

"That's my guess, and it leaves us with fifteen people, assuming we're right. As unlikely as it is, there's still the chance someone got in," Giovanni said from behind him.

"Shit, you're right. Go. Make sure they stay in the study and know I'll be there shortly."

"We will," was all I got before they disappeared.

I rushed to put on the rest of my clothes and brushed my hair and teeth. The last thing I did before I ran out the door was to tuck my gun into my waistband and my backup into my boot. It didn't take me long to get to Travis's study on the first floor. Ben and Jae were alert. When they saw me coming, they gave me chin lifts and moved so I could knock and call out.

"Travis, Hadley, it's Griffin. I'm coming in."

"Please do," Travis answered back.

"You guys stick around," I informed Jae and Ben.

"Got it," Ben said.

Opening the door, I hurried inside. As I shut it behind me, I scanned to see how they were doing and, as always, looked for threats. It was automatic for me after all these years. They were sitting on his sofa. He had his arm around her, and her head was hanging down. My worry increased as I went to them. I sank down on my knee beside her.

"Hadley, I need you to look at me, please."

When she did, I didn't see what I thought I would. I expected fear or even tears. What I got was fire. She was pissed. Travis was the one who appeared to be worried. "Are you alright?" I asked.

"Hell no, I'm not alright! Some son of a bitch was in our house and tried to get into my bedroom. It wasn't by accident. They knew where the cameras were. I wanted to help find them, but I was told I had to sit in here on my ass like some damsel in distress. I want to be out there finding whoever it was," she snapped.

Seeing her so fired up made my desire for her burn hotter. It took all my restraint not to kiss her right there in front of her dad. Instead, I smiled at her, which surprised her. "Darlin', if you keep this attitude up, I might have a job for you after this is over with," I teased her.

She looked surprised for a second or two, then she laughed, and her body relaxed. "You couldn't afford me. I don't come cheap."

"We'll have to negotiate then. Okay, seriously, did you see or hear anything?"

"No, I was dead asleep, then suddenly that alarm Jae installed and told me to engage at night when I go to bed went off like a bullhorn. It damn near gave me a heart attack, and the way whoever it was ran, it did him too."

"Was it a man?"

"I think so. I mean, I don't know for sure but I just can't see it being a woman. Please tell me the guys have found something."

"So far, no, or they would've called me. If you two are alright, I'm going to leave Jae and Ben here, and I'll go join the hunt. They'll keep you safe."

"Go, we'll be fine. We're armed as well, and I promise we don't shoot without knowing who or what we're shooting at," Travis assured me. I wasn't thrilled having them armed, but I couldn't tell them no. It was their right.

Reluctantly, I got to my feet. After one last look, which was mainly at her, I left them. After I ordered the guys to remain there, I hurried outside and called Undertaker. I wanted to know where they were so I could search somewhere else. Whoever did it would pay for invading their home and trying to go for her. She was wrong. She was the target, not her dad.

We combed the estate for hours. Everyone who lived on it had to be woken up. All denied hearing or seeing anything. There was no way to know if they were lying or had left their homes. Damn it, we needed more eyes. It was too big with too many people for us to monitor it all.

It was almost dawn when we returned to the main house. I knew they were probably anxious to have an update, so we went straight to the study. All of us gathered there. None of the regular guards were invited. This had to be between us and the Gerards. As we'd searched and came up empty, the more convinced I became that we had to make a change. This only illustrated why. I hoped they felt the same, but if they didn't, I'd have to find a way to change their minds. I'd pulled Undertaker aside before we went inside and told him my thoughts. He was a hundred percent in agreement.

"Did you find anything?" Hadley asked as soon as we entered. She was pacing the room. Travis was sitting slumped on the sofa. He looked tired and pale.

"Let's sit down, then we'll tell you," I suggested.

Surprisingly, she went to sit by her dad without an argument. We all found a spot to sit or stand. Undertaker nodded to me when I looked at him. I guess he was leaving this to me. I was fine with taking point.

"We searched the entire estate. We found no one. There was evidence of some crushed shrubbery along a section of the stone wall in the southwest corner. It's possible whoever it was came in and went out that way. We spoke to all the staff who live on the estate, too. They all claim to have been asleep and didn't know anything was wrong until we woke them up."

"You sound like you don't believe them," Travis stated.

"I don't know if I do or not. At this point, I'm suspicious of everyone other than our men, which brings me to what I need to talk about. I want to separate you two. Alone, you're a big enough target, but together, it's too much. Plus, this property is too vast to keep secure. We have holes, as we found, even with all the extra cameras and alarms we installed. The fact the person knew where the cameras were suggests insider knowledge. They could work here or know someone who does."

"Where would we go?" Hadley asked.

"I have a spot in mind that I think would be ideal for you, Travis," Undertaker said quietly.

"Where?"

"I don't want to say where. Just know it's remote, off the grid, so to speak, meaning no one would tie it to me. It has security and can be defended. It's a cabin."

I was surprised he was offering his refuge. Since he and Sloan had gotten together, he had purchased a cabin, which they used as their getaway when things got too much for him. He was right. It would be ideal.

"Okay, if I agree to go there, where will you take Hadley?" Travis asked. I knew he'd be more worried about her than himself.

Undertaker glanced over at me, and I took my cue. "I have a place."

"Back in Hampton?" Travis asked.

"No, somewhere else. I'd want to take her where I'd have help protecting her without anyone guessing she'd be there," I explained.

"Can I know where that is?" he asked.

I shook my head. "No, like you, it's better if you don't know exactly. I can assure you she'll be safe, and it'll be no more than a day's travel away unless it becomes too dangerous and we have to go further. I know you don't like the idea, but we don't know how else to tighten the protection. You have all this, and then there's the corporate office. Hadley, do you have to go back for anything hands-on again?"

She thought for a minute or so before she answered me. "Technically, no. The engineers can handle it. I just prefer to be there, but as long as I can check it out before we deem it ready for testing, then I don't have to be there. That gives you a month, maybe six weeks, by my calculations."

"Make the arrangements. When do you need us ready, and how are we leaving so we aren't followed?" her dad asked.

"Where's your pilot? We saw the helicopter pad and the hangar where you keep two helicopters. That would be the best way, at least, to get you to a staging area and then take you from there, so even the pilot won't know where you went," Undertaker said.

The two of them exchanged grins. "That won't be an issue. Both helicopters can be taken, and no one will be the wiser," Travis told us.

"How? You have more than one pilot?" I asked.

"Yes, although we do employ a pilot, both of us are licensed pilots as well. I can fly one and Hadley the other. If we do that, I assume the other Patriots will return to your headquarters."

To say I was stunned was an understatement. We weren't expecting this, but after the past several days, I should know that this family was full of surprises. "That would be perfect. How quickly can you get some of your things together? We'd like to be out of here before noon. We'll need to make a few calls to get things set up. Try to do it quietly so no one will know we're leaving until the last minute. If they ask where you're headed, tell them you aren't sure. I wish there were another way, but I can't think of one."

"Honestly, I can't either. I hate leaving those who are trustworthy without answers, but since we don't know who it might be or how they're getting their information, we have to treat everyone as a suspect. I can be ready by ten. Hadley, do you think you can be ready by then?"

"Dad, I can pack in a hurry. I do have to call in and check with the others at the lab, but I'll act like it's a regular check-in and not say anything about going anywhere. If we're doing this, we need to eat breakfast as usual so no one suspects, and then we can pack and be ready to go. The helicopters should be gassed up and ready for takeoff. It's only a matter of doing our preflight checks. Who's flying with us versus driving back? I assume you're riding, Mark."

"I will, but I'll meet you, Travis, in Hampton, at Dark Patriots headquarters. I'll take you from there. We have a hangar nearby where you can store your helicopter. I'll have Ben fly with you."

"It works for me. I have the address. We'll need to clear our flight plans, too."

"Good, now who's going with me?" she asked.

"It's you and me. We'll be flying directly to our destination. I'll give you the specs in private so you can clear your flight plan as well. We won't need anyone to go with us. We'll have plenty of protection once we land."

She seemed to tense at my words, but then she relaxed. With this in place, we got started. I went with her to her office, which I'd only discovered she had, and I gave her our destination. I saw her surprise. I hoped that meant no one would guess. Soon afterward, I left her to do her thing while I made my calls and packed my stuff.

Hadley: Chapter 9

I had no idea exactly where we were going when Griffin gave me the flight plan. I knew the airport was a smaller regional one in eastern Tennessee, and I would be able to have the helicopter stored there. How far it was from our final destination, I didn't have a clue. All he told me was when we got there, there would be more people to keep me safe. I tried to suggest he send Dad to this place and let me go to the cabin, but he refused. He said Undertaker and some of their men would be more than adequate to keep Dad safe. I hoped he was right.

After landing and taking care of the helo, he led me to the airport's parking area. That's when I found out who was helping him. To say it was a shock was an understatement. Sitting there was an SUV surrounded by several motorcycles. On those motorcycles were leather-clad bikers. As we approached, they came off their rides. One stepped ahead of the others. I could tell, even with their sunglasses on, that they were all studying me. I tried not to squirm.

Undertaker had been intimidating, and these men had the same vibe—not that Griffin didn't—he did. It was just different. I couldn't explain why. The one in the lead stopped a few feet in front of us.

"Griffin, it's good to see you, man. It's been a while. You said you were bringing a guest and that you'd need a place to lie low and help to protect her, but you didn't tell me you were bringing an angel, and she was my future old lady." His gruffness changed to a low chuckle at the end. He took off his sunglasses, and I was caught by the greenest eyes I'd ever seen.

I could see the mirth in those eyes. I automatically smiled back. He held out his hand to me. "Hello, gorgeous, I'm Jinx. Welcome to Tennessee and our neck of the woods. Who might you be?"

"Jinx, lay off the charm. She's not here for you to play with. She's here for us to keep her safe. This is Hadley Gerard. Hadley, Jinx is the president of the Ruthless Marauders motorcycle club, as if you couldn't guess that. They're friends with us and several others."

"Oh, so you know the Warriors. Hello, it's nice to meet you and thank you for helping us out. Sorry, we dropped in uninvited. Hopefully, we won't have to impose for long," I replied as I shook his hand. He gave it a nice squeeze and then held on to it.

"Hadley, you could never be an imposition. You're welcome to stay as long as you want, with or without this one. In fact, is forever too long?"

I laughed at his flirtatiousness. It did my ego good to be admired by a good-looking man. Before I could hit him with a comeback, another biker stepped up and took off his sunglasses. He was smiling, too.

"Out of the way, she's here to see me. Hello, Hadley. I'm Animal, the VP of this motley bunch."

I had to tug to get Jinx to let go of my hand so I could shake Animal's outstretched one. Damn, all of them were easy on the eyes. "It's nice to meet you too, Animal. I like the name, by the way."

He grinned wider. From there, the remaining ones came forward to introduce themselves. There were three more—Sinner, Rage, and, lastly, Sarge. He was introduced as the enforcer, whatever that was. I thought I had an idea, but I didn't want to ask in case that was a no-no.

"If you're done flirting, can we get on the road? I don't like standing out here with her exposed. We can explain more once we're at the compound," Griffin said gruffly.

"Sure, we can do that. This is Tony. He's one of our prospects, and he'll drive you in the SUV," Jinx explained as he pointed to a guy standing quietly beside the vehicle surrounded by the bikes. Tony gave us a chin lift, but he didn't say anything.

"Prospect, stow their gear, then let's go. I want to get home so I can start to get to know this lovely creature," Jinx said.

Tony hurried over and took our bags, hauled them to the back of the vehicle, and loaded them. Animal opened one of the back doors for me. I was a little surprised by their manners, to be honest. I guess I had a lot to learn about bikers, or at least the ones the Patriots called friends. By the time we were ready to go, they were on their bikes with the engines running. The roar of them as they revved them made me long to be on one.

Griffin stared out the window with a slight scowl on his face and didn't say a word, so I kept quiet. I wondered if he was regretting being the one to come along with me. I wasn't sure why he didn't send one of the others. Or he could've gone with Dad and let

Undertaker come with me if he thought one of the bosses should be with us.

As we headed out into the countryside, I checked the scenery. There wasn't much color to see, but that wasn't unexpected in the dead of winter. Most of the plants were bare of leaves other than the evergreens. There were tracts of homes here and there, along with large open fields and plenty of woods. I wondered where this compound was. Did bikers have them in town or outside? I'd never been to an actual motorcycle club's headquarters, compound, or whatever they called them, so I had no idea.

It didn't take us long before we were pulling up to a large tract of land enclosed in a chain-link fence with a gate. A guy came running out to open the gate and move it out of the way so we could drive inside. My question was answered. The Marauders were outside of town. We followed the bikes in front of us to a large metal building that stood more than two stories tall. From the outside, it looked like a large garage, the kind you keep big semis in or like the metal hangars at the airport.

More bikes were parked out in front of it. Beyond it, I saw a few other buildings scattered around. They were much smaller than the first one. As Tony parked, I turned to Griffin. He was watching me.

"This place looks huge. Are most motorcycle clubs like this?"

"I don't know about most. The ones we know, yeah. They're mainly big ones when it comes to their property. I haven't been to the Horsemen of Wrath's compound in Florida or the one the Pagan Souls have in Lake Oconee, Georgia though. I recall Jinx telling us at one time that this used to be the property of a trucking company that went out of business. This big building is their clubhouse. They converted the two-story main garage into it."

"It reminds me of a garage or even the hangar where we left the helo. How many guys are part of this club?"

Tony answered me as he glanced over his shoulder at us. "Right now, it's average-sized. There are a dozen patched members, and counting me, there are two prospects. The other prospect is Micah. He's the one who opened the gate for us."

Tony hopped out and opened my door. Getting out, I looked around. The guys we followed were getting off their bikes. Suddenly, I felt a tad anxious about going inside. I had no idea why. I was usually someone who didn't get nervous about meeting new people. The portion of the Marauders I had already met seemed nice, and I hadn't been nervous with them. Jinx reached us as I was thinking. He took my hand and placed it on his extended forearm.

"Come with me, and let me introduce you to the rest of the club and show you around your future home," he said with a wink.

"Lead on," I said back with a wink of my own. His teasing set me at ease.

As he led me toward the clubhouse door, I heard a low growl from behind us. Glancing back, I found Griffin following us, and he didn't look happy.

God, don't tell me he thought I was trying to sleep with Jinx and his guys just because I teased him back.

I honestly didn't know why he thought so little of me. I quickly turned back around so he wouldn't see the sheen of tears in my eyes. I wouldn't let him see that his attitude was hurting me.

"What's wrong, pretty girl? You went from smiling to looking like you might cry," Jinx asked softly so no one but me could hear him.

"It's nothing. I got something in my eye. I can't wait to see your club. How long have you been a part of it? Has your clubhouse always been here?" I gave him my best fake smile.

He studied me intently without saying a word. I was getting more nervous. Suddenly, he nodded. "I know exactly what to do to help with that thing in your eye. While you're here, you're gonna smile, I promise. Now, as for how long I have been a part of the club, really, all my life. My dad was in it, so I grew up in this club. I patched in at nineteen. He was the president before me. I was voted in as the president at twenty-five when he was killed in a motorcycle accident. We acquired this land and moved the club here five years later."

I gave his arm a squeeze. I couldn't imagine losing my dad. It was hard enough not to have my mom. "I'm sorry you lost him. It's tough, I know, no matter how old you are. My mom was killed when I was nine. I still miss her every day."

"Sweetness, you're so right. I do still miss him and that was almost twelve years ago. I'm sorry you lost your mom. You say she was killed. Do you mind if I ask how?"

I guess Griffin hadn't told them our family story.

I shouldn't be surprised. He had a rather closed mouth. However, if they were trustworthy enough to help hide and protect me, they were trustworthy enough to know my history.

"Do you know who I am? I mean, other than some woman named Hadley Gerard? Did Griffin explain why I was here?"

"All he said was you needed protection and asked if we'd help. He did say he'd explain when you got here."

"Then I think we should gather your men and explain. If, in the end, you don't want to let me stay, I won't take it personally. He should've told you what you were getting yourself into."

Jinx laughed, which got the attention of those around us as if they hadn't already been staring. "Babe, I don't see us kicking you out, but if it makes you feel better, then let's do it. First, though, let me introduce the rest of the guys. They're salivating to meet you, can't you tell? Bunch of damn beasts. They make Animal look tame."

I laughed with him because Animal was far from tame-looking. I felt Griffin's presence come up behind us. It was like his energy reached out to touch my body. I fought not to shiver. Jinx gave a sharp, piercing whistle to get everyone's attention and settled down the chatter.

"I'm making introductions, then we're gonna sit down and have a chat. Everyone out except members while we do," he said, scanning the room. It registered that there were some women in here—very scantily, slightly trashy-looking women who were hanging on to a few of the guys or sitting at the bar having a drink.

They gave me unhappy looks. Tony didn't appear fazed by being told to get out. He headed for the door without a word.

The women, on the other hand, didn't appear to be in a hurry to leave. They either remained where they were or were super slow to move. I jumped when Jinx shouted. "I said to get the fuck out in case you didn't understand me being polite. If you women want to be allowed back, I suggest you move your asses. Now!"

This got them moving. They scrambled for the door like their asses were on fire. They had the room cleared within a minute. As the door shut, Jinx escorted me to a table and pulled out a chair for me. I sat down gingerly.

"What can I get you to drink, Hadley?" he asked.

"Any kind of soda if you have it, as long as it's not a diet. If you don't have that, water is fine."

I was surprised when Sarge went behind the bar to get it. Jinx sat next to me. More guys came over with their drinks in hand and took seats at the table. I shouldn't have been surprised when Griffin sat on the other side of me. He was still scowling. Sarge smiled at me as he sat a bottle of Dr Pepper in front of me.

"Thank you, Sarge."

"You're welcome, honey," he said before he took a seat.

The room was quiet, and I was the center of attention. My nerves were flaring up again. There was no way I was letting that happen. I'd tackle this head-on. "Hello, thank you so much for opening your home to me. I'm Hadley Gerard for those I haven't met. I understand from Jinx that you don't know much about me or why I'm here."

"I planned to fill them in once we got here. Why don't we let her rest, and we can talk?" Griffin asked.

"I don't need to rest, and I think I should be here for this. I don't need to be coddled. Jinx, would you do the honors and introduce the rest of your guys?" I asked sweetly, ignoring Griffin. I was tired of his attitude.

"Of course I will. Starting on my right is King. Next is Mad Dog, Thrasher, Styx, Beast, Crow, and lastly, Cujo. These two are our newest members. You met Tony, so that only leaves Micah. He's our other prospect who opened the gate. You'll meet him later."

"It's great to meet all of you. Now, I think I should tell you about myself. As I told Jinx, if, after you know who I am and why I'm here, you don't want us to stay, I'll totally understand. You don't know me, nor do you owe me anything."

There were muttered grumbles from around the table as they exchanged glances with each other. "Hold on. You think we'd make you go? Honey, I don't know what kind of people you're used to being around, but we don't abandon women to defend themselves. Griffin assured us you needed help. That's enough for me," Mad Dog said.

His irate tone made me want to smile, so I did. "Mad Dog, I thank you, but I still would like to explain."

Jinx was relaxed in his chair, watching everyone. When I glanced over at him, he gave me a chin lift. "Go for it. The floor is yours."

"How many of you have heard of Gerard

Industries? They make weapons and other things mainly for the US government. In fact, they're the biggest US defense contractor."

"I have. Although it may be because I was in the military," Sarge said.

"Me too. Same reason as Sarge," Mad Dog added.

There were a few nods around the table, indicating more knowledge of our company. Beast sat forward. "Gerard, your name is Hadley Gerard. Shit, you're related to the people who own that company."

"Not just related to, she's the daughter of the owner, Travis Gerard," Griffin told them. A low whistle came out of Beast. There was more speculation in their eyes.

"It's true. My father owns Gerard's, and he's always a target, as you can imagine. We're in the middle of trying to complete something new for the government, and they want it yesterday. A couple of weeks ago, my father received threats, which resulted in him bringing in the Dark Patriots for our protection."

"What kind of threats?" Styx asked.

"The kind that if he didn't do as they asked, they'd take Hadley and make her wish for death before they gave it to her and sent her back in pieces. We're not gonna let that happen. Can I finish telling them the rest?" Griffin asked me. I nodded.

"Travis has kept Hadley's existence a secret for the most part. Very few people know she exists, so you can imagine getting a threat against her is a big concern. It had to be someone who knows about her, or they were told by someone who knows. It may've been purely by accident. We don't know."

"Why keep her a secret?" Animal asked.

"Because my mom was kidnapped and murdered when I was nine. After that happened, my dad was scared the same thing would happen to me. He made sure I was kept out of the media," I explained.

"Christ," someone muttered. There were a few more swear words uttered.

"Okay, I can understand why. You obviously haven't figured out who. Since it's been a few weeks, why the sudden move here? We're not complaining at all, just curious," Jinx asked as he drummed his fingers on the table.

"Last night, someone attempted to enter her bedroom at their estate. We had them secured there with not only their guards but extra from us. Beau, Ben, Heath, Justin, and I were there first, then we brought in Undertaker, Giovanni, Aryan, and Jae. It was because of Jae we knew about the attempt," Griffin told them.

"How?" Beast asked. I noticed he had his phone out, and he seemed to be dividing his time between it and us.

"He rigged up a special alarm to her room and her dad's, which only we and they knew about. They activated them before going to bed at night. When whoever it was opened the door, it triggered the alarm, and they ran. We know for sure it was someone with inside knowledge or help because they knew where the cameras were in the hallways, and they avoided them or turned them away. It's too big with too many people there to keep them safe, so we decided to divide them up.

"Travis is in a cabin where no one knows he's at. Undertaker is with him. I decided to bring Hadley here."

"Why us? Don't get me wrong. I'm not saying we don't want her, but you usually go to the Warriors," Jinx asked.

"You're right, and anyone digging into us would likely find that. They were too obvious. You guys are close, more than capable of helping, and I knew you'd do it. We can't afford to let anything happen to her or her dad."

"So are they hoping if they take her, he'll stop working on whatever he's developing? Is it likely that would be enough to stop him? What about a ransom? Maybe she'd be held for that," Thrasher stated.

"The men who took my mom asked for a ransom, and my dad paid it. They killed her anyway and sent him her finger before they did. If something happens to me, my dad will lose his mind."

"Could it be the same person or persons?" Sinner asked.

"No, because he made sure he had them found and taken care of," I told them bluntly.

"Damn, okay, so back to the question. If you're taken, will that cripple the project or at least slow it down?" Thrasher asked again.

"It would since she's not just his daughter. She works for the company and is one of their lead inventors slash scientists. She's the lead on the project, not Travis, as everyone thinks. She's been doing it for years, and she has two doctorates to show for it," Griffin admitted before I could.

This brought all eyes back to me, and they had gleams of respect and interest. I didn't know how to react. A faint blush heated my cheeks.

"Well, hot damn, you're not only beautiful and luscious, but you're smart too. That's even sexier. How would you like to get married and have a bunch of brainiac babies?" Beast asked out of the blue.

This got the guys' attention. They began to protest loudly.

"Hell no, she's not for you."

"Over my dead body. We don't need any kids with your computer smarts and hers taking over the world."

"I already called dibs."

"She doesn't want you ugly bastards. She wants me."

Their remarks made me laugh and then giggle. They were so outrageous, and it was funny. I could tell they were having fun with each other and me. I didn't take them seriously, but it was a nice tension-breaker.

"Thank you, but how would I ever choose? I'll have to admire you all from afar, I'm afraid," I joked back.

"There won't be time for admiration from either side. This is serious," Griffin snapped. They all quickly sobered up.

"Chill, Grif, we've got this. She'll be safe here. How well did you cover your tracks, getting them out of there? Is it likely someone followed them?" Jinx asked.

"Followed, no, because we took separate

helicopters, but if they checked for a flight plan, they could get to the general area," he told them.

"Not after I get done with it. Tell me where and when her dad landed. I know where she did. I can go in and totally change it so anyone trying to find them will think they went to the other side of the country," Beast said with a smirk.

"You can do that?" I asked.

"Babe, I can do amazing things. Just remember, brainiac babies. I'll be right back," he told me with a wink.

"What about the pilots? Will they tell if asked?" Rage asked.

I smiled. "Nope. Since Dad and I flew the helicopters, they won't. Can Beast hide where we stored the helos?"

"We won't log the one at Patriots' headquarters, but the one you had to leave at McGhee, we'll have to ask him. I bet he can. If not, he'll ask Smoke or Everly to do it," Griffin said.

"What're you asking Everly and Smoke to do?" Beast asked as he came back and retook his seat. He was frowning.

As Griffin explained, Beast shook his head. "I can do it. Don't give my work away, or Jinx will think he can live without me."

Jinx snorted. "Brother, there's no way in hell that'll ever happen. Don't get me wrong, I love Everly and Smoke, but you're still my favorite. Although, if you steal Hadley here to have those brainiacs, I might have to reconsider."

"Oh my God, you're all crazy. I do admit you're good for a woman's ego, but settle. As tempting as your offer is, Beast, I'm not sure I would want to release our spawn on the world. Not to sound prideful, but I'm considered a genius," I told him with a flutter of my eyelashes.

"What ages were you when you got your doctorates that Grif mentioned?" he asked.

"Sixteen for the first one and nineteen for the second one. Why?"

"Goddamn, my dream woman! Nope, I can't do it. I'll have to change your mind. Since you probably have all the money and material things in the world, I'll have to find ways to satisfy your other needs and wants." He wiggled his eyebrows.

"Enough!" Griffin shouted as his hand came down on the table. I jumped. The guys, rather than appearing startled or upset, seemed amused.

"Griffin!" I admonished.

"We have shit to get in place and your protection figured out. We don't have time to mess around. Do I need to take her to Dublin Falls or Hunters Creek?" he asked them.

Jinx gave him what I'd call a steely look. "No, you do not. We're ready to protect her. Don't let our easygoing and teasing attitudes fool you. We have shit in place, and we'll kill anyone who comes looking for her. If you want, you can go back to Virginia. We'll keep her safe, and you can work with the others to find out who's doing this."

"Like hell, I'll leave. She goes nowhere without

me, understand?" Griffin snarled back.

I was getting worried they might get into a fight, which was ridiculous. They were friends, and my being here shouldn't have affected that. I had no idea why Griffin was acting like he was, other than he was afraid I'd sleep with them, and it would cause problems. I shouldn't have flirted back with them like I had, but it was fun and a relief for my tension. Only it backfired on me, and now he felt like he couldn't trust me with them. I doubted it was really due to him not trusting them with me. I got to my feet.

"There's no need to argue. If no one minds, I'd like to rest for a bit. Also, is there a way I can talk to my dad? He'll be worried, and I know hearing my voice will reassure him. I don't know how long we'll have to be here imposing on you. I thank you for offering your sanctuary to me. I'll be sure you're compensated accordingly. Now, can one of you show me to my room? I assume in a place this size, you have some extras. As long as it has a bed, I'm good."

Griffin opened his mouth, but Jinx beat him to saying anything. "Yes, you can rest, and if Grif doesn't have a secure phone, I know Beast can get you one. You're not imposing, and we won't take your money to help. It's our pleasure. As for your room, there are several here in the clubhouse, but I don't believe they'll be quiet or private enough. My house is available, and I have rooms for both of you. If you're ready, I'll take you there and get you settled. The tour of this place can wait."

"It's not necessary for us to stay in your house. We can find rooms here," Griffin told him.

"I insist. Come. We need to take a car since the houses are a bit of a walk. While you're here, the SUV Tony brought you here in is at your disposal."

"Thank you," I told him sincerely.

The guys all got to their feet and told me they'd see me later. I followed Jinx out to the car. Griffin was the silent presence behind us. Tony came hurrying up, and he was told to drive us. We got in the car while Jinx got on his bike.

I understood why we drove as we followed him. Behind the clubhouse and the other buildings I saw were thick woods. The road from the gate ran through the middle of them. On the other side was a big open area. I was surprised not only to find Jinx's house but also to find several more, eight in fact. Tony was nice enough to point out whose houses they were. The one dead center in the back was where we stopped.

I loved the layout. The houses were grouped in a loose circle, and in the middle of them was a huge, almost communal yard, which was the backyard for some and the front for others. A small building sat in the middle of it. We came to a stop in the driveway. I sat there admiring the peacefulness of it. What I wouldn't give to sit here with my eyes closed and just be still and not hear anything.

Griffin: Chapter 10

I was kicking myself for coming here with Hadley. For one thing, this would put me in close proximity with her most of the day. At least back at their estate, I could distance myself with the training sessions, the perimeter checks, and such. Here, there wasn't nearly as much I had to do. Unless I hid out, we'd be seeing a whole lot more of each other.

Hiding wasn't an option because if I did, I had no doubt the Marauders would jump all over the chance to spend time with her. The way they'd flirted and teased her had put my teeth on edge. I wanted to plant my fist in more than a couple of faces, which wasn't my place. She didn't belong to me and had every right to flirt or do more with anyone she pleased.

Yeah, that's what a logical person would say, but I wasn't feeling logical. I was feeling possessive and becoming more so by the hour. That was a revelation to me. I wanted to tell all of them she was mine, and if they dared to touch her, I'd remove their hands with a dull, rusty hacksaw. Not something you wanted to do to men you considered your friends. You tended to have no friends or, in their case, you got yourself killed.

We settled into Jinx's house yesterday—or, I should say, she did. I spent my time walking their perimeter and becoming familiar with their layout, security, and more. I then called and had a long chat with Sean and Gabe. They assured me Mark and Travis had made it to their hideaway without issue.

Later, we went back to the clubhouse so we could get the tour and hang out. It was the last thing I wanted, but somehow, I made it through it and then spent the night tossing and turning. I got up at least a half-dozen times to check everything was secure. Every time I walked past her bedroom door, I had to resist opening it and going in.

That was yesterday. Today was a new day, and it wasn't any easier than the last one. I couldn't fault Jinx or his crew. They were on alert and taking this seriously, even if I accused them of not doing so yesterday. They had cameras that monitored the fence line. Beast had done his magic and somehow hid where we landed as well as where the helo was being stored.

Sean and Gabe were having some of our people back at headquarters working to see if they could figure out who was behind the threats and the attempt on Hadley's room. They told me Jae was taking it personally that whoever it was had slipped by his cameras. I even went as far as to call him myself to reassure him it wasn't his fault, but he wasn't letting it go. It had become his mission to find whoever it was himself.

For the bulk of today, I spent my time holed up in my room going over the reports and information we had, even though none of it was new, hoping something would jump out at me. When I wasn't doing that or the perimeter walks or talking to Jinx or one of his guys, mainly Beast, I kept myself wherever I knew she wasn't.

Which turned out not to be necessary since she'd

been shut up all day in her bedroom. I did check a couple of times to make sure she was alright, but all I got was her calling out that she was busy with work and she was fine. I could hear the murmur of her voice whenever I passed her door, but not what she was saying.

Jinx had been around on and off. He made sure to show us where everything was and let us know if we couldn't find it in his house, to let Tony or Micah know, and they'd either tell us where we could get it or go get it for us. However, it was now evening, and everyone was back from work and gathering at the clubhouse, which meant we were expected to join them. In fact, Jinx beat on our doors and said to be ready to head over to the clubhouse in ten minutes. They were bringing in dinner.

Coming downstairs, I found Hadley had beaten me there. She was talking to Jinx in the kitchen. They were laughing. My gut tightened seeing them. She seemed so relaxed with him yet tense with me. I knew the way I'd been acting probably didn't help her feel more at ease with me. When she saw me, her smile faded, and she moved away from him.

Shit, I had to get myself under control. I gave them what I hoped was a believable smile. "Sorry if I kept you waiting. Ready to go?"

"No worries, I just got down here a minute or two before you. I'm ready if you guys are," she said.

"Then let's go before the food gets here and those damn animals eat it all. I warned them if they did, I'd let you use them for target practice tomorrow," Jinx said with a grin as we headed for the door.

This was the first I'd heard about target practice.

Outside, our ride was waiting for us in the driveway. He opened the front passenger door for her. I walked around to the driver's side and got in. I was surprised when he opened the rear door and climbed in.

"Hey, you can drive if you want. I thought you'd take your bike," I offered.

He waved off my offer. "Nah, you can drive. I haven't been chauffeured for a while."

I started it, and we were off. As we made the short drive to the clubhouse, I asked about what he said. "What's this about target practice tomorrow?"

"Hadley told me she needed to practice her shooting, so I told her we could do it tomorrow. We have an area set up on the other side of the compound from the clubhouse. Some of the guys heard me talking to her about it, and they wanted to come, too. You're welcome if you can spare the time."

She wasn't going without me, by God. No way. "Sure, I wouldn't mind going. Should I assume you already know how to shoot, Hadley? As much other self-defense stuff that you know, I assume your dad had taught you this too since you had a gun the other night."

"He did. Believe it or not, Dad was my shooting instructor. He's an avid gunman and hunter. He started teaching me when I was probably six or so. The biggest mistake someone can make is to assume that because he's wealthy, he can't and won't defend himself or others."

"I think that's the case for both of you," I said with a grin. She laughed.

"Are we going to get a chance to see you in action

only with guns, or maybe we'll get to see your fighting skills, too?" Jinx asked.

"If you're good, then yeah, I might show both. Griffin hasn't seen what I can do yet. I didn't get a chance to work out with the guys before we had to come here."

"Then we'll have to make it happen. Just promise to be gentle with us," he said. We'd made it to the clubhouse, and I'd parked. Again, he got to her door before I could after he hopped out.

When I rounded the car, she was smiling at him. I walked up and subtly put myself between them as she responded, "I make no promises. Every man or woman for themselves. So, you didn't say what we were having for dinner tonight."

He gave me an amused glance before going ahead to open and hold the door to the clubhouse for us. I pretended not to see it. Inside, the roar of voices wasn't terrible, but there was a lot of chatter. Checking my watch, I saw it was already six, which meant everyone should be off work. When we were spotted, they all shouted out greetings. I saw their eager faces as they watched us approach, or I should say as they watched her.

"Make room for the lady. She gets first dibs on the food. Make sure to get enough because if you don't, there's no guarantee there'll be any left for a second round," Jinx hollered over the chatter.

"If I want a second plate, I can take it off one of them. I'll fight them for it," she responded back with a chuckle.

"Babe, you don't need to fight me for it. A kiss will do," Styx said.

I clenched my hands and took a deep breath. Having all these men around her and vying for her attention was pushing my buttons which wasn't something I was used to. I couldn't ever recall being truly possessive toward a woman.

"Enough flirting. It's chow time," Jinx told them. He motioned toward the kitchen we'd been shown yesterday. I gently directed her that way with my hand on her back. I felt her stiffness for a moment or two then she seemed to relax and she didn't move away. I let the jolts of awareness run up my arm. They went from my hand to my chest and then straight to my groin. It was hard to hold back my groan as blood filled my cock.

I dropped my hand and moved to stand so the counter blocked the view of my crotch. I pretended to be interested in the food laid out before me, but I was no longer hungry. Or at least not for food. *Stop it. You've gotta stop thinking shit like that,* I chastised myself.

Hadley moved to stand next to me. Her brushing against me and the smell of her that filled my nose didn't help me to regain control. I desperately checked over the selection. I was chuffed to see it wasn't the typical pizza, wings, or pasta. There was an array of burritos and soft-shell tacos made with chicken, carne asada and carnitas, along with a bunch of different toppings plus chips, salsa, guacamole, Mexican rice, and refried beans. Smelling the aroma and seeing the variety made my mouth water.

Hadley moaned. I glanced over at her. She met my eyes. "Why Mexican food? Why?"

"Don't you like Mexican?"

"I love it, which means I'll eat too much. You'll have to roll me out to the car and then into Jinx's house. You know what, never mind. Just leave me here. If I can't get out of my chair, just let me sleep there. I'll be in a food coma, so I won't hear a thing they do."

"You can have my bed," Sinner told her.

"And let me guess, you'll be in it, too. Sorry, but I'm not that crazy, Sinner."

"Come on, you might just love it," was his comeback.

"Dirt naps suck," Jinx said.

I saw all the guys get surprised looks then they gave him a chin lift. I watched as they stayed friendly but didn't make any more suggestive remarks to her. As we ate, I waited for them to start up again, but they didn't. I was puzzled. What was that dirt naps suck remark code for? They all seemed to know what Jinx meant.

It was a while before I got him alone where I could ask him. "Hey, I have a question."

"Sure, shoot."

"What did your dirt naps suck remark mean? The guys all seemed to react to it like they knew."

"It meant to lay off the flirting and suggestive remarks unless they'd like to find themselves dead and buried. What did you think it meant?"

"That's what my mind went to, but I didn't know why you'd say that unless you're staking a claim."

"I won't lie. Hadley is an intriguing woman and

she's gorgeous. If she wasn't already claimed, I might just have to see if there would be a chance with her."

"Claimed? She's not claimed."

"Really? So you weren't getting pissed at us all for coming on to her? If we'd like to see if she's in for some fun or something more, you won't mind?" he asked with an innocent expression on his face.

Instantly, my hackles went up, and I didn't cut off my reaction fast enough. The bastard laughed at me and then slapped my shoulder. "That right there is why I warned them. We've been around enough possessive friends, they should've picked up on it. I think they weren't thinking you'd be like us bikers. We weren't around when Undertaker and Gabe got with their women, and Cassidy and Sean were already obviously into each other when we met them."

"We're not together. She's a free agent."

"Bullshit. You want her so damn badly you can barely see straight. Why're you fighting it?"

"Can you see a woman like her with someone like me? Come on. She's rich beyond belief. She can have anyone she wants. She's the kind to be with a successful businessman who can help her run her daddy's company one day. She's a freakin' genius on top of it. I know when I'm out of my league."

"Did you ask her what she wants? Is that the kind of man she sees herself with?"

"No I didn't, but it's a given. She might go slumming, but in the end, she'll stick to her own kind."

"Hmm."

"Hmm, what the hell does that mean?"

"It means if you got this all figured out and there's no way you two will ever work, then you need to step back and let someone else give it a try. I don't see her being stuck to a certain type. I don't know her, of course, but she strikes me as the kind who's more interested in who she can have the life she wants with and who'll love and support her. Money has nothing to do with it. If you want her, then don't waste time on doubts. Ask her what or who she wants. If she doesn't say a rich man, then I'd go for it. The worst thing is to look back and regret that you let someone perfect walk away because you were a fool."

"Have you done that?"

"I've seen it and it's fucking miserable."

We didn't stay away from the others long after that. When we returned, it was hard not to focus on what he said. When we finally called it a night and went back to his house, I went to bed not long after we returned but I didn't go to sleep. I had too much to think about.

It was afternoon before the guys were able to get free and back to the compound. Last night as we talked about the plan to go shooting today, the rest of them got excited and wanted to come with us. I thought having a bunch of people there might make her nervous, but she said the more the better.

We all planned to meet at the range. I was on a call with Gabe, Mark, and Sean, so she went ahead with Animal. Jinx hung back to bring me. I hurried to get through my call. It was frustrating.

"We're no closer to figuring out who made the threat and then got into the house. It's someone with inside knowledge we know, but everyone has been questioned again and still nothing. The only thing of interest is how Rockwell is reacting according to Ben and Beau," Sean said.

"Oh yeah, and how's that?" I asked.

"He's losing his shit, demanding to know where they went. They told him it was none of his business. He's making threats to call the police and report them as kidnapped by us. Beau told him to do it and see what happens. He insists Hadley wouldn't leave without telling him. The fucker is too attached to her. If nothing else, this threat has broken her away from him. I hope she'll stay away and not have him back as her main guard after we solve this issue," Mark uttered.

"If that little prick calls the law on us, I'll beat his ass. Did you tell Travis what he's saying?" I asked.

"I did, and he called him on a secure line. He informed him that they didn't have to tell him or anyone else shit. They left for their safety. He was threatened with his job being kaput if he called the cops. Rockwell tried to get Travis to tell him where they were, but he shot him down. He wasn't happy when they hung up." I could hear the happiness in Mark's tone.

"Good. How's it going with Travis?"

"Other than wanting this over with and missing his daughter, he's doing great. We went out yesterday and had target practice. That man can shoot." The admiration in his voice told me a lot. It took a lot to get that out of him.

"Yeah, well I'll be finding out here after I get done with you guys if he's passed that skill onto his daughter. We're going shooting with the guys. She told me he's an avid shooter and hunter and he taught her since she was little. Not what you think of when it comes to a billionaire."

"No, it's not, but he's been telling me how he grew up. His father inherited the startup money, but not until Travis was older. He's not as pampered as we thought."

"How's it going with Hadley?" Sean asked.

"It's been fine. We've stayed in the compound. She's been working a lot in her room. I've been making sure we have the bases covered here, which it seems like they do. Jinx and the crew have been good so far."

"If that's the case, then what's up with the tone? You said it's good, but your voice doesn't sound like it is," Gabe pointed out.

I didn't want to get into what Jinx and I talked about last night or the hours of thinking I'd done, not just the past couple of days but since I had met her. "No, it's good. I'm just tired. I haven't gotten a lot of sleep." I played it off.

"Wanna try again?" Sean asked with a raise of his eyebrow.

"I have no idea what you mean."

"Cut the crap. You know damn well she's got you tied in knots and you don't know what to do. Talk to us. What's the problem? You like her. I know that. I swear she likes you too," Mark added as he exchanged smirks with our brothers.

"It's not that simple, goddamn it. Yeah, she intrigues me but there's nothing about me to intrigue her. She's not what I expected. However, a woman like her is meant for a man like her dad. Could you see Travis being thrilled that his daughter was hooked up with a guy like me, even if she was interested?"

"If you love her and take care of her, making her happiness a priority and don't try to change her, he's all for it," Mark said.

"And you know this how? You suddenly got ESP or something?" I mocked him.

"No, fucker, I asked him. He doesn't have a problem with you or your background, man. I made sure."

I stared at him stunned. My mouth was hanging open and all I could do was blink at him. He had a self-satisfied twist to his mouth. Sometimes I hated being on video. The other two just sat there laughing. This was one of those times I wish at least one of them was in my shoes and still single.

Finally, I got my voice back. "Motherfucker, I can't believe you asked him that! We're here to protect him and her, not for one of us to try and steal his daughter," I snapped.

"Cool your jets. He knows we're professionals who'll do the job. We can't help when we meet the one meant for us. He said he knew his wife was the one for him the moment he saw her. They met and were married a couple of months later. She's still the love of his life. All he's ever wanted was for Hadley to find someone like that. He said to tell you to treat her right, love her, be there for her no matter what, and to let her be herself. He'll be happy to give you his blessing, assuming she feels the same toward you."

I couldn't respond to that. They took pity on me, which was a surprise, and we wrapped up the call soon afterward. They left me with parting food for thought. All three insisted I needed to talk to her and find out where her head and heart was. I hung up thinking about it. That was four people in less than a day who told me essentially the same thing. Maybe I should listen. If I wasn't scared she'd tell me it wasn't happening, I might've told her this morning. Damn. When I joined Jinx in the kitchen, I didn't say much.

The drive to the shooting area wasn't long, and he kept the talk to idle chatter, nothing serious. I couldn't have done it otherwise. When we pulled up to the shooting range, I saw they'd done more than just make it a spot with places to hang targets. They put thought and effort into it.

They used a natural hill and built a berm behind it to create a safe shooting location. The berm was U-shaped, so it had sides. I knew they did that so they could shoot at targets without worrying about the splatter that can occur when projectiles break apart when they hit steel or the debris that could travel.

They had both paper and steel targets. They had them in front of a backstop of dense wooden logs in front of the berm, creating a two-layer backstop. The steel ones let us see and hear when the bullets hit, and we didn't need to walk down to change out the targets, although they did have some of those to one side. I had no doubt the steel targets used were AR-500 or rifle-rated so as not to ruin the targets.

Some might think it was fun to shoot glass bottles and stuff, but those can shave fragments that become projectiles, and you didn't want any of them coming at you. The steel ones were at least the required ten yards away, whereas the paper ones were set from point blank to as far out as you could hit them. The steel ones were staggered at different distances so the flash of one wouldn't hit and damage the others.

They had constructed a long, covered pavilion-like building with a concrete floor. It had benches so you could sit and shoot or stand, and there was a waist-height counter so you could load and even help stabilize the guns if you chose.

The others were gathered, and I saw a huge number of gun cases and ammo boxes laid out on the counter. Hadley was intently talking to Cujo and Crow, who were holding guns in their hands. I got my weapon bag out of the back of the car and walked over to them. I planned to stick close to her, even if she was capable on the range.

She smiled at me, which made my heart skip. "Do you see this? I love it. Dad and I need to rethink going to a range and just have one built at home. He'd love this. I wish he were here."

"Well, if it makes you feel better, he went shooting yesterday with Mark, and they had fun. You can take pictures of this one and send them to him. Your phone is secure, just like your laptop is. Jae made sure of it before we left."

"I know. He told me. I'll do that. Are you ready to

be beaten, Wraith?"

"Sweetheart, I was a SEAL. You might not wanna challenge me. I have no doubt you can shoot, but I'm not sure you can outshoot me. A few of these guys were in the military, too. Just sayin'."

"Who?" she asked curiously.

"Sarge, Mad Dog, and Styx were," Cujo supplied.

"Hmm, is it usual for men who've been in the military to join groups like yours and motorcycle clubs, or is this just a coincidence?" she asked me.

"I don't know for sure what it's like in all clubs. All the ones we're close to, yes. Quite a few were. I think the freedom from certain rules and the desire to make your own decisions without having to adhere to ones you disagree with might have something to do with it. Also, the desire to help others never goes away. Despite what most people think, lots of clubs help those who need it. As for the Dark Patriots, we wanted to continue to serve, just not where we have no control. Now, when the government wants us to do something, we have a say in whether we do it and how."

"So helping my dad was something you wanted to do and not something you were forced to do?"

"We were never forced, Hadley. Your dad, and now that we know about you are national treasures we must protect. Even if not, we would've still taken the job once we were told that kidnapping and shit was threatened."

"Shit is right. Any luck on finding out who's doing this?"

"Not yet. Listen, why don't we just relax and have

fun? Besides, you need to concentrate if you have any hope in hell of beating me," I teased to lighten her mood. The mention of protecting them had taken the smile from her face.

She grinned. "Challenge accepted. Hope you take defeat well, Wraith."

"Wraith?" Jinx said as he came up to us.

"Yeah, it's his military nickname. You didn't know that? The guys he brought with him to our house used it," she told him. Soon, everyone knew, and they started calling me Wraith. I didn't mind, but it seemed I'd have to get used to hearing it a lot more.

The Marauders were unpacking their guns, so I got to it. I'd brought a bag with several of mine. What stunned me was apparently she did, too. She unzipped a bag that I thought was just a regular piece of luggage. It was cleverly disguised. I could see where it would come in handy. I'd have to find out where she got it.

When she unloaded it, she got the attention of the whole club. Not only was there ammo and several handguns, but she also had a takedown AR-15 packed in there. That was just a fancy way to say her AR-15 could be broken down into smaller pieces for easy storage. We watched as she expertly put it back together, checked the slide and everything before loading it, and then proceeded to check and load her other guns.

She looked up when it got silent to find us all watching her. "What? Never seen a woman load guns?"

"Oh, we've seen it, and we know a lot who know what the hell they're doing, too. The old ladies in the clubs are no slackers. It's just not what we'd expect to see out of someone…" Animal petered off.

"Out of a rich spoiled brat like me? Don't worry, you can say it. Hell, Wraith still thinks I'm one," she said with a shake of her head.

"I do not."

"Well, you did."

"If I did, I don't anymore, and they're right. The old ladies can all shoot, now that I think about it. If they didn't know when they got with their men, they soon learned. Now, are we done jabberin' and ready to do this?"

"I think we should have a contest and a prize for the best shooter. Everyone does better when there's one. Bragging rights are one thing, but let's make it more interesting," she suggested with a gleam in her eyes. That made me wonder just how good she was.

"What do you have in mind? I don't mind competing," Thrasher said.

"There's always money, but I find it boring. But if you want, we can do that. Or, we could do something better." The gleam got brighter.

"I know I'm gonna regret asking, but what do you have in mind?" I asked slowly as I glanced at the guys.

"The losers have to get up and sing and dance for the top three winners. It has to be for a whole song and the song is picked by the winners. And there's none of this half-assed standing there and swaying from side to side. I mean full-out dancing with ass shaking, the whole nine yards," she told us gleefully.

There were plenty of protests. She stood there

with a smirk on her face. After some arguing, I watched as they gave in. I knew it was because they were confident they could outshoot her along with a few others, so they'd be safe. Of course, based on the numbers, they were wrong. As they agreed one by one, I knew I couldn't say no, so I agreed, too. This would be the most interesting shooting contest I'd ever done, and I'd done several over the years.

When you were out in the field and bored, or even here at home, it wasn't unusual to decide to have one, and unique bets went with them. I wondered if she'd done this particular bet before. It had easily come to mind. This should be fun.

Hadley: Chapter 11

I tried to keep the smile off my face as they all agreed to the bet, but it was impossible. This was gonna be hilarious. Even if I did lose, the fact that so many of these big badass men would have to get up there with me to sing and dance made it the perfect bet. I'd done this once before, and it was always worth the entertainment, no matter if you were the winner or loser. Of course, I'd never done it with a group of bikers. In the past, several military guys had joined in, not knowing what they were gonna get.

Daddy had not only been my first and main instructor in firearms, but, like everything else, he ensured I had the best trainers. I'd been put through training equal to what a sniper in the field and survivalists would get. I'd had special forces men, top survival experts, and even an Olympic gold medalist teach me.

Since we couldn't all shoot at the same time, we had to do it in two groups. It was agreed we'd get three shots to sight in our guns and then five shots that would count as done. Paper targets were the only way to make this doable, so Micah and Tony went to put them up down range. I was in group two.

I had to admit the first group was good, but my confidence didn't dwindle. And group one didn't have any of the military-trained guys. I wasn't sure if that was intentional or not. It was King, Crow, Micah, Cujo, Sinner, Rage, Beast, and Animal in that group. When they were done, the targets were gathered, and then it was our turn.

The feel of the gun in my hand felt great. Dad and I tried to go shooting at least monthly, although lately, that hadn't happened. It was kinda intimidating yet thrilling to go up against four military men plus badass bikers. After sighting in our guns, I breathed and cleared everything from my mind. I took control of my breathing, which was key, and let everything else fade away as it came down to me, the target, and my gun. I vaguely heard the order to shoot. Even the pound of bullets, which you could still hear through the protective ear gear, was distant for me.

We'd agreed we could have up to five minutes max to fire all five shots so we could sight in and give our best shots. I heard them firing fast. I took my time. I knew how to rapid fire and I practiced it so it would be muscle memory, but when I did that, it was to simulate going for a body shot, not precision like now. This was like sniper work, where you could take your time to shoot your target.

They were all standing there waiting for me when I fired my last shot. I cleared my gun and laid it down. We all went to get our targets. When we got back, it was hard for sixteen of us to gather around to see the targets spread out with our names on them. It took a while to compare them. It had been agreed that the four military guys would be the ones to judge.

When they eliminated all but six, I was thrilled. Mine was one of the six. The eliminated targets were good, don't get me wrong. Whoever they shot would be hurting, if not dead, which seemed likely. It wasn't easy to eliminate them. They studied the six more intently. Finally, they removed two. One more. I was still in the running to be a winner, which I was kinda shocked to see. I was good, but they were experts with real-life experience. It was down to me, Griffin, Sarge, and Styx.

I held my breath. In the end, two were set aside. "These are definite winners, but these other two are too damn close to pick. We need these two to shoot three more rounds to determine the third winner. Hadley, Wraith, get to it," Sarge ordered.

I gulped. Shit, it had to be him. My life sucked. As we got new targets up and ready, I debated. On one hand, I wanted to win something fierce. My pride as a shooter and even as a woman was riding on it against these guys. On the other hand, if I beat him, would it make him even more standoffish with me? Although why I cared was stupid.

My attraction toward him hadn't abated a bit. In fact, it was worse. The way he was avoiding me gave me little hope he'd suddenly find himself interested in me, but a girl could hope. However, if I beat him at this, would his male pride make sure there was zero chance? I argued with myself as I got ready. In the end, I had to fight to concentrate. I took several deep breaths and held them to steady myself and slow down my racing heart.

This time, the shots were over faster and I was shaking when the targets were grabbed by the prospects and brought to the table. As I leaned over mine to look, a hand on my back rubbed soothingly. I glanced around to find Animal standing there. He smiled.

"Honey, relax. No one is gonna be pissed for real if you win, let alone Griffin."

"Yeah, you say that, but he doesn't like me as it is," I whispered so no one else would hear me.

He gave me a knowing smirk as he replied. "Babe, he's far from disliking you, believe me. That man wants you, and he's fighting it for some damn reason. If you want him, then go get him. Make sure he knows you're interested. If you're not into him, then there are plenty of guys here who wouldn't say no to a chance to see if something permanent could grow."

"And would you be one of those men?"

"I would, but only if you're interested, but I think there's already a man who has your whole attention. Don't let him slip away out of fear. What's the worst he can say? He's not interested, and you already think that."

I nodded but didn't say anything. I'd have to think about it. While we were talking, the judging had happened. Jinx announced the three winners: "Alright, the winners are Styx, Sarge, and... Griffin."

I couldn't hold in my groan of disappointment. Griffin gave me a sympathetic smile. "It was damn close, Hadley. You have nothing to be ashamed of. I'm damn impressed. You'd give Harlow a run for her money, and that's saying something."

The others all chimed in with how great I did and agreed about this Harlow chick. I felt jealousy flutter in my stomach. Who was this woman he was admiring? She had to be someone significant if they all knew her.

Maybe Animal was wrong. I had no idea if Griffin had a woman he was involved with. I swallowed my new disappointment and forced a smile on my face. Years of practice made it convincing, I had no doubt.

"Thanks, guys. It was great fun. I didn't think I'd win. If you don't mind, can I stay and shoot some more? I promise later tonight when it's time to pay the bet, I'll be there." I couldn't contain my curiosity, though. "So, may I ask who this Harlow is you all mentioned? She sounds interesting."

"You don't have anything to worry about," Animal whispered in my ear. I ignored him although I saw Griffin frowning at him.

"She is. She's Terror's woman. He's the president of the Dublin Falls Archangel's Warriors. She's his old lady. Her dad is Bull. He's the president of not only the Hunters Creek Warriors' chapter but the whole Warriors' charter. She's the first old lady in all the clubs, well not counting Sherry. Harley started the whole settling down epidemic. She's a badass. Before she married Terror, she was a Marine sniper. She's one woman no one wants to mess with," Jinx explained.

Admiration for her was clear as well as affection. She had to be special to get that kind of response from these men. My jealousy over thinking Griffin was involved with her settled, but my desire to have this bunch or ones like them seeing me the same way hit me. I guess I was still trying to find people who liked me for myself and not who I was. It was rare to find ones who knew my identity, and the small number over the years who did, I could never trust they wanted or liked me.

Even men in my past wanted things from me,

even if they didn't know who I was. I worked in a very desirable setting. I had money, even though I tried not to be obvious about it. The men I'd been involved with had tried to figure out how I had it or to get me to get them a job at Gerard's. Eventually, we would break up since I couldn't tell them the truth. If I'd found someone who wanted only me, I would've told them the truth. Not that there had been a ton of men, but there had been a few.

Case in point, my last relationship ended when the guy got mad at me for not getting him into Gerard's. He accused me of being afraid of competition. He then went on to tell me how there was no way I could be anything more than a secretary because everyone knew women weren't smart when it came to science. I'd told him I was a scientist, but he didn't believe me. He thought I was lying, and if he got a job there, he'd know it. He was gone from that moment.

Oh, he tried to come back and say he was kidding, and he begged me to take him back. I'd been pissed enough to have him over one more time, and I introduced him to Dad, although he had no idea he was my father. Dad told him I was a scientist at Gerard's and the best they had. Yeah, petty, but it felt good. It took a while for him to give up trying to get me back. but he finally did. The last I heard, he'd moved outside the States and found a low-level job in a similar industry.

Thinking of him made me wonder. Surely, after all this time, he wasn't still butt hurt, but what if he was? I needed to add him to the list of possible suspects. I added him to my mental list to talk to one of the Patriots about later. Maybe I'd get Dad to mention him to Undertaker.

"Oh, we're not done shooting yet. Come on, let's try out more of these guns," Styx hollered. I got lost in the comradery of it and had a blast. Griffin tried to talk to me a couple of times, but I was with the other guys. I wondered why.

It was a couple of hours before we headed back. We had time to get ready, and I was going to spend it doing some soul-searching before the big dance and sing-off. Back at Jinx's, I excused myself as soon as I got there. I told him and Griffin I needed a shower and to work.

❧❧❧

Walking into the clubhouse hours later, I felt like I was ready. Not only was I ready to pay the bet, but I planned to have a talk with Griffin. Animal was right. What did I have to lose? As I walked in, I held my head up high, and I made sure I was dressed for my performance. I might've lost the shooting match, but I was determined to win the dance and singing part. I saw the reaction I got from Griffin and even Jinx when I came out of my bedroom.

I hadn't packed much other than comfy clothes, but for some reason, I'd thrown in a pretty dress, like you'd wear out to a nice dinner, and this outfit. It was one I'd gotten a while back but hadn't worn, and I hadn't gone anywhere appropriate to wear it.

It was a pair of tight leather pants and a top that had crisscrossing straps across the chest, coming from the shoulders. It showed my cleavage through a keyhole opening. To top it off was a pair of strappy four-inch heels. Everything was black, with silver studs placed tastefully. It made me think of a biker chick.

I left my hair long and just curled the ends. My jewelry was black and silver, and I put on makeup tonight. It had an edgier look to it. There was lots of black and gray in the eyeshadow, and my lips were dark rather than neutral like I typically wore. There was no need to get fancy at work or around the house.

The whistles I got when I walked in told me I pulled it off. I smiled and turned in a circle so they could see all of me. When I was done, I had to say something smartass. "I know I'm gonna smoke your asses at this dancing and singing bit, but it never hurts to dress up. Now, we've all got leather on. Well, except Griffin."

"We can't have that. Grif, hang on a minute," Jinx said. He hurried out of the room. As we waited for him, the guys mobbed us and were talking excitedly. They teased Griffin about his leatherless state and me about the performance. Jinx was back in a few minutes. In his hand was a leather cut. He handed it to Griffin. It didn't have any patches on it yet.

"I just got a few new ones in and haven't sent them off to get patches put on them. That way, no one can say you're lacking."

Griffin laughed and slid it on. "I like it. Okay, how about we get a drink and then get this show on the road? I want to see how they do," Griffin said.

It took a bit for us all to get a drink, then actually drink it and get the music cued up. I found out the winners had conferred at some point, and they had a song ready to go on the stereo system in the common area. All of us who lost gathered in the middle of the room where we'd have plenty of room to dance. I could tell some of them weren't confident.

As the song started, I laughed. It was an old song by Aerosmith. "Janie's Got a Gun" filled the room. It wasn't the fastest song, but it fit the bill. The guys all hooted. I threw myself into dancing to it and singing my heart out. We weren't all on key, but it didn't matter. The guys didn't shake it much, well, except for Mad Dog. He shocked me with how good he was. The man was a hot-ass dancer. Soon, we were in a dance-off against each other.

When that song stopped, a new one came on, and we kept going. This one had a much faster beat. It was "Never Again" by Nickelback. Mad Dog shook his ass and then grabbed me to dance seductively when the third song started. It wasn't until after that one that the music was cut off. I glanced around. The room was quiet. Griffin didn't look happy. The others appeared to be slightly stunned. Finally, it was Sarge who broke the silence.

"Hot damn, Mad Dog. How many years have we known you and never knew you could dance, especially not like that? Shit."

"He's great. He's the best partner I've ever danced with, to be honest. That was fun. Thank you," I said. I gave him a hug. He squeezed me. As he let go, I was stunned when Griffin got up and came over to me. He grabbed my hand.

"If you want to dance, I'll show you dancing. Give me a minute to get something cued up." He walked off to the stereo before I could say anything. I caught Animal's eye. He winked at me.

When Griffin came back, he took me in his arms, which surprised me a bit. He tugged me close, and his eyes bore into mine. My temperature spiked at the heat I thought I saw there. When the music started, I gulped. It was "Pony" by Ginuwine. His hands landed on my hips, and he started to sway.

It was all I could do, not to moan and melt. I had to fight to pay attention and move. As he held my gaze, he began to sing the words to me. My nipples hardened, and I could feel myself starting to get slick down below. I had to work not to rub my thighs together. Shit, I had no idea he would even know this song.

As he sang and we danced, his hands slid further down to cup my ass. He tugged me hard against him, and I felt his erection. Oh my God, he was turned on by what we were doing. Knowing we needed to talk but unable to resist, I rubbed against him harder. He stumbled over the words, which made me smirk. The song seemed to last forever, yet at the same time, it was done too quickly. As the music stopped, the room was dead silent.

Suddenly, I was whisked toward the door. He didn't let me look around or say anything. When I hit the cold air outside, it was a relief—until he pushed me up against the side of the clubhouse and kissed me. The way he took command of my mouth spiked my desire again. I grabbed the back of his neck and kissed him back.

Our teeth clashed and our tongues were frantically trying to twist around each other. In between the tongue movements, he nibbled on my lips, and I did the same. I had no idea how long that lasted before he broke away. He was breathing hard like I was.

"Fuck, Hadley, I shouldn't have done that. It was a mistake."

"What was? The dance, the singing, or the kiss? If you just need someone to get off with, then you're right. I'm sure they can find you someone to fuck tonight," I said before I turned my back and began to walk off. I was instantly mad and sorrowful. I'd walk back to Jinx's and then find some alcohol to drown my sorrows. For a couple of minutes, I could've sworn he felt the same way I did. Guess I was an idiot. Any woman would've done it for him. No thanks, I wasn't that desperate.

I was whirled around and then slammed into his chest. His arms wrapped around me, and he held me tightly against him. I went into pissed-honey-badger mode. I tried to shove him so I could get room to punch or kick him. When I couldn't, I yelled at him.

"Let go of me, Griffin! I'm not in the mood for any more of your games. I'm going to the house. I suggest you stay and get laid."

"I'm not staying and getting laid by some random woman who might show up later. Calm down and tell me why you're acting like this."

"Because you're an asshole. You do all that then you have the nerve to be sorry. You know what, fuck you, I'm staying. You might not want to get laid, but I do. I've been guaranteed there's more than one taker in there. Maybe I'll see if more than one will be up for it tonight," I snarled.

I was startled when he let out a roar, then I was in the air and landing over his shoulder. I tried to kick, but he had my legs pinned to his front. Not having a choice, I pounded on his back with my fists. He was moving as I screamed at him. "Put me down right this minute!"

"Not on your life. If you think I'm gonna stand back and let you go in there to fuck one or more of the Marauders, you're delusional. Now settle. We need to talk, but it's not gonna be here."

"I don't wanna talk to you!"

"Well, that's too bad." He smacked my ass. It stung, but it also felt good. *Get your head out of the gutter. You're pissed at him, remember? Stop thinking of jumping his bones and riding him raw,* I reminded myself.

My devil side argued, *"Yeah, but just imagine if you could work off all your frustration with him? I bet he's an animal in bed."*

But you don't just want meaningless sex, my angel side argued back.

I got so caught up in arguing with myself I didn't realize what was happening until my ass landed in the car we used to get here. He didn't put me in and then go around to get in on the other side either. No, he slid me in from the driver's side and followed me. He didn't let go of my wrist, so I couldn't go out the other side. I yanked on my arm.

"What's your problem?"

"You and I are solving it tonight. You can fight it, but we're gonna talk without an audience," he growled as he started the car.

He didn't let go of me the entire time. When we pulled up in front of Jinx's, I tried to get loose to run inside ahead of him, but he had me secured. He pulled me out of the vehicle on the driver's side then I was up and over his shoulder again. I decided to save my strength. He'd have to let go at some point, then I'd kick his ass and be done with it.

He didn't slow down as he headed to the porch. Damn man, why couldn't he be struggling to carry me or something? He acted like he wasn't even carrying anything. It pissed me off more.

He didn't put me down until we entered the house and he got to the living room. When he did, my feet barely touched the floor before I swung. He wasn't expecting it and it landed square in the side of his face. Of course, it was rock hard, like the rest of his head, and it hurt like a mother. I refused to cry out, though. I'd break my hand before I let him know it hurt. I swung again. This one, he stopped by grabbing it in the palm of his hand.

He looked at me sternly. "Stop it, Hadley. I don't want to fight. We need to talk."

"No, we don't. You need to learn not to haul women around like we're a sack of potatoes. Just because you're stronger doesn't make it okay to use it against us!" I shouted.

"I'm sorry, but you have it all wrong, and I need you to listen."

"What do I have wrong? You're looking for a fun time. You can get that at the clubhouse. I've heard the stories about the women who come to party and sleep with bikers. Don't tell me you've never done it when you've been with your biker buddies before."

He remained silent. I had my answer. I didn't

know why it bothered me so much. It wasn't like I expected him to be a virgin. I wasn't, but it made me feel unhappy, and I wanted to cry. It was either fight with him or cry, and whenever that was the case, I'd rather fight.

"That's what I thought. Go back and do whatever you like. I'm going to bed. Tomorrow, we'll talk about the new plan."

I turned my back on him to leave, but the suicidal man grabbed my arm. I swung at him when I whipped around. He used my momentum against me, and I slammed into him. His arms came around me and secured me tight against him again. He was scowling.

"What new plan? You're not making sense, and it doesn't make sense why you're so upset."

"It doesn't matter. Forget it. I'm tired."

"No, you're not going anywhere until we resolve this."

"Fine, let go of me, and I'll tell you."

He studied me for a few moments before his arms eased. As soon as I could get loose, I did. I took a seat in the one chair in the room, which left him on the couch. He sat, too.

"I don't like to be used and messed with. That's why I'm upset." He opened his mouth to argue, but I stopped him. "Let me say what I have to say, or I'm done," I warned him. He shut his mouth.

"On top of it, your displeased attitude around me is wearing on my last nerve. First, you can't stand me, then you dance with me and kiss me, then get upset that you did. I don't have to put up with it, nor have

I done anything to warrant it. The new plan is to have someone else from the Patriots stay with me. If it can't be here, I'll go wherever they think is safe. Hopefully, this will be resolved very soon, and we won't ever have to see each other again. You can go back to your life, and I'll go on with mine. There, that's it, end of story. We can hash out the details tomorrow."

I went to stand, but his words stopped me. "Now that you've finished, I have some things to say. Let's start first with your new plan. There won't be a changing of your bodyguard or location. There's no need." He paused. I wanted to argue, but I kept quiet.

"I don't have an issue with you, Hadley, like you think. I don't want to get rid of you. That's the last thing I want."

I couldn't help it. "Bullshit" slipped out before I could stop it. I bit my lip, not to say more.

"It's not bullshit. I couldn't let someone else guard you even if I wanted to. I have to be the one to ensure your safety."

Again, I slipped up. "Why?"

"Because you've fucking invaded my every thought and even my dreams. Not being near you or able to keep you safe is impossible for me. And being around all these men who'd give their arm for a chance with you is making me insane. I thought this was the best place for you, and from a security standpoint, it is. From a personal standpoint, I want to scoop you up and run. Find a remote cabin like your dad is in and keep you there with me alone. I said I shouldn't have kissed you, not because I regret it. It's because it made me want you even more, and I don't even know if you'd want a man like me. What can I give you? You have everything."

To say I was stunned and speechless would be an understatement. I sat there trying to process what he had just said. I couldn't believe it. He thought he had nothing to give me, but what did he see in me? If you stripped away my wealth and who my dad was, I was a boring research scientist and engineer who liked to travel, read, and learn new fighting skills. I was decent-looking, but I wasn't a beauty queen. There were women much better looking with great things about them. Why not be with one of them?

I must've been quiet too long because he came to his feet. He was scowling. "See, that's why I shouldn't have said anything. It's not possible, and I know it. I swear, despite my attraction to you, I can keep this professional and protect you. I don't want you to get a new guard. I wouldn't be able to leave anyway. I promise I won't touch you again or do anything to make you uncomfortable. I'm sorry. I think it's best if I get out of your hair and go have a drink with the guys. Goodnight."

As he went to walk away, I launched myself at him and grabbed his arm. He jerked to a stop and turned his head to stare at me. I gulped. Was I going to do this? I was crazy because the answer I gave myself was to *go for it*. What did I have to lose? At least I knew he was attracted to me. No one said it had to be a forever kind of thing. He hadn't mentioned that was what he was looking for. Maybe it was time not to get involved with a man whom I only thought long-term was an option. None of them worked out anyway.

"Don't go. You didn't let me respond to what you

just said."

"There's no need. Your silence said it."

"No, it didn't. God, are you going to make me beg you to stay and hear me out? Do you want me to plead on my knees?" I asked a bit snarkily, and then, to make my point, I sank to my knees.

The groan he let out sounded tortured. That's when I realized what I had done. I was at the perfect height to give him a blowjob, and based on his groan and the way his crotch was growing, he was thinking the same thing. It was naughty of me, but I couldn't help but tease him a bit. I slowly licked my lips before I glanced up at his face. His eyes were burning.

"Will this work?" I asked.

"Hadley, I swear to God, if you don't get up off your knees, I'm gonna lose it. You can't do this to me. I'm only human."

"And so am I. I can't seem to make you listen, so I thought this would help."

"All it'll help is to find yourself naked on a bed with me tasting and touching your entire body and making you scream," he growled.

He said it like it was a deterrent. I had news for him. It wasn't. The thought spurred me on, and I smiled at him.

"Good," I said.

He frowned. "Good? What the hell does that mean?"

"It means we might get on the same page if that happens. You said you want me. Well, I want you, too.

I'm not asking you to promise me forever or anything. You affect me like no other man ever has. As for you not having anything I need, and I have it all, you're wrong. I want someone to want me for myself, not my job or the fact I have money, even if they don't know why. The few who knew who my dad was wanted me for what it could get them from him. I'd love to be the center of a man's world, but it's not realistic, so I don't expect it. I want someone who doesn't lie, cheat, be abusive, or use me."

He was the one to go quiet this time. After a couple of moments, he held out his hand. I took it, and he lifted me to my feet. As I straightened, I was surprised when I was tugged against him. His hand came up to grip the back of my head, and before I could say a word, he kissed me. I thought the one outside the clubhouse was amazing. This one was even better.

The fire he lit inside me made my entire body burn. My skin tingled, my legs trembled, my nipples hardened, and my panties were dampening again. His hand tightened and tugged on my hair a little, and it made me hotter. I moaned long and low as our teeth and tongues battled to conquer each other. Suddenly, his hand dropped, and the next thing I knew, he grabbed my ass and hoisted me up. I reflexively wrapped my legs around his hips and my arms around his neck. He kneaded my ass.

I felt him move, then I was on my back on the couch, and he was over the top of me. My legs fell open, and he lay himself between them. He didn't crush me with all his body weight, thank goodness, but he did press his lower half into me, which had the lump in his pants pressing into my heated pussy. I tore my mouth away to cry out.

"Am I hurting you?" he asked hoarsely.

I shook my head hard. "No, you're not."

"Good," he said, then he went back to kissing me.

I have no idea how long we kissed, but it seemed like forever in one way and only a second when he lifted away again. I whimpered and tried to follow his mouth. He shook his head.

"I need to tell you something and then ask something else. First, I love that I affect you like no one else ever has. You do the same to me. Second, I know you're not asking for forever, but I fucking want it, and I pray this is the beginning of that for us. All those things you said you want. A man who wants you for yourself, not your money, job, or your family connection, I can give you. I don't give a shit about your money or fame or whatever you call it. I won't ever lie, cheat, or use you, and I most certainly won't abuse you. You might think it's unrealistic to be the center of a man's world, but, baby, I can promise you, if you're mine, that's exactly where you'll be. There would be nothing I wouldn't do except hurt innocent people to give you what you need and to keep you happy."

My heart stuttered. This was what I dreamed of a man saying to me. The expression on his face, I would swear showed him as being nothing but honest. I ran my hands up his chest until I could cup his face. Staring at him hard, I said, "Then I'm yours."

"You mean that? I can't have you change your mind tomorrow."

"I won't," I promised.

"Then come with me," he said as he eased away from me. I shakily let my legs down with his help. Holding my hand, he led me up the stairs and down the hall. We passed my bedroom and didn't stop until we were standing inside the one he'd been given. Seeing the bed made me suddenly nervous.

He saw my look and must've known what I was feeling because he reassured me. "Baby, nothing has to happen other than I need you to sleep in my arms. I'd love to continue to kiss you and do more, but we have time. I just can't face sleeping alone again. Will you stay in here tonight with me? I should've asked you first, and if you agreed, stopped to get you some things from your room."

"I'd love to stay here with you, and although my things would be nice, I don't have to have them. I assume you'd lend me a shirt if I needed one, wouldn't you?"

"Yes, I can lend you one to sleep in."

"Or I could just sleep naked. That wouldn't offend you, would it?"

"Only if you're ready for me to lay full claim to you. If not, putting something on is required."

"Well, I guess I have my answer. Do you mind if I use the bathroom?"

"Go right ahead. I'll get you that shirt."

I didn't say anything while he rummaged in the drawer and found me a T-shirt. As he handed it to me, I saw the way he was checking out my body. I felt desired as I strutted to the bathroom. Closing the door, I began to strip off my clothes.

Griffin: Chapter 12

What was I gonna do when she came out, and who was I kidding? Even wearing a shirt would test my control to the limits. I tried to calm myself as I stripped and pulled on a pair of gray lounge sweats. I got into bed and pulled the covers up over my waist. I worked to calm my mind.

I hadn't totally lied to her. I did want to kiss her more and hold her in my arms. The idea of that excited me. I'd never wanted a woman to stay all night therefore, they didn't. When the sex was over, we went our separate ways. With Hadley, there was zero desire to let her leave. I wanted her as close as possible.

The taste I'd gotten tonight had me so on edge that I should probably send her to her room and go sleep at the clubhouse, but I couldn't. When she fell to her knees, it took every ounce of my control not to unzip my pants and have my cock in that pouty mouth of hers. When she licked her lips and made her suggestion, I had to grit my teeth and pray so I wouldn't come.

The thought of her hands and mouth on my cock or any part of my body made me want to howl. The things I wanted to do to her were intense and almost animalistic. Besides tasting and touching her entire body, I wanted to mark her with visible tokens of possession and my scent. That way other men would know to steer clear of her. She was mine, and if she went through with allowing me inside of her at some point, it would be a done deal.

These kinds of thoughts were foreign to me. I liked sex a certain way and found women who were of like minds, but I never had the need to mark them or fight others to stay away. It was all Hadley. She was like my mate. Is this what Mark, Gabe, and Sean felt? Or the guys we knew in the clubs? If so, they hadn't adequately explained it at all. This was all-consuming.

My thoughts were interrupted by the bathroom door opening. I steeled myself to see her in my T-shirt. I knew it would only increase my possessiveness. My whole body froze, and my breath caught. I couldn't believe it. Standing there without a stitch of clothing on was the most alluring and beautiful woman in the world. The revelation that she was mine—my future wife, the love of my life, the owner of my soul, and the future mother of my children hit me as my body reacted. My half-erect cock went full-on steel hard.

She stared at me with a slightly apprehensive expression. She stood in the doorway, holding onto the doorframe. When I didn't say anything, she looked embarrassed. She turned away, and that broke my trance. I threw back the covers and bounded out of bed and over to her in a couple of leaps. I grabbed her shoulders and whipped her around to face me. She gasped.

Her wide eyes looked up at me. I did the only thing I could at that second. I kissed her. It was a hungry, seeking, and dominating kiss. I ravished her mouth, and thank God, she followed my lead and did the same. It wasn't long before I had her pressed tightly against me. The feel of her soft, naked, and warm skin against mine made my erection rage even more. I knew she felt it because she wiggled against it. I moaned into her mouth.

Not breaking our kiss, I lifted her. She automatically encircled my hips and shoulders with her legs and arms. This put her pussy directly against my cock. I hissed as she moaned. She was so damn wet and hot.

In a lust-filled haze, I walked her to my bed and laid her down. I followed her down, not breaking our connection. She spread her legs to make room for me as I lay between them. I thrust against her wet core. She whimpered.

There was so much I wanted to do and say. I wanted to spend hours bringing her to release, over and over with my hands, my mouth, and if I had toys, those too before I finally got her to come on my cock, but I couldn't do it. The methodical Griffin who could hold back for hours to tease a woman was gone. My beast side was all that was left, and it wanted only one thing at the moment. To be buried to the root inside of her pussy. To be pounding her into climax after climax until I exploded. The image of what that would look like and then the one of her being big and pregnant hit me.

I tore my mouth away so I could speak. My voice was hoarse and shaky when I did. "I'm sorry. I've never been like this, my beauty, but I need you. Now. Please say yes. If you aren't ready for this, then you need to run."

Her answer made me swear and see stars as she raised her head to kiss me. As she did, she shifted then her hand was around my cock, guiding it to her entrance. I didn't even recall either of us lowering my pants. As the head touched it, I gave up the fight, and I thrust inside of her. I was able to hold back enough to do it slowly. I wasn't small, and she'd insinuated it had been a while. Plus, I was bigger than her in general. As her pussy reluctantly let me inside, I groaned long and hard. She moaned along with me. She was unbelievably fucking tight, so damn hot and drenched. God, I'd never felt anything like her.

When I bottomed out, I paused. I broke our kiss to stare into her eyes. She was panting and squirming. "Is it too much? Am I hurting you?" God, I hoped not. Right now, I didn't ever see myself wanting to leave.

"No, you're not hurting me. Yes, you're a lot, Griffin. God, I feel so full. Move, please. Hurry," she said in a panicked way.

Taking her at her word that I wasn't hurting her, I lifted so I could watch as I pulled back until only the tip was still inside. My cock was glistening with her honey. Pausing for a moment, I snapped my hips forward, driving myself back into her. Watching her pussy take my cock made me groan.

"Jesus Christ, you have no idea how goddamn amazing you feel, Hadley. No idea."

"If it's anything like what you're making me feel, then yes, I do. Lord, don't stop. I want you to take me hard and fast. I can't wait this time. Do whatever you want as long as you make me come. Fuck me!" she screamed as she flexed her insides, tightening herself around me even more, although that should be impossible.

I growled like a beast and snapped. I took her fast

and hard. Her cries only drove me to go deeper, faster, and to mark her as I did. I left bite marks on her skin. I wanted to get my hands and mouth on her gorgeous breasts and explore the rest of her, but that would have to wait. First, I had to make her mine and, if I was lucky, plant my seed. It vaguely registered moments ago when I saw her honey on my cock that I wasn't wearing a condom, and I had no idea if she was on birth control, but I didn't give a shit. Impregnating her would ensure she was mine.

She suddenly tightened around me and came screaming my name. As she milked my cock, I was able to hold on by some miracle and not come. It was hell not to. I kept thrusting and twisting my hips. When she came down and relaxed, I jerked myself out of her. She whimpered and gave me a questioning look. Her eyes were on my cock.

I smacked the side of her hip. "Roll and put that ass in the air," I ordered, stepping out of my pants that were at my knees.

As she weakly turned over and then presented her ass in the air like a fucking enticement, I attacked her again. I spread her ass cheeks and kneed her legs apart so I could see her. Her swollen, wet, and bright pink pussy beckoned to me, but I was momentarily distracted by her tight little asshole. Fuck, what I wouldn't do to be sinking my cock into her ass.

That was for another day, maybe. As I notched the head and then pushed back into her pussy, I told her my fantasy. "Hadley, baby, you have the prettiest little asshole. Babe, I don't know if you're into anal, but if you are, I want this ass. God, I can't imagine how tight it is.

Your pussy is insanely tight," I panted.

She thrust back to meet my stroke. We both moaned. Shit, it felt so much deeper. As I paused for a second to keep my cool, the minx wiggled her ass and tightened her inner muscles. She glanced over her shoulder at me. Her face was full of hunger. My hands gripped her hips hard.

"I've never played that way, but if you want to, I'm game. But that'll have to be next time because right now, I need you to make me come again, and I need you to come, too. Come on. Show me how out of control you can be, Griffin. Don't hold back. You won't hurt me. Show me you."

"You asked for it. Tell me if it's too much," I muttered darkly before I grabbed a fistful of her hair.

As her head came back and her back arched to relieve the strain, I leaned down to bite her ribs. None of my bites had broken skin, but they left red marks and, in a few cases, ones that might bruise. Growling, I fucked her harder. It was like a beast mounting and coupling with its mate. The grunts, growls, and groans coming from me sounded like an animal was in the bed with her. The moans, whimpers, and begging from her told me she was loving it as if the amount of honey running down my balls wasn't enough of a clue. Or the way she thrust back hard over and over to meet my thrusts.

Wetting my thumb in her copious cream, I rubbed it around her asshole. She faltered for a moment or two but then resumed her thrusts. She didn't tell me to stop, so I pushed the tip inside. She made a hissing sound and tensed but never stopped moving. I worked it deeper as I kept fucking her. Once it was into the farthest knuckle, I began to counter-thrust my finger with my cock. She went crazy. I was right, too. Her ass was a vise.

"Please, oh God, please. I'm so close. Fuck!" she cried out.

I let go of her hair and slid my hand to the front to grip her throat. I didn't choke her too tightly, but I did squeeze as I snarled at her. "Then come. Take your man's cum. Ugh, that's it. Squeeze that pussy and that ass. Come. Now," I roared. I was right there, and I didn't want to come without her.

Her scream made my ears hurt, and the way she gripped my cock and finger made me gasp. Then I was coming, and I came harder and longer than I ever had in my life. My cum flooded her pussy, and it wouldn't stop coming. I don't know how long it was before she stopped milking me and slumped to the bed with me groaning as the last jerk stopped, and I lay beside her. I'd rolled so she was spooned from behind, and my depleted cock was still sorta inside.

We were both breathing like we'd run a race. Our skin was soaked in sweat, and I could feel her shaking. Growing concerned, I raised up on my elbow so I could see over her shoulder. She had her eyes closed, and there were tears running down her cheeks. My heart stuttered in fear.

I pulled out and rolled her onto her back. I frantically wiped away her tears. Her eyelids fluttered open. She had an unfocused look. "Hadley, honey, are you alright? Did I get too rough? Shit, baby, I'm fucking sorry," I told her remorsefully.

I'd never let go like that before, and based on

her reaction, I'd never do it again. If she ever gave me a chance to touch her again, that is. Panic and horror began to choke me. She focused on me. A frown spread across her face. She put her hand up to run it across my forehead.

"Why would you say that? Griffin? You didn't hurt me, honey. You made me forget my name and feel like I had an out-of-body experience, but you didn't hurt me."

Relief swamped me. I laid my head on hers for a few moments. When I raised it back up, she was smiling at me and shaking her head. "Crazy man, as if I'd let you hurt me. If I didn't like what you were doing, you'd know it, believe me."

I chuckled. "Well, I hope so. I never want to hurt you or make you do something you don't like or want. I may get crazy for you like I just did, which I've never been like that, just an FYI, but I will never be so far gone as not to listen."

"I know that. However, I have one complaint."

"What?" I asked worriedly.

"How long will my legs be unable to hold me up?"

Her serious expression morphed into a grin. I burst out laughing. I gave her a passionate kiss before I answered her. "That depends on whether I can get better or not. I think I'll use that as a gauge to see if I'm improving."

"Oh dear Heavenly Father, no! If you get better, it'll kill me. As if you need me to tell you that."

I rolled, bringing her over to lie partially on my chest. I ran my hand up and down her back. "I need to know that I'm able to satisfy you like no other. If you're not, then I won't be either. As for your past lovers, I don't want to know who they are or the details, but I do want to know if there are things you hate or enjoy or if you want to try something."

"I don't want to know the specifics either, but like you, I do want to know if you like things or not, if there's a certain way it feels better for you, and if there's anything that's a hard no."

"I can do that. I love to be in control, but that's not to say you never can be or that you can't ask for something. I love playing and trying new things like toys and such. I admit, the whole biting thing was new for me. I never have wanted to mark a woman like I did you. I wanted my marks and scent all over and inside you. That's why I did this," I admitted before I put my hand between her legs and gathered our combined cum on my fingers. She moaned softly. I held up my hand and waited to see what she would say.

She gazed at my hand for a couple of seconds, blinking, and then I saw understanding begin to dawn on her. As it did, her eyes widened, her mouth fell open, and her breathing sped up. She shot up into a sitting position and grabbed my wrist.

"Griffin, oh God, I can't believe this! We didn't use a condom. How could we be so careless? Oh my God," she finished softly.

"Are you saying this because you're worried about us giving each other something? If so, I can guarantee you that I'm clean. I never forget to use a condom, and I get tested every few months. My last one wasn't long ago, and I've not been with anyone but you since I took it. Is there reason to be concerned for you?" I didn't think there was, but maybe I misunderstood how long it had been for her.

"No, it's not because of that! But there's also a risk of pregnancy too. That's the flip side of using condoms and birth control. We weren't smart and should've talked about it before we lost our minds. You don't want a little Griffin running around in nine months," she said with a frown.

I eased up to sit next to her. I took her hand and laced our fingers together. "Baby, if there's a little Griffin or a little Hadley running around in nine months, you won't hear a fucking word of objection out of me. I'll happily take either or both. I didn't intentionally go bare, or if I did, it wasn't done consciously. However, the thought did pop in my head of you being pregnant after the fact, and it made me want it," I confessed.

She was back to staring at me in shock. I stayed quiet and let what I said sink in. It was a good three or more minutes before it did, and she was able to respond. "Griffin, are you hearing yourself? You just made it sound like you're trying to get me pregnant. Or at the least, that you want a baby."

"I know what I said, and like I said, consciously, I didn't do it before I was inside of you, but afterward, I realized I was bare, and I didn't stop. I didn't care if you got pregnant. In fact, I wanted it. I'm sorry I didn't stop to ask you. That was a fucked-up thing to do. As for having kids now, if you're the mom, then hell yeah, but I won't take away your choice either. We can go get one of those pills, and from now on, use condoms or whatever you prefer."

I didn't want to do that, but I would for her. I had to make her happy so she'd stay with me. Making decisions for her was the wrong way to go about it. I slid out of the bed and went to grab my pants. As I tugged them on, she straightened up.

"What are you doing?"

"I'm going to the drugstore. One should still be open. I'll be back as soon as I can." I glanced around to see if I could see the shirt I had taken off earlier. My wallet was on the dresser with my keys, and I had shoes in the closet.

Next thing I knew, she was out of bed and pressed up against me. Her nakedness made my brain go haywire. She pressed her hands on my chest. I backed up and sat on the bed since it seemed to be what she was trying to do. She straddled my legs.

"Let me make sure I've got this straight. You didn't take me without protection on purpose or not at first. When you thought of it, you wanted me to get pregnant or at least you didn't mind if I ended up that way. You want kids even if this first time results in one, but since you didn't give me a choice in the matter and you believe I don't want them, you're going out in the middle of the night to find me one of those morning-after pills. Oh, and we can use whatever I prefer going forward for contraception. Did I miss anything?"

I shook my head. "Nope, that covers it. Now, I need you to get up before I forget what I'm supposed to be doing and I take you again." I couldn't help my hands landing on her naked hips and I caressed her outer hips and up to her ribs. I stopped short of her breasts. As hard as I came, she had me getting aroused again already.

She moved closer rather than getting up, and there was a slight smirk on her lips. "Baby, what're you doing?" I asked.

"Well, I'm trying to keep you here and get you out of those pants again. Don't get me wrong. That first round was phenomenal, but I didn't get to touch and explore you. I want to do that."

"And I want to do the same to you, but we have to take care of the other thing first. Then, I promise we'll both explore to our hearts' contentment."

"There's no need to do that. I should've explained first that I'm covered on the pregnancy front, but hearing you say all those things makes me want to say the hell with it and see if we could have a baby right now, which is nuts of me. I'm a planner. I don't do things spontaneously. Everything about you makes me do the opposite of what I typically do. Better be sure or I could forget to take my shot next month and then bam, you might end up a daddy after all," she teased me.

I fell back on the bed, taking her with me, so she was lying on top of me. I growled as I kissed up her neck. "Hadley, there's no need to think about it. Don't renew the damn shot unless you're not ready for a baby because I'll take one now. You've given yourself to me. There's no escaping. Time to reconsider is gone. You're mine. I'll tell you right now, I want it all. You, us, a house, kids, marriage, everything. I don't know what you see in me, but I'll make sure to never make you regret it. Say you're mine. Say it," I said insistently.

"I'm yours if you want me, Griffin Voss, and we can get rid of the shot next time if you still want me to," she whispered, then kissed me. I got lost in the taste of her mouth. My heart was about to explode with happiness.

As our passion grew, I had to tell her something. "Babe, if you want a chance tonight to do any exploring or tasting of your own, you'd better go first. If you don't, I'm making no promises."

She sat up and rubbed her naked pussy back and forth on the bulge in my sweats. She was wet. I could feel her through my pants. As she gazed down at me, I saw the heat growing in her eyes.

"Then I need to get these pants off you, although it's a crime. We women love a man in gray sweats," she told me before hopping off me and starting to tug on the waist of them. I raised up my ass, but I had to ask as she worked them down.

"Why is it a crime?"

She tsked at me as she shook her head. "Lover, you don't know? Women love to see a man in a pair of light gray sweats because they cling so deliciously to all this." She cupped my balls and cock in her hand and squeezed gently, making me moan before she continued. "We can see the whole thing without actually seeing it. Our imaginations go crazy and the fantasies about what you look like underneath the fabric start. You can never wear these outside the house or if there's anyone of the female persuasion over to the house. This is mine."

She rolled my balls in her hand then let go to stroke up and down my length. I moaned again. She made my moan turn into a groan as she stood from taking off my pants and pushed my legs apart. She settled between them and laid on her stomach so she was hovering over my cock which was standing upright begging for her attention. She gripped the base firmly then stroked up and down a couple of times. When she got to the head, she swirled her thumb over it and worked the precum leaking out down my length.

"Mmm, I've gotta taste you, honey," she whispered before she engulfed my head with her hot, wet mouth. I cried out as she sucked tightly. She hummed which sent jolts through me.

Now, I'd had plenty of women go down on me and I couldn't recall any that were awful, but not a single one of them ever felt like this that I could remember. Within a couple of pulls of her mouth, she had my head ready to blow. I gripped the sheet under me to keep from shoving my cock down her throat and fucking her throat and mouth until I came.

I blinked as she found my one hand and lifted it away from the sheet and put it on the top of her head. She glanced up at me as she pressed it down. Hoping I was reading this right, I gripped her hair and pushed her down on me, sinking my cock to the back of her throat. When it got there, she swallowed, hummed harder and even though she gagged, she let it slip deeper.

"Fuck! Hadley, baby, I won't last like this," I warned her.

She sucked me harder, thrashed me with her tongue and took me deeper. Letting go of my objections, I began to work my cock in and out of her mouth. It didn't take me long to be there. "I'm coming," I shouted a few seconds before I exploded and saw stars as she sucked me dry. Jesus, this was what heaven looked like and I'd never get tired of her or it.

Hadley: Chapter 13

Stretching my body, I wanted to groan. My body was sore, but it wasn't in a way that I would regret or not find delicious when I thought about the cause. Griffin had made love to me twice last night, and I thought it couldn't get better than the first time, but I was wrong. After he got off in my mouth, he explored and played my pleasure points like he'd known my body for years. I lost track of the times I came before he shocked me by getting hard a third time and taking me again.

As I reluctantly opened my eyes, I saw the hazy morning light coming in around the curtains. I buried my face in my pillow. No, I was staying in bed all day, and no one could make me get up or do anything. I was on strike today.

Heat hit my back a second before I felt a hairy chest rubbing against me, then a leg thrust gently between my legs. A low, growly voice whispered in my ear. "Good morning, darlin'. How did you sleep?"

His rough-sounding voice made me shiver. My body reacted to it. The man could command my whole body with a few words. He had no idea how truly far I'd fallen under his spell in such a short time. When I thought about it, I was totally stunned. Insanity was the only word for it, but I wasn't seeking help to stop it. His lips and teeth nibbled on my ear.

"Umm, that's not the way to get me out of this bed, Griffin. I slept great, although the thought of staying in bed all day does seem like a good one."

"What would we do if we did that? Maybe there's something we can do to keep ourselves entertained," he said with a chuckle.

"There is. I planned to sleep. There's nothing better to do," I smarted off.

His teeth latched onto my earlobe, and he growled. I squealed, then found myself flat on my back with two hundred pounds of muscular man straddling me with a gleam in his eye. "Oh really, you just want to sleep, do you? I guess I have to accept that challenge and do better than I did last night if that's how you feel."

"Kidding! I was joking. I swear, Grif, last night was amazing. You have nothing to prove. You're the best lover on the planet."

"Hmm, I still think I should make sure you're not just telling me that to spare my feelings," he muttered. He was lowering his head to kiss me when there was a loud banging on the bedroom door. I jumped. He didn't.

"Hey, enough messing around in there, you two. Get your asses to the kitchen. Breakfast will be ready in five minutes. Don't let it get cold," Jinx yelled through the door. I could hear amusement in his tone.

"Go the hell away, Jinx," Griffin yelled back.

"Nope, if you don't want me coming in there to get you, naked or not, you better be there. The clock is ticking," was his response, and then we heard him walk off whistling.

"Would he do that?" I asked.

"Come in here? Probably. As much as I want to stay in bed with you, baby, I won't chance it. If he came in and saw you like this, I'd have to kill him, and that would cause a war between his club and the Patriots, and then our friends would have to take sides. It would be a clusterfuck. I guess we'll have to put this on hold until later," he said with a deep sigh and a remorseful expression.

I burst out laughing. This caused him to attack and kiss my neck, so in the end, I barely had time to throw on clothes, brush my teeth, and run a brush through my hair before hurrying downstairs. When we entered the kitchen, we found Jinx wasn't the only one there. How we didn't hear them, I don't know. The whole club was gathered in his living room, kitchen, and dining area. It was one huge room.

Everyone looked at us. There were a few smiles, a couple of smirks, and the rest were speculative glances. As we came to a stop, they began to clap.

"About goddamn time, you two stopped circling each other," Sarge said.

"Yeah, we were about to lock you up in a room and not let you out until you stopped this bullshit," Sinner added.

"Personally, I hoped she'd shoot him so I'd have a chance," Thrasher said with a wink.

"You don't have a chance of that. Not after what I heard last night," Jinx said with a chuckle.

My face grew hot, but I didn't let him get away with embarrassing me. I let go of Griffin and rushed toward Jinx. He put up his hands as if to surrender as he grinned. I took my chance and feinted a punch to his jaw. When he raised his hands higher to block me, I landed a punch to his ribs. I pulled it enough not to do damage, but he felt it. He huffed out air as I smirked at him. He gave me a surprised look.

"That was a love tap. Keep it up, and I'll let you have the real thing, Jinx. I know what I'm doing. Broken ribs and pissing blood for a week doesn't sound like fun, does it?"

"Jesus, get your woman away from me, Griffin. She's mean. I thought she liked me, but I guess not," Jinx pouted as he said it.

"If I didn't like you, you'd be nursing several hurt spots. I just want to keep you in line," I told him sweetly.

"I'm in line. Truce," he said then he added a wink at the end.

I laughed, and the next thing I knew, he was giving me a hug. I hugged him back, which got the others lining up for one. Griffin tugged me out of Styx's arms. "Get your own woman."

"We're trying, but they all get snapped up by fuckers like you and the other guys first. What the hell? We're gonna have to host a damn party or something for all the eligible women within the nearby six or seven states," Rage grumbled.

"I refuse to believe for a second that any of you have trouble finding women," I scoffed.

"We're not saying we don't have sex. We do, but most of us want more than that. It's all those damn Warriors' fault. We were carefree bikers living the good life, oblivious that there was more out there or that we wanted it until we became friends with those bastards. Suddenly, we meet all these gorgeous, strong, interesting women, and they're all taken by the time we meet them. Then the Patriots start the same thing, along with the Punishers and Pagans. I think they owe it to us to help us find women," Mad Dog stated firmly. He was staring hard at Griffin.

"Hey man, don't look at me. I stumbled across Hadley by accident, and from what I know, so did all the others you're bitching about. Go out and rescue some women, walk the town, or meet one through one of your businesses. I don't think a party will do it. You'll get more of the same kind you get now," Griffin advised.

"While you're all debating, the food is getting cold. Hadley, ladies first. Make sure to get as much as you want because these assholes won't leave any for a second round," Jinx gestured to the food. Knowing they'd wait on me if I didn't. I picked up a plate and got started. As I went down the long counter with the different selections, I had to ask.

"Where did you get this? It looks great, by the way. I'm starved."

He smirked, so I gave him a warning look. He didn't say anything about why I was starving. I didn't know I was that loud, but then again, I'd been so caught up in what we were doing.

"I made it. Where do you think I got it?"

"You made all this?" I didn't mean to sound astonished, but it wasn't what I pictured a biker, especially one who was the president, to do.

"I did. I'm more than a handsome face, a hot body,

and a badass. I have other skills. You need to promote that to find me the right woman. I can be somewhat domesticated. Put it on my resume," he joked.

"Do you clean and do laundry?" I asked.

"I can and would split the work. You don't get to be my age without learning shit. So when you go looking for the women Mad Dog mentioned, find mine first."

This got loud objections from the others. I had to laugh as they got more insulting, and the threats grew wilder. It was loud, chaotic, and so much fun to eat with them. I laughed so much it was hard to eat, but I snuck in bites. Jinx had done a really good job, and when we were done, there wasn't a morsel left. I watched in awe as the guys, without saying a word, got up and began to clean up. Sinner saw my face.

"We know if we want Jinx to keep cooking for us, we clean up. It's the least we can do," he explained as he cleared the table.

"Does he do this often?"

"At least once a week if he can. It's not always breakfast. Sometimes, he makes dinner. It relaxes him, he says."

I glanced over at Griffin. He shook his head. "I'm sorry, beautiful, but I don't cook. It's not because I won't. I've tried, and it always ends in disaster. You can ask the guys and their ladies. I'm banned from all their kitchens other than to chop stuff or clean. I can do that. Do you cook? If not, no big deal. We'll hire someone to make meals for us or do the mail-order meals that's become popular in the last few years. We won't starve or have to eat out every night."

I pasted a mournful look on my face. I couldn't help it. I had to do it. I shook my head. "I'm sorry, Griffin, but that's a deal breaker. Jinx, I guess you and I should talk." I winked at Jinx when I said it. Griffin couldn't see it. A wicked smile spread across Jinx's face.

He pretended to puff up as he replied to my suggestion. "Babe, not only will I do all those things I told you, but the sex will put what he did to shame."

I took a step toward him. I squeaked, which wasn't dignified, as I was hauled back against Griffin, and his strong arms caged me in.

"Over my dead fucking body, you'll take her."

"Hey, you heard the lady. She wants a man who can cook. Don't be a sore loser, man," Jinx said.

I felt Griffin moving, and the next thing I knew, he had out his phone. We all watched him, wondering what he was doing as he pressed a button. I could see his screen, and I saw the name Mark. He hit the speaker button. It rang a couple of times before Undertaker's gruff voice answered.

"What's up? Is everything alright with Hadley?"

"Other than a bunch of bikers who want to steal her, she's fine."

Undertaker barked out a laugh. "You can't trust a damn biker. Have I taught you nothing? They're a bunch of horny fuckers."

The guys all laughed and nodded.

"I knew that, but damn, Jinx is tempting her away with his cooking."

Undertaker groaned. "Man, don't lie to her and say you can. It's too ugly to contemplate your cooking. Hadley, honey, don't even ask him to try, please. I beg you."

"But I really had my heart set on a man who could cook," I pretended to whine.

"See, that's why I'm calling. I need you, Sean, and Gabe to order an assault team against them. I'll get her out of here. The only way to keep her is to eliminate the competition."

I turned my head so I could see him. He was staring intently at me. "I can't believe you called him to joke about this."

"Who said it was a joke? I have news for you, woman. You're mine now. Last night sealed the deal. I'll fight and even kill to keep you."

His macho words made a part of me melt. I know it wasn't all modern to want a man to take control, but in certain instances, it appeared I loved it. I was shaken from that feeling when Undertaker answered him.

"If you mean what I think you do about last night, about damn time. As for an assault team, how soon do you want them, and do you want them to give Jinx special treatment?" he chuckled darkly.

"Mark, don't you dare encourage him! We're just playing with him. Touchy damn man." I elbowed Griffin in the stomach.

"Hadley, I'll always back a brother, especially to keep his woman or protect his family. The Marauders are friends, but he's my brother."

Aww, that was sweet, especially coming from a

man like Undertaker. This led to Jinx protesting. This went on for a couple of minutes before Griffin ended the call by telling his brother to hold off on the assault.

I shook my head at him. "Crazy ass man," I muttered.

He turned me around to face him. "Anything for you," he said before he kissed me. The hoots and shouted encouragement were a faint noise in the background as I got lost in him.

❧❧❧

The fun continued with Griffin and the Marauders for the rest of yesterday after his call to Undertaker. Some of them went to work, but others stayed at the compound. I got to do more exploring when I wasn't working. Even if I was away from the lab, I still had things I had to do. We were at critical points in the project. I was really encouraged that it appeared we'd make the deadline Dad had set.

It was aggressive, and I'd been asking him why, but all he said was the government wanted it. That wasn't unusual, and he'd always pushed back when they got too pushy in the past. There was something he wasn't telling me. I even had a call with him earlier when I updated him and then asked again why the push.

"Honey, I told you. They just really need it, and this time, I thought we could do it faster. We're not going to cut corners and not thoroughly test it, but it needs to meet the deadline. Now, enough of that. Tell me, how are things going there? Are Griffin and the Marauders treating you okay?"

I knew he wouldn't say more, so I answered him. "It's going really well. The area is peaceful, and no one is too close to their compound. It's been interesting to be here and to meet them. They're not exactly what I imagined, but they've been more than welcoming and helpful. They make me laugh a lot. What about you? How's it being with Undertaker in the woods?"

I didn't want to tell him about me and Griffin over the phone. It was a face-to-face conversation. I wasn't worried he'd think he wasn't good enough or anything. I just knew he'd have lots of questions and would want to talk to Griffin and observe us.

"Mark has been wonderful. He's not the most talkative guy, but we get along well. He has a great mind and we've been talking about things needed to protect us and our men and women in the service. I want to get all the Patriots and those who work for them together to pick their brains. Why I haven't done something like that before, I don't know," he grumbled.

"Dad, you've more than helped to protect them and this country. I think it would be fun to have a discussion with them, though. Any more shooting sessions in the woods?"

He went on to tell me what they'd been doing. Our call lasted an hour before I had to hang up to do a conference call with the team back at Gerard's.

Today, I was working on figuring out why one of the components wasn't working the way it should. Everything had been performing perfectly until this morning when, bam, it was as if it was totally offline, and no one knew why. What happened between yesterday and today?

I could do things remotely via remote access to the lab computers. I was doing that now, trying to trace the problem. Griffin was off doing something. He'd known without me telling him I needed to concentrate.

Hours later, I had my answer. It wasn't one I expected or wanted to contemplate, but there was no other explanation. With shaking hands, I grabbed my phone and texted Griffin. He was still out somewhere on the compound.

Me: Need you here, please. We need to call Dad and the team.

It wasn't more than thirty seconds before I had his response.

Griffin: I'm coming. What's wrong?

Me: I'll explain when you get here and we have Dad and the others on the phone.

Griffin: I'll be there in a couple of minutes.

I paced the office. Jinx had been sweet enough to let me use his home office to work from. I was impressed with his setup. He had told me about all the club's businesses and how he had the ultimate responsibility and oversight of them. They ran the club like a company in many ways.

When Grif arrived, he wasn't alone. Jinx and Animal were with him. They were all frowning. Grif came to me and hugged me. "What's wrong? You look sick."

"I'll tell you, just get Dad and your team on a video call. Please."

He let go and went to the computer. I paced as he got things organized. Jinx left the room. Animal had taken a seat. A couple of minutes later, Jinx was back, and he had a glass with what looked like whiskey in it. He handed it to me. "Drink this. You're pale as shit and agitated. No matter what's wrong, we'll take care of it."

I didn't argue. I took it and drank the whole finger of alcohol in a gulp. It was whiskey. It burned, but in a good way. "Thanks," I told him when it was gone. I didn't usually drink like that, but this warranted it.

It was amazing how fast Griffin got the others together. He waved me to take the desk chair. He stood at my side. Jinx and Animal sat in other chairs.

"Sweetheart, what's going on?" Dad asked worriedly.

"I got a message this morning from the lab team. One of the components that had been working perfectly suddenly stopped working. They discovered it when they came in this morning." Dad already knew it, but I was bringing the others up to date.

"Okay, so what did they expect you to do about it?" Sean asked.

"I'm able to remote access into the computers there and certain other things. I've been working on it all day, trying to figure out what's wrong. I finally did, and that's why I wanted this call with all of you."

"And?" Gabe asked.

"The only explanation I have is that someone sabotaged it. There's no way it broke on its own. It's been tampered with. The team didn't touch it once they figured out it wasn't working. I designed it so they knew I'd want to be the one to fix it. We need to get the security footage from yesterday showing the time from when we stopped working on it until they called me this morning. Someone was in that building. I want to know who and how. The ones with access are extremely limited."

I felt sick to my stomach as I told them my conclusion. The people in our lab I'd worked with for years were more than just employees. I would've never, in a hundred years, thought they'd do this. As I waited for us to all be together for this call, I racked my brain to think who would do it. None of them stood out.

There was swearing, and Dad exclaimed in shock and disbelief, "Hadley, that can't be. No one at Gerard's would do that. There has to be another explanation."

"If there is, I can't find it from here. Dad, I don't want to believe any of them could do this either, but we have to consider it. Here's my next dilemma. In order to gain access to the security footage, we have to ask our head of security for it. What if he's part of this? It would tip our hand that we're onto what was done. I don't know how to access it. Do you?" I asked my dad.

He shook his head. "No, I don't. Damn it, why didn't I think of that? I don't know how else to get it other than to ask PJ."

"It's not your fault. I didn't think of it either."

"We can get in and get what you need. Don't worry. Let's not jump to conclusions until we view it. Give me a minute to get Makayla on it. If she can't get in, then we'll call the big guns, Smoke and Everly. I'll be back," Gabe said before getting up to walk out of the room.

"Who's Makayla?" I asked.

"She's our newest addition. She's a computer

expert, and she likes to get into impenetrable systems," Sean explained.

I knew who Everly and Smoke were. Griffin had talked about the other clubs and their members. While we waited for Gabe to get back, I told Dad what I'd been doing and found. I knew it was all gibberish to the others, but he and I knew what it meant and how serious it was.

When I was done, Gabe was back. "She's on it. She said to give her an hour. If she can't break in with what you provided us before, Travis, then I'll call Smoke."

"Thank you. I really hoped I was mistaken, but I'm sure I'm not. Short of me going to Gerard's and tearing it apart, it's the only explanation."

"You can't go there. If you do, whoever is behind this has a chance to get to you. In fact, that's probably why it was done," Griffin said sternly.

"I agree. It's likely a ploy to get you to show yourself along with your dad. You both need to stay where you are," Undertaker seconded.

"It may be, but if it derails us from completing this on time, that's not going to be acceptable. You know how unforgiving the government is. It's fine for them to make you wait but not for you to make them," I reminded them.

"Yeah, their double standard of hurry up and wait for us and gimme now for them," Jinx muttered.

It was true. Not wanting to get off topic too much, Sean brought us back to the task at hand. "I know this isn't what you want, but why don't we get off here and come back in an hour? That'll give us time to work on things. I'll send out the invite. Okay?"

We all agreed and ended the video call. I got up and paced the office. The three with me were watching me closely. "You don't need to stay. Jinx, I promise not to wear a hole in your wood floor. I just can't sit still right now. I need to be doing something, but I don't know what?"

"Take a walk with Griffin. Get out of the house for the next hour. You've been cooped up here all day. I'd say go sex her up, but then we'd never see you again today," Jinx said with a grin. As tense as I was, I had to chuckle. I knew he did it to ease the tension a little.

"Hush, no talk about our sex life, remember?" I reminded him.

"If you go for a walk, I'll hush."

That's how I ended up taking a long stroll. Grif purposefully wouldn't let me talk about the situation. Instead, he told me more about his home in Virginia. I had to admit when we returned for the follow-up call, I was a bit more relaxed.

Hadley: Chapter 14

When we took the second call, we didn't gather in Jinx's office. We were in the clubhouse in the room they used for church. They'd educated me the other night about what church was. And it wasn't just the five of us. The others were there, too. I had no idea why they were home in the middle of the afternoon. My puzzlement must've been evident.

"I sent out a text asking anyone who could come to get their asses here. I cleared it with the Patriots. The more eyes and brains we have on this the better," Jinx explained.

"Thank you," I told him.

"Anything for you sweetheart. Put that in my pro column," he teased. He was still adding things he said should sway me to him. He made me laugh especially when Griffin got in on it and listed all the creative ways he could torture him.

Beast prevented me from saying anything more by bringing up a large screen on the wall with the rest of the Patriots and Dad. I saw that Sloan and Cassidy were with them, along with a woman I didn't recognize. I knew it wasn't Gemma. I'd seen her before.

"Okay, we're back, and we have the security footage. Everyone, let me introduce Makayla. She's our newest find. Makayla, this is the Ruthless Marauders

MC. You know Griffin, and that's Hadley Gerard. The gentleman with Mark is Travis Gerard, her father." Sean made introductions.

"Hello. I wish we were meeting in person and for a more pleasant reason. Hopefully, we will soon. I know you're anxious to see what we have, so I won't waste your time. I got in quickly and perused the footage. At one forty-seven a.m. today, someone entered your lab. Here's what the cameras caught."

She tapped on a laptop in front of her. On our screen appeared the footage. A figure dressed all in black with a full ski mask entered the secure lab. The way the person moved told us that they knew the layout—no surprise there. That he or she quickly made their way to the camera recording this, and it was covered with something, was. Everyone cursed.

From there the screen kept quickly changing scenes. They were from other cameras in there, but none were directly focused on our prototype. We caught glimpses of the person moving around but not what he or she was doing. They were there for about fifteen minutes then the covering on the camera was removed and they left.

I was frustrated. This didn't help us a bit. I still had no idea who it was. The way the figure appeared hunched, it could be a man or woman. Excluding me and Dad, there were seven others with the codes and ability to enter the lab. Retinal scans and fingerprints guaranteed that.

There was silence then Griffin broke it. "Whoever it is, they had to get past the retinal scan and the fingerprint scanner."

"Which means it can only be one of seven. You met all of them the day we went to the lab," I reminded him.

"I did, but that's not the only way to get past the security. If you know what you're doing, you can fool the retinal and fingerprint scans," he dropped on us.

"How?" Dad asked.

"The fingerprint can be picked up with tape and transferred into a machine that will produce a replica that can be worn over your finger. As for the retinal scan, there are ways to map the retina to get a scan. Have either of you recently been to the eye doctor and had them do a retina check for glaucoma?" Gabe asked.

"How do you know that?" I asked.

"We can't say, just know it's possible. If anyone who works for you is tech savvy or has connections, they could do it, which unfortunately opens up our suspect pool. We can't afford to rule anyone out. So far our background checks have shown no one with suspicious histories, emails, or unexplained large amounts of cash," Sloan added.

"Cash?" Dad asked.

"Yes, we're also checking that whoever came to your house wasn't being paid to do it by someone else. Sabotage by other companies wouldn't be out of the question. Those who want the government contracts Gerard's has. You've been the primary defense contractor for years. That has to piss off people," Undertaker said.

I groaned and laid my head on the table. "This is hopeless. This means it could be anyone. How do we figure out who, with these kinds of odds?"

"Unfortunately, unless they leave us a clue, not very fast. We have lots of manpower hours working on this. We know it's frustrating and scary, but we will find out who it is and why, and we'll stop them," Griffin said confidently. I wish I had his certainty.

"And if we don't? Playing devil's advocate here, we can't stay hidden away forever. We have a company to run and a project to finish. Also, this isn't the only thing we're working on right now. We have obligations and not fulfilling them might mean having to let people go. Our employees don't deserve that. I'm gonna have to return to the lab soon to do more hands-on work," I informed them.

"You can't go back and let someone kill you! Your employees won't want that," Griffin snapped.

"Grif, I've lived under the threat of the possibility of someone kidnapping and killing me since I was nine years old. Hell, even before that. Despite doing everything Dad can to protect me, someone found out who I am. I'm not living my life in hiding."

"You will until we catch this psycho. You hired us for our expertise. Use it. Listen to us," he said, mostly to my dad.

"I hear you, and I agree, but I also agree with my daughter. We have to think of the employees and their livelihoods, too. I'm terrified of losing Hadley, but eventually, we will have to come out of hiding. The board is getting more and more antsy. I get daily emails asking where we're at and when we are coming back. I won't be able to hold them off forever."

"Which ones are bugging you?" Sean asked.

"All of them, but especially Ansel Dewitt, not that I'm surprised. He and I have been friends for years. He's worried about not only the company but me and Hadley."

"Yes, Ansel has been like an uncle to me for as long as I can remember. He can be a bit abrasive, but he means well. I can't recall a week going by that he and Dad didn't talk or meet. It must be driving him nuts."

"It is. Plus, our security guys are getting restless. They don't like not doing their jobs," Dad added.

"The security guards are reaching out too?" Gabe clarified.

"Yes, they are." I verified.

Griffin's head whipped around to me. "You've been in contact with them? I told you not to do that."

"Hang on, I haven't answered them, but I get their messages. Ortiz, Sanders, and Rockwell have all asked if I'm alright and when I'm coming home. They're worried about their jobs, Griffin. Wouldn't you be?"

"Their jobs are to keep you safe. If you staying in hiding and not communicating does that, then they should shut the fuck up. Let me guess: Rockwell has been the worst. I need to see your phone," he snapped.

I was all for him being demanding in the bedroom, but not out here. His attitude made me get defensive. I glared at him. "I'd change my tune if I was you. I don't take orders. Your attitude about Rockwell is why I didn't mention it."

"Of course, I have an attitude, as you call it. He's

not worried as your guard. He wants you, damn it. If you think for a minute I'm gonna let him get near you, then you don't know your man, babe."

I fought not to groan as he said the last part. I should've warned him not to say anything in front of Dad. And yes, Dad immediately caught on. I saw him perk up on his screen. Shit!

"Her man? Babe? Is there something you want to tell me, Hadley Marie?"

This made Grif grimace. He gave me an apologetic look. I opened my mouth to explain, but Grif beat me to it.

"Yes, Travis, you heard me right. We'd like to talk to you about it but we want to do it in private. If you'll bear with us, as soon as we're done with this, we'll talk to you together."

"Yes, we will," was all Dad said.

The rest of the call was basically them discussing increasing their manpower to look into our people and their insistence that we had to stay hidden. I gave up arguing for the moment. When they ended the call, Griffin and I excused ourselves to go back to the house to call my dad from there. No one objected. As we headed there, he apologized.

"I didn't mean to out us to your dad. It just slipped out. I know I get a bit crazy when it comes to Rockwell, but he wants you, and I can't stand it. I don't want him texting, calling, or even looking at you. I know that's over the top, and I'm trying to work on it."

"Good, and while you do, you need to work on not bossing me around. What I allow and even like in the bedroom doesn't mean I want that to be my life outside of it. If you think something needs to be done, we talk it out, and you have to listen to my side and consider what I'm saying. You just dictating won't get it. We won't become anything other than temporary lovers, Griffin, if it's like that."

We'd made it to the house by then. He pulled me into his arms. "Babe, temporary isn't in our vocabulary when it comes to us. I promise to work on it, but you have to give me some slack. I'm new to this whole relationship stuff. All I can think about is making sure you're safe and mine. I can't lose you. It took me years to find you."

I sighed and put my head on his chest. "I don't want to lose you either. All I ask is you work on it and I'll do the same. Okay, enough talk. We have to call my dad. God, can I have a drink?"

He laughed. "No, you're not getting drunk. Why are you so worried? Do you think he'll hate it because I'm not like you?"

"If you mean the money, no. Will he hate it? I don't think so, other than he'll want to know everything about you and ask you a million questions. He's never really been able to do that as a dad in the past."

"I can handle it. Come on, no more procrastinating." He tugged me along behind him to Jinx's office. He made me sit then he pulled a chair around to sit beside me. He was the one to place the video call. Dad answered right away.

"What took so long?"

I explained, "We had to get from the clubhouse to Jinx's house so we could have privacy."

"Fine. Tell me, what's going on? When I sent her with you, I didn't expect you to start a sexual relationship with her. She may be an adult, but she's still my daughter. That isn't very professional. Do you often get involved with your clients? I won't have my daughter used to stave off your boredom." There was a bite to Dad's tone.

To say I was shocked would be an understatement. "Dad! What in the world?"

"This is between me and him, Hadley. You and I will talk when I'm done with him. What's wrong? You don't have anything to say for yourself?" he asked Griffin.

I started to say something else, but Grif stopped me with a hand on my arm and a shake of his head. "Baby, don't. He's right. I need to talk to him. Travis, would you prefer to do it alone?"

"I would like to, possibly, but at the end. Tell me what you expect to get out of this, whatever it is. Hadley is a very rich woman and will only get richer one day. She's smart and could have anyone. She's going to change the world even more than she already has. What she needs isn't someone who wants to have a good time for a few weeks and then leaves."

"I have to stop you right there. I know she's smart and will do great things. She's also beautiful and giving, and she cares about people. You've raised a wonderful woman. However, letting any man use her is not to be tolerated. I can assure you that's the last thing in the world I plan to do to her."

"What then? You're gonna see if dating works, and you can maybe have a real lasting relationship?" Dad's tone was slightly less biting. It was so hard not to interrupt them, but I held my tongue.

"No, we're not going to date." I saw Dad's face tighten when Grif said that. He continued. "This is as serious as it can get. I'm working to make sure your daughter is mine for the rest of our lives."

"Does that mean you plan to get married one day?"

"Yes, marriage, house, kids, the whole thing. Hell, I want dogs, too, and the sooner, the better. I know it sounds too fast, but when you know, you know."

I couldn't tell if Dad was astonished, relieved, happy, or a mixture of the three. He didn't say anything for a few moments, then his gaze shifted to me. "Hadley, what do you have to say to all of this? Do you feel the same? How serious is it?"

"Dad, it's very serious, like Griffin said. We're both on the same level about this. Yes, it's super fast, but it feels right and in a way I've never experienced. You know how my past relationships have been. This is the first time a man knows everything about me, and he's not intimidated, nor does he seem to care about those things."

"What about you and Gerard's and your status as my daughter and with the company? You know, once this threat is over, the days of hiding who you are are done. I won't do it anymore. I need the world to know about you and to accept you're my heir and that Gerard's will be yours when I'm gone. Also, they need to know you're a brilliant inventor and scientist in your own right and have been doing it for years. This will make you a bigger target and bring even more people into your life. Where will you live? How does he feel about you working?"

We hadn't exactly talked about those things yet, but Griffin knew I wouldn't give up my dad's company. "We haven't figured all that out yet, but he knows the company is part of me. I won't part with it, and I don't see him asking me to do that."

"She's right. I know, and I wouldn't. As for her being a bigger target, I'll ensure she's well-protected. I would hope she'd be willing to move at least closer to Hampton so we could both split our time between our companies. Like her job, I'm committed to Dark Patriots. Mine may be a bit more flexible than hers. I believe I can do more remote work."

"As long as you talk about those things and figure it out together, that's all I ask. Combining your lives will take effort. If you're not willing to work at it to make it work for both of you, then don't go down this path. It'll only end in hurt feelings and resentment."

"Dad, I'm willing to put in the work, and I don't expect him to do all the compromising."

"Travis, I'm more than willing to do the same."

"Good. Now, Hadley, would you be so kind as to leave so I can speak to Griffin alone?"

"Dad, be nice." I made sure he could hear the plea in my voice.

He smiled. "I will, I promise."

It was with great reluctance that I got up to leave. However my man didn't let me go until after he gave me a kiss to take my breath away. He did it right in front of the monitor, so Dad saw it. I walked out a bit dazed when he let go of me. I think I might've wavered on my feet. When I got to the living room, I found Jinx there. He gestured for me to come to him. I went over and plopped down on the couch across from him.

"Talk to me. Tell me what your dad said and why Griffin isn't out here," he demanded, so I slowly filled him in.

Griffin:

As the door closed behind Hadley, I gave Travis my full attention. I wouldn't disrespect him by only half paying attention. I needed him to believe I was fully committed to his daughter and meant every word I said. I saw his grimace as his smile faded. Goddamn, here it comes. He's gonna threaten me to leave her alone. I thought Mark said he was alright with us being in a relationship. I had news for him, there was nothing he could do to make me give her up. The only way that happened was if she didn't want me, and from what I'd experienced so far, that wasn't happening.

"Griffin, I need you to listen very carefully to me. I need you to understand what I'm about to tell you. And I don't want you to say a word to Hadley. Do you agree? I want you to swear on the life of your best friends you'll keep this private."

"Travis, I can't promise that. If you think threats or bribes will make me leave her alone, you're mistaken. I won't do anything like that to her and lie about it. She's too smart to fall for it anyway."

"You're right. She's too smart. It's her smartness that's made this so hard to do. I swear it's not me trying to separate the two of you. It's information so you know what you're up against and so you can protect her. Will you agree for this reason? At least for now, it needs to be a secret." He sounded tired, and I heard the pleading in his tone.

"Why don't you tell me, and then we'll see? I can't blindly promise. I'm sorry."

He sighed and nodded. "Okay, here goes. You know this project is on an accelerated timeline."

"Yeah, Uncle Sam is impatient to get it. I understand why and the amount of work it's going to take to make it happen—or at least as much as I can as a non-scientific person. I don't have your or her brains."

He gave me a faint smile. "I lied. The timeline wasn't imposed by Uncle Sam. It was all me," he said bluntly, which stunned me.

"Why would you do that to yourself and her?" was my first question.

"Because I had to make sure it would be completed in time."

"In time for what? Is there a threat coming we don't know about?"

"Yes, I guess you could call it a threat. I don't know how much more time I have, Griffin. Time is running out."

"Running out? I don't understand."

He paused, then blew my mind. "I'm dying, Griffin. I'm dying and I need this to be done before I do. I need time to have nothing distracting us so she and I can spend as much time as we can once it's done without focusing on another project. I want to spend my last weeks or months with her."

My stomach dropped, and a sick feeling filled me. I might not have known them long, but I knew how much she loved her dad and how much he loved her. It would kill her to lose him. I grasped at straws. “Have you gotten a second opinion? Maybe your doctor is wrong.”

He shook his head. “No, it’s a certainty. I’ve consulted with the top doctors in not only the country but the world. They’re all consulting on my case, and so far, they’ve helped me to hide it and slow it down. If it became known I was sick, the company would potentially falter. The public could panic, and so could the board. I can’t let my legacy to her be an empty one, but even more than that, I can’t bear to watch her suffer, knowing I’m dying. She’d try to give up her life to take care of me, and I don’t want her to.”

“You have to tell her. I can’t keep this from her.”

“Please just wait until we catch whoever is making the threats and who broke into our home and the company. Knowing you as I do from Anderson, I have every confidence you and your company will figure it out soon. If it’s not done in the next two weeks, then I’ll tell her.”

“Why only two weeks?”

“Because that’s how long it’ll take for all the legal things I’ve put into play to be finalized. By then, the company, all stocks, all rights, and property, everything will be hers as well as she’ll be the one to make my medical decisions if I become incapacitated. Plus, it’ll give you time to help me get even more security in place for her. I need her to be safe, son.”

“I’ll make sure she’s safe no matter what. Do you mind if I ask how much time they gave you and what’s your diagnosis?”

"Time can be a few months to a year max, although it isn't likely to be a year. I have myelodysplastic syndrome, MDS, which is a fancy name for a group of disorders that affect my bone marrow. It can no longer make normal blood cells. My marrow isn't making red blood cells to move oxygen throughout my body, clotting cells, or white blood cells to help me fight infections.

"Isn't that what leukemia is?"

"Those with MDS are at risk of having it progress to acute myeloid leukemia, AML. Some debate AML is the natural progression of MDS, not a separate disease. Regardless, mine is very advanced, and yes, I have AML. They suspected I had it for many years, but it was never found. The symptoms I dismissed as normal weren't. My hectic and stressful lifestyle explained most. Fatigue, sometimes getting weak, short of breath, and lightheaded. I would bruise easily. I ignored it and brushed it off. Even when I'd get sick with an infection, I'd just say it was due to stress lowering my immune system."

"How long have you had it? How do they know it's not treatable?"

"I've known for a year. They said it's more common in people aged fifty-eight to seventy-five, which is where I fall. They tried the typical treatments. I've had growth factors that were to help my bone marrow make my blood cells and platelets. I had injections for a while, and then after that were blood transfusions. Eventually, we tried immunotherapy. It was hard to hide the effects of those. By the time we decided those weren't working, chemotherapy, a bone marrow transplant, or a stem cell transplant weren't viable options, and I was tired. I don't want to spend the last few months of my life in worthless treatments."

I had to close my eyes for a moment. This was going to devastate Hadley. How could I keep this from her for even two weeks?

"I know what I'm asking you, and I wouldn't if I thought it wasn't important. She should be done with the project by then, too. If she knew now, she'd be too distracted to work on it, and I'd be too tired to do it. We can't let our service men and women down. This will save lives."

"I agree it's important, but so is your daughter's knowledge of what she's soon to face. You have to tell her. Now."

He shook his head. "No, I can't. You have to give me two weeks. I'm begging you. If you do, I won't voice a single objection to your relationship. I know that might not mean much to you, but it does to her. Please."

I sat there in agony for I don't know how long. I debated all the pros and cons of it in my head and even aloud with him. It was with great reluctance that I finally gave him an answer. "I'll keep it from her for two weeks max, but I have to share it with my team. I need their help to prepare her security and to help support her when the time comes. If I do this, then I need a few things from you."

"Anything."

"You'll stop work immediately and come to Hampton once this is over. I want her to have a chance to see where I live and if she can live there or not. She won't do it if you're sick and in Fairfax, and I wouldn't blame her. You'll come with her and let us take care of you. There will be no bullshit out of you. You'll give her this. I'll ensure your safety and help her to cope."

"Done."

"I'm not done. I plan to ask her to marry me. If she agrees, then I want to have the wedding as soon as possible. I know she'll want you there, and if you're able, you can walk her down the aisle. If you can't walk, we'll wheel or carry you. You'll give her away and into my keeping."

"If she agrees to marry you, then yes."

"You need to know before we get married. I want her lawyer or yours, whichever, to draw up a prenuptial agreement that will protect all her money and assets. I want nothing she has, and I don't want anyone to think I married her for any of it. Our children will inherit everything."

"You plan to have kids?" I heard the excitement in his voice. I smiled and nodded.

"You probably don't want to hear this, but if I could get her pregnant tomorrow, I would. We've already discussed it. I'm thirty-eight years old. I'm ready for a family. I didn't know it for sure until I met her. I can promise you I'll love and cherish her."

Tears filled his eyes and streamed down his face. It made me feel bad to make him cry but by the expression on his face, they were tears of relief and happiness. I could handle those. "I couldn't be happier. Deal. Now, let me get myself cleaned up. Then we need to call her back in here to reassure her we're good.

Thank you. You have no idea how much this means to me."

"I can guess. I just hope she forgives me for not telling her."

"We could lie and say I never told you."

"Nope, I refuse to lie to her even to spare her feelings or me her wrath."

"Good. That's the answer I was hoping for."

Griffin: Chapter 15

I was finding it hard as hell to face Hadley and not tell her that her dad was dying. On one hand, I could understand why he wanted to wait, but on the other, I could see it from the perspective of being his child. I know she thought I was upset over something her dad said to me in private, which I kind of was. She kept asking me to tell her and I kept telling her nothing was wrong. It had placed a slight strain on us.

I was trying to stay away more so I wouldn't slip up. I used the excuse that I was working on stuff and didn't want to interrupt her, which wasn't a complete lie either. The project was at a crucial point, and she was spending hours on her computer and talking with the team—the team we couldn't trust to be the ones who hadn't sabotaged it.

They had gotten the problem fixed, thanks to her. Watching her work told me how brilliant she was. She was years ahead of me in every way. I'd always seen myself as a rather intelligent person, but compared to her, I was an idiot. When I told her that, she was appalled and begged me not to think such a thing. See, sweet as hell, too. How I'd gotten so lucky to capture her attention, I'd never know. Hopefully, our kids would take after her but not leave their daddy in the dust. They'd probably bypass me by the time they were five.

It had been three days since we found out about

the sabotage. We still hadn't eliminated or confirmed anyone as responsible. Everyone on my team, her, Travis, and even the Marauders, was on edge. Jinx and his guys were on edge, not because they were worried they couldn't protect her, but because they had taken a liking to her and were feeling ultra-protective.

There had been no more nighttime visitors to the lab. We had someone monitoring it. I wanted her to finish the project without delay so Travis could tell her what he was hiding, and I could stop feeling guilty for not telling her.

She was working in Jinx's office while I was working at the clubhouse. They'd given me an empty room and were nice enough to move in a desk so I could use my laptop and tap into their internet and printer. I was typing away when there was a knock. Glancing up, I found Beast standing there. I went on alert. He had no reason to seek me out unless he'd found something. He was spending his spare time trying to track down the culprit like my team was.

"Did you find something?"

"Not exactly. Can I talk to you for a minute? I need more information."

"Sure. Have a seat."

He sat in an extra chair I had put in here. "I need to know more about the bodyguard, Rockwell. From what we've heard you say, you don't like him or trust him. Tell me why."

"It's mainly because he's too interested in Hadley. He's been her main guard for the past four years. He's with her full-time, and he even lives on their estate.

Now, he's not the only employee who does, but still. You should've seen how he hovered over her and how pissed off he got when anyone was taking her attention. He wants her."

"Do you think he could be the one who issued the threat to her dad?"

I'd thought about it and I just didn't see it. I shook my head. "As much as I'd like it to be him making the threats, I can't see him hurting her. Yeah, I know obsession can turn dangerous, but I didn't get that vibe from him. He wants her but not in an 'I want to put your body parts in a jar' kind of way. He sure hated having me anywhere near her."

"I bet. Was there anyone else who you were around who made you feel wary?"

"Not really. You could tell the security people were worried about their jobs with us coming in, and they weren't thrilled to take orders from us, but who could blame them? We didn't have a lot of contact with the other staff, and those at the lab I only met once. That's when we found out Hadley is more than just Travis's daughter and is an actual key person in the company. Why? Did you find something?"

"Not exactly. It was the way you talked about Rockwell that made me focus on him. I've been digging, and he's too boring."

"Too boring? How?"

"From what I can see, he has no damn life. He's a young, attractive guy. He doesn't work twenty-four-seven, but there's been no indication he's been with a woman or even a man in the past five years. He has a small social media footprint, and there's nothing on it other than a few photos of him over the years and a random post here and there. He doesn't have memberships in a bunch of groups or anything. He doesn't seem to spend much of his money. It just made me want to know more. We're men. Don't tell me he hasn't needed sex in five years. Of course he could be paying for it and using cash. He does occasionally pull out a decent amount of money," he mused.

"He could, but I'm not sure if he would. You're right, as much as it pains me to say it. He isn't unattractive, which didn't help my dislike of him being so close to her. Of course, he might not be as enamored with her after she beat his ass at the physical challenges we had them going through."

"I've gotta hear this," he said eagerly, so I quickly told him about it. He laughed himself silly.

"Oh my God, I would've loved to see that. It serves him right and should be a reminder to us all. Women will always surprise us, I think. Now, don't kill me, but I want a woman just like her. Someone who can lean on me when she needs to but still has inner strength and will stand up for herself and others."

"No killing today. Did I help you?"

"I think so. I'll still keep looking, but he doesn't sound like one to threaten to torture and send her back in pieces. If they hadn't found the men who did that to her mom, I'd be tempted to say it was the same person or persons."

"So would I. Well, let me know if you have other questions."

"I do have one, and it's not on this topic. You might tell me to go to hell, but I gotta ask."

"Go for it."

"What're you hiding from Hadley? The last few days, I can see it. You're not as comfortable with her, which usually means you're hiding something. She's picking up on it, too."

His calling me out surprised me. I thought I was hiding it better. Shit, what if Hadley knew I was hiding something worse than her dad not wanting us together? I didn't answer him at first as I thought of what I should or shouldn't say. I'd told my guys what was up. They'd been worried about it like I was, but I hadn't said anything to any of the Marauders. He sat there staring at me.

Finally, I gave him an answer or at least a partial one. "You're right. I am hiding something from her. I'm not telling you what, but I know if I tell her, it's gonna hurt her, and I just can't do it. She has enough on her mind as it is. I promise once this assignment is over, I'll tell her. I should've never done it, but it's too late to have regrets. Now all I can do is live with what I did and fix it as soon as I can."

He shook his head. "I hope you know what you're doing."

"Me too."

We talked for a couple more minutes about mundane things before he excused himself to get back to work. After he left, it was hard for me to concentrate on what I'd been doing. I needed to talk to someone. I closed and locked the door so I wouldn't be disturbed, then I called Mark. He was with Travis and would have a better idea of how he was doing and maybe how to help me. Not that Gabe and Sean couldn't, but Mark often had a different take on things, especially after his five years of being "dead."

I dialed my phone. It didn't take long for him to answer. "Grif, is everything alright?" was how he answered. I heard the edge in his voice. I swear, I don't know if the man totally relaxed anymore. If he did, it was when he was alone with his wife and son.

"Hadley is fine. I need to talk to you about the secret Travis has me keeping from her. Do you have time to talk?"

"Sure, let me close the door. Travis is resting in his room. I noticed he's more tired even in the short time we've been here. Okay, it's closed. Hit me."

"It's tearing me up to keep this from her. It's gotten to the point I'm avoiding her some. She thinks it was something Travis said about us, and she wants me to tell her. I assured her he didn't do that, but she wasn't convinced. Then, a few minutes ago, Beast was in here and he called me on it. Asked what I was hiding from her. What the hell? I don't want to break my promise to Travis, but she's the woman I love. I hate doing this when I know it'll hurt her when she finds out, and she may never forgive me."

"The woman you love, huh? That's the first time I've heard you say that."

I jerked as I realized I'd said it. I thought about it, and even though it was damn fast, it was true. "Yeah, that's what I said. Don't ever tell her I told you before I did her. Fuck, okay, help me with the other."

"My lips are sealed. About the other, think about this. Do you want to risk pissing him off and having him possibly actively talking to her about not being with you? Personally, I don't think he'd do that, but I can't say for sure. Do you think she'll be so pissed she won't eventually get over it? It's all about what you can live with. Losing his respect and support of your relationship or losing her trust and possibly her?"

"That's easy. I can't lose her. I hate the idea he'll spend the little time he has left disliking me, but it's better than her walking away from me. I plan to marry her and have a family. The sooner, the better. I told him this. In fact, I want it soon so he can be here for it and be there to give her away on our wedding day."

"And he agreed?"

"He did. He wants two weeks for all the legal and other stuff to be finalized. He's also hoping we will have solved whoever is making the threats."

"Maybe there's a way to do both. What if you talk to her and tell her you're in a hard place, and it's killing you? Tell her he made you promise and how you don't want to break his trust but you don't want to do the same to her either. Let her know the time limit and that regardless of whether he wants you to tell her when the two weeks are over, you're primed to tell her everything. She'll see you being honest yet willing to keep your word. She strikes me as a woman who would appreciate it."

"Damn, why didn't I think of that? Has anyone told you you're more than muscles and tattoos with a furious glare?" I joked as my heart lightened. It was a good idea.

He barked out a laugh. “Only Sloan. I like to keep my amazingness hidden. Otherwise, people will want to spend too much time with me, and I don’t like that. My fans would become legions,” he joked back.

I laughed. “Keep telling yourself that. You’re great and all, but you’re never gonna be that damn approachable. Thanks, man. I’ll do what you suggested. Before I forget, is everything quiet there?”

“All’s quiet here. Not to borrow trouble, but I’d enjoy a bit of action right now. I love the cabin, but too many days and I get antsy. Plus, I miss Sloan and Caleb. FaceTime isn’t enough. They’re planning to come up at the end of the week. Travis seems to be enjoying it. Since you told us what he said, he and I talked about it and I’ve got him resting more. You gotta feel for the guy. He’s lived years without the love of his life, and now he’s soon to leave his daughter. He loves her to death.”

“He does. You know, if you need a break so you can go home, we can get someone else up there.”

“I know, but I don’t want to do that. We’ll survive.”

“But how will you give me another nephew or even a niece if you and Sloan aren’t together to make one?”

“Not you, too! Cassidy is after us, so I told her we’re waiting for her and Sean to have the second one before we do. Noah is getting close to two and a half. However, with you finding Hadley, that means you two should be having one in the next year or so.”

“Yep.”

“Really? That’s all I get? You’re ready for a kid

already?"

"Were you ready when Sloan got pregnant with your son?"

"Hell yeah. It was one of the happiest days of my life."

"We've talked and agreed it may be sooner rather than later, but don't tell your wife, Cass, or Gemma that, or I'll have to kill you."

All the bastard did was laugh. We talked for a few minutes about a couple of other work assignments, then signed off. I sat back in my chair to organize my thoughts on how to broach the subject with Hadley. I had to do it today. There was no way I could go another day with this weighing me down.

Hadley:

I dropped on the bed and let my tears out. How could I have been so stupid? I let a man sweet-talk me, and I fell for his lines. I really had no skill in figuring out when men were liars, I guess. Well, this would be the last time it happened. From now on, if I got the urge to be with someone, I'd either take care of it myself or if that weren't enough, I'd find a man I could tolerate and have a night or two of sex until the urge subsided. No way would I risk a relationship.

I knew something was wrong the last few days, but I thought it was something Dad said to Grif. He'd voiced more reservations about us or maybe made his version of threats. Griffin had kept denying it or that there was anything wrong, but I felt it. He'd been spending more time away from me. Regardless, I now knew I'd been way off-base.

I'd gone to find him at the clubhouse. I wanted to see if he wanted to have lunch with me. Boy, I'd gotten an earful. His words kept playing over and over in my mind. *You're right. I am hiding something from her. I'm not telling you what, but I know if I tell her, it's gonna hurt her, and I just can't do it. She has enough on her mind as it is. I promise once this assignment is over, I'll tell her. I should've never done it, but it's too late to have regrets. Now, all I can do is live with what I did and fix it as soon as I can.*

My insides felt like they were being ripped to

shreds, and I was bleeding internally. How could he do this to me? I thought from the way he talked we wanted the same things, that we were on our way to spending our lives together. I guess his talk with my dad made him realize it wasn't what he wanted, but he was too chicken to tell me. He probably thought I'd cry, beg, and scream. Well, I had news for Griffin "Wraith" Voss. No man would ever make me act that way. I had too much pride for that.

I let the tears and pain out for a few minutes then I sucked it back in. Nothing would be accomplished by feeling sorry for myself. Getting up, I went to the bathroom first and rinsed my face in cold water. Once I was done, I grabbed the items I needed. Back in the bedroom, I got my bags out of the closet. I put them on the bed and opened them so I could pack my stuff. No way I'd stay here with him. It was time to stop hiding. I was going home and facing this danger. Whoever was behind it had to make a move soon, and when they did, I'd shoot the motherfucker myself. I was done having my life dictated by whims and threats.

I was almost packed when Jinx walked in. I'd forgotten to close the door. He looked confused. "Where are you going? Griffin didn't say anything about moving you."

"That's because this doesn't involve him. I planned to stop in and tell you thank you and goodbye before I left. I can't thank you and the club enough for making me welcome and for giving me a place to think, but it's time I go home. Since you're here, can you tell me who I should call around here to get a ride to the airport so I can get my helo? I'd like to get home today."

"Wait, what the hell? Hadley, this doesn't make any sense. Why're you leaving, and why doesn't it involve Griffin?"

I finished putting the last piece of clothing in the bag. I zipped it closed before I answered him. I was trying hard not to cry again. As it was, I had to keep my back to him and fiddle with moving my bags.

"The Dark Patriots are no longer my protection detail, so there's no need to involve him."

"That's fucking bullshit, and you know it. You and he are together, Hadley. He's not gonna just accept you firing them and leaving him."

"There is no me and him. It was all a mistake, a lie. Now, will you tell me who to call for a ride or do I just start looking online myself?"

He frowned and studied me for a few seconds, then sighed. "Fine, I'll get you a ride. Stay here, and I'll be back. There's no need to call someone."

"Don't go running to Griffin and tell him anything. You can't tell him," I warned him.

"I won't tell him, I swear. Give me five minutes to get a vehicle."

I didn't know if I could trust him, but I nodded anyway. I did one last walk-through to be sure I hadn't overlooked anything. I had my bags together and was waiting by the door when it happened. Instead of Jinx coming through it, it was Griffin. He appeared confused and upset. Sonofabitch, I should've known Jinx would run to him. I saw him in the hallway. I glared at him.

"Liar," I snapped at him.

"I didn't lie. I said I wouldn't tell him, and I didn't. I told Beast, and he told him. There's no goddamn way we're letting you run off into danger or leaving without talking to him. You two need to settle your shit. Anyone with eyes can see you're meant to be together. I'm heading back to the clubhouse. Don't kill each other. I did this as much for you as for him, Hadley," he said before he walked off.

I snorted. Yeah, right, he did. Ignoring Griffin, I picked up my phone. I guess I'd find my own ride. I gasped as it was snatched out of my hands and thrown on the bed. I whipped around to glare at him. "How dare you do that!? Get out. I have nothing to say to you. As you know from Beast, I'm going home. You're fired, or at least as far as my protection detail. It's up to Dad if he wants you."

"Over my dead body, will you leave here!"

"That can gladly be arranged," I hissed at him. My pain was swiftly becoming anger.

"What the fuck has gotten into you? Talk to me."

"Like you've talked to me every time I've begged you to? Forget it. I'm over the games, and I want to go home. I don't have time for this or you. You've got what you wanted, so why do you care?"

"What I wanted? Like hell I did. You leaving here and me is the last thing I want!" he yelled.

"Don't lie to me, Griffin. Just be a man and tell me the truth."

He went silent.

"Fuck this, I'll walk," I muttered as I shoved to get past him. The next thing I knew, I was grabbed and pushed up against the wall next to the doorway. I went into fight mode. Since he had a hold of my upper arms, I lashed out with my knee. Unfortunately, he expected it and blocked me.

Next, I tried to free my arms, but his grip tightened. “Stop it and listen,” he said.

I answered him by trying to head butt him, but the bastard was too tall for me to reach his face. I wanted to break his nose. I twisted, tried to punch, kick, and anything else I could think of. Finally, I sank my teeth into his upper arm. He howled, and then I was airborne. He had me wrapped tight in his arms. I heard a door slam. I was screaming and swearing at him.

“Put me down, you cocksucker. I swear to God, when I get loose, I’ll kill you. You and your company are done. I’ll make sure no one will ever use you again.”

He pinned me to the bed. He was red in the face and breathing hard. “You need to calm the hell down, you little hellion. You need to explain what this is.”

“You want to know? Okay, I know, Griffin. I heard what you said. I know what you’ve been hiding from me for days.”

He swallowed and looked defeated. He closed his eyes for a moment or two, then opened them again. I saw the pleading in them. I steeled myself against it. There was no way he could spin it to make it not hurt.

“Baby, I’m sorry. I didn’t want you to find out that way. Please, let me explain. I didn’t want to do it.”

“Then why have sex with me in the first place? You could’ve gotten it at the clubhouse like I suggested. You didn’t have to fuck me, make promises you won’t keep. At least if you'd been honest, this would've ended a lot better than this."

"Sex? Promises I won't keep? What the fuck are you talking about?"

"Come on. I know you've been hiding the fact you should've never started anything with me. You say you didn't want to tell me because I have enough on my mind, and you know it's gonna hurt me. I know how you should've never done it, and you planned to fix it as soon as this assignment was over. Well, there's no fixing anything, and for you, the assignment is done. I don't need any man to feel sorry for me or have sex with me out of desperation, boredom, or pity."

His face flushed red again. "You think I slept with you because of those things? Woman, you're so damn wrong you have no idea. I wasn't saying any such thing when you heard that. It was something else."

This took me back. "Then what was it?"

"Oh no, we'll get to that, but not before I address this. I don't for a second regret us. I'm not trying to get rid of you. I'm not letting you walk away from me, ever. If you keep fighting me and trying to leave, I'll tie your ass to the bed, and I'll keep you here, with me making love to you until you know without a doubt I want and need you," he panted.

I stared at him with my mouth open. I was stunned and not sure if I should believe him or not. Maybe my threats to have the Patriots blackballed had scared him. Apparently, I took too long to say something.

"Fuck it, you need to be punished for doubting

me," he growled.

I was suddenly free, but only long enough for him to flip me onto my stomach, and then his hand landed on my ass. It wasn't a light love tap, either. It was a hard one, which hurt. I squirmed and tried to get away, but he had my arms and my lower legs pinned, so I couldn't.

"Griffin, stop!"

"Not until you learn a lesson. You will never doubt me again." Smack.

"You will never try to leave me." Smack.

"You will talk to me, and we'll work out any issues or disagreements we have." Smack.

I wiggled, but it wasn't just to get away from his smacks. It was because we were in the middle of a serious moment, and his spanking was making me wet. Who in their right mind got like that at a time like this? He landed another one, and a small moan escaped despite how hard I was biting my lower lip. I prayed he didn't hear it, but it was in vain.

Suddenly, he was pressed flat against my back. His hot breath was rushing over my neck and ear. "What's wrong, baby? Do you like that ass being spanked?"

I refused to answer him. When I didn't, he chuckled darkly. "I think I should check."

He eased away, and then my pants and panties were being yanked down my thighs. "No!" I cried. I tried to get away, but again, he was too strong for me to do it.

I cried out but in pleasure as his fingers slipped between my folds and rubbed up and down my slit. I was so wet. There was no way to hide my arousal. He groaned. "Goddamn, you're fucking soaked. Does my baby need to come?"

He kept rubbing, and I couldn't stop myself from nodding. He worked my clit and thrust a finger in and out of my pussy fast and impatiently. I ramped up so damn fast. It seemed only to take a minute for me to crest and come. As I screamed, I clenched my eyes shut. I vaguely felt him shifting and heard a faint sound, but I couldn't concentrate on that. All I could do was ride the wave of my orgasm.

My eyes flew open, though, when I felt a harder probe at my entrance, then I was being filled with his thick, delicious cock. I bucked my hips, driving him deeper. We both groaned together. His hands shifted to grip my hips, and then he slammed himself all the way inside. As he growled, I whimpered. It hurt a little, but mostly it felt amazing.

A hand raised up to grip my hair as he rode me hard and fast. He was breathing heavily as my ass met his pelvis, making loud slapping sounds. There were no words as he hammered me into the mattress, and I loved every second of it. I was almost there again when he spoke.

"That's it. Take that cock. This is mine. This pussy, your whole body, your fucking heart and soul. Mine. I'm never giving you up. I'll kill anyone who tries to take you. You're mine. MINE!" he screamed right before I detonated, then he grunted and stuttered in his movements. I felt his warm cum filling me as he gave me his seed, and I took it happily.

Griffin: Chapter 16

I felt lightheaded as I came down from the high of my orgasm. I hadn't intended to take Hadley. I was scared when Jinx told me she was packed and planning to leave. I raced over to the house as fast as I could to find out why and to stop her. The things she said made no sense to me until she said she heard. At first, I thought she'd heard what I said to Mark. When I realized she heard what I said to Beast and her assumptions about what I meant, I got angry.

Spanking her that way wasn't what I'd ever done before to a woman or thought of doing. Sure, spanking could be fun but I'd never done it as a punishment. When I heard her moan and it dawned on me that she was getting aroused by it, I had been driven to touch her. The feel of her wetness and tightness on my fingers made me instantly hard. Finger fucking her to come had only made it worse. I'd been in a haze when I shoved my cock inside of her.

The feel of her, the smell of her, and the sounds had driven me to go insane. All I could think was she was mine, and I had to prove it. Shouting the word mine as I emptied myself deep inside of her had filled me with a deeper sense of ultimate possession, or maybe it was relief.

However, now that my mind was clearing, I became afraid again. What had I done? As I eased out of her, she remained limp underneath me. Her face was buried in the mattress. I felt cold as I lost the heat of her body. I hesitantly touched her shoulder. That's when I realized she was shaking like she was crying. I let go and moved away from the bed. That's when it fully hit me. God, I was no better than a rapist. My stomach heaved, and it was all I could do not to puke. I didn't know what to say. There was nothing I could say to make this right, but I had to try.

"Hadley. Jesus, I'm so fucking sorry. I never meant to do that. You have to believe me. I've never done that to a woman before. Fuck, do you need medical attention? Tell me what to do. I swear, I won't touch you again, baby. I just can't leave you like this. I'm calling Sean and the others to have someone come here to protect you. I understand you'll want to call the cops. I won't run."

Tears were burning my eyes. I'd ruined the best thing to ever happen to me. No way she'd forgive or forget this, and I couldn't blame her. It was a terrible thing to find out about yourself. That you'd lose control so badly you'd hurt a woman. I felt filthy. I had to cover up. I still had on my clothes. I hadn't even bothered to remove them. In disgust, I yanked my underwear and pants back up and secured them. She rolled over onto her back. I couldn't meet her eyes. I kept my head down.

"Griffin, what the hell are you talking about? I know you've had sex before. And why would I need medical attention, or would you call the cops?" Her voice sounded weak.

I had to turn my back to her as I answered. "Because I was a fucking animal. I forced you to have sex with me. I struck you hard. I didn't ask if you wanted me. I assumed, and then I took you roughly. I'm so goddamn sorry. I've never raped a woman before, but that's not a reason. Please, tell me I didn't injure you."

I heard rustling sounds, but I didn't turn around. If I were her, I'd take a gun and shoot me. I wondered where hers were. A bullet to my head would be too quick and merciful. I wouldn't fight whatever she wanted to do. Knowing her, she'd probably want to beat my ass first. I felt a hand on my arm, and then I was abruptly yanked around. I had no choice but to look at her then.

I saw tears on her face, which gutted me. Along with them, I saw confusion. Her brow was wrinkled. "Say that again," she ordered.

So I repeated what I said. When I was done, she grabbed my other arm and shook me. "Are you kidding me right now!?" she shouted.

I shook my head no. "No, I'm not."

"Sit down. We need to talk. Give me a minute." I watched as she straightened her clothes. My remorse got worse. I stumbled to sit on the edge of the bed, making sure to sit as far away from her as possible. When she was done, she began to pace. I stayed quiet. After a few times of going back and forth, she stopped and faced me.

"You really believe that you forced yourself on me? That you abused me before that?"

I nodded.

"My God, Griffin, I can't let you think that! Yes, I was pissed at you, and we fought. I hit you, so that means I'm guilty of abusing you."

“No, you’re not! If I hadn’t manhandled you, then you wouldn’t have needed to fight back. It was all me,” I protested.

“Then if what I did wasn’t abusing you, then yours isn’t either. As for having sex with me, I might not have verbally said I wanted it, but if I didn’t, I would’ve fought you, screamed for help, and done everything I could to get away. I didn’t do that because even as upset as I was, I wanted you. Was it wild and out of control? Yes, but I loved it. I was crying because it was the best orgasm of my life, not because you hurt me or forced me. All the ones I’ve had with you have been the best. It felt like my soul left me.”

I had a hard time believing what she was saying until she came over and straddled my lap. She hugged me. “I don’t want to hear you say such a thing again. Was the spanking a shock? Yes, but it was such a turn-on, too, once I got over the surprise of it. Couldn’t you tell by how wet I was and how easily you had made me come?”

Relief filled me. I hugged her back hard. “Thank God. I felt sick, baby. I never want to hurt you.”

“You didn’t. And I’m sorry I jumped to conclusions like I did. That was unfair of me, but I do need to know what it was you were referring to.” She leaned back so she could see my face.

As relieved as I was about the other thing, her reminder made me tense. What if this was what she couldn’t forgive? Fuck, I wish I had never agreed to hide it from her. I had to tell her.

“You’re right. I do need to tell you. I want you to listen to me completely first before you react, okay?

Please."

She studied me for a couple of moments, then slowly nodded.

"You were right. I have been acting differently these past few days, and it was because of my talk with your dad, but it wasn't about what you think it was. I didn't lie. He never said anything negative about us. He just warned me not to hurt you, which any father would do. It was something else he told me and begged me not to tell you. He wanted a couple more weeks, and then he planned to talk to you about it.

"He wanted things to be official with some legal things he's got in motion. When he told me everything, I told him to talk to you now. He pleaded with me not to tell. I went against my better judgment and agreed. Honestly, I did it so I wouldn't make him turn against me as your man. That's not a good enough excuse, but it's the only one I have. In the end, I gave him two weeks, then ready or not, I was telling you if he didn't." I could tell she was fighting not to interrupt me to ask what it was, so I stopped beating around the bush and told her.

"Baby, I hate to tell you this, but your dad is sick, like majorly sick. He has been for a while and he's been hiding it and making arrangements. I'm sorry."

Tears filled her eyes, and I saw denial on her face at the same time. She was shaking her head. "No, no, it can't be. He wouldn't do that to me. You must have misunderstood him."

I held her closer. "No, I didn't. He told me his diagnosis and everything."

"You said arrangements. What kind of

arrangements? And what have the doctors been doing to cure him?"

"Sweetheart, I think we should call your dad and let him explain. It's really between you two. Will you forgive me for not telling you?" I was afraid to ask, but I had to.

"I'm not happy you did it, but I'm more unhappy with Dad for putting you in that position. He should've never done it. I'm hurt, but I'll get over it. And as for this being between him and I, no, it's not. He made you a part of this by telling you. And I need you."

"Babe, I'll be here no matter what comes or what you need. That includes what he needs. I already made a few demands of my own with him when he asked me not to tell. One of those was regardless of where we end up living, he'll move there so we can take care of him. I hope you'll like my area of Virginia, but I know you have Gerard's and will need to be nearby to work there. We'll figure it out."

"Wait. Where we end up living? You want us to live together, now?"

"Hell yeah. You don't think I can live without you, do you? You're stuck with me."

"Hmm, and what else then do I have to prepare myself for, Mr. Voss?" she asked with a smile on her face.

"Well, let's see. Living together means marriage and kids, too. We already talked about those in passing. The second one means a wedding."

"Whoa, you sure want it all. How soon for those?"

"Is next week too soon for all of them?" I half teased.

Her eyes widened. "You're joking, right?"

"Nope, but I know it's not likely to happen. We have to figure out who's threatening you and your dad. Then, we have to figure out where to live, get a house, or build one. A wedding will take some planning. There are the legal documents to have drawn up. I guess I should back up and ask you if you want all those, too."

"I do. I'm just shocked, I guess. This is moving so fast. We should be cautious and take our time, but I don't want to. And what legal documents?"

"The ones protecting your money and assets. You're a very rich woman. I don't want you or anyone else ever thinking for a second I'm with you due to that. Your money will be yours. I want no claim to it."

"Wait up, that's not how a true relationship works. Or not in my mind. If we're together, we share. Or are you thinking we might get a divorce one day?"

"No, I don't. When you and I marry, it's forever. If we have issues, we'll work them out. I have plenty of money of my own from Dark Patriots. I don't need yours. Besides, I don't see the board or your family lawyers not insisting on one."

"Screw the board and our lawyers. They can demand all day, but this is my choice. We'll talk about this more later. I know we need to iron out details, and I hate to cut it short, but I need to talk to Dad."

"Of course. Do you want to call him from here or Jinx's office? I'll give you privacy."

"Here is fine, and I want you with me."

It made me feel good that she wanted me with her, so I smiled and nodded. She got off my lap and sat beside me. She got into her purse on the bed and got out her phone. I saw her hand shake a tiny bit as she found Travis's name and hit the call button. I heard it ringing, so I knew she put it on speaker. He answered promptly.

"Hello, honey. I'm so glad you called. How's things going?" His tone was cheerful, but I could sense tiredness, too.

"Hi, Daddy, it's going fine. What about you? Is it all quiet there with Undertaker?"

He chuckled. "It is, although thinking of him by that name makes me wonder what I'm thinking, being alone in the woods with a guy named Undertaker."

She laughed as I grinned. "True, but then they don't know him. He can be scary, no doubt, but he's also protective, so I'm not worried. Hey, I want to let you know. You're on speaker. Griffin is with me."

"Oh, hello, Griffin. Are you taking good care of my girl?"

"Yes, sir, I am. Always."

"Since Griffin is on the call, is there something I should know? Have you found out anything about who's doing this?" I heard hope in his voice.

"No, not yet, but we haven't given up. We have some of the best computer and investigative people on it," I assured him.

"Damn, well, you can't blame me for hoping. So, what's up? Are you calling to give me some other good news?" he hinted.

He knew my plans to marry her. If I'd had time, I would've gone out and gotten her a ring, but I didn't want to be away from her in case something happened.

"No, Dad, nothing like that. Give the guy a break. He just told me he wants to get married and move in together. Give a girl a minute to process. There is a reason we did call, though. We had a big misunderstanding earlier, and I was packing to leave."

"What!? Why?" he asked in alarm.

"Because I overheard him talking to one of the guys here. He said he wasn't able to tell me something and was worried I wouldn't forgive him. I jumped to conclusions and thought he meant he regretted us, and I was hurt. I packed my bags and was about to leave when he found me. We fought, and then once things settled down," she paused to wink at me, "he told me what he really meant. I think you know what it was."

His deep sigh was easily heard over the phone. He didn't answer her right away, so we waited. Finally, after several tense moments, he did. "Yes, I do. I'd hoped to tell you myself."

"You should've told me a while ago, I think. You were wrong to ask him to keep it from me, Dad! He's been struggling with it, and it put a barrier between us before today's fight. He didn't go into details. I need you to tell me. Don't leave anything out. I need to know everything."

He didn't disagree. It took him a few times starting and stopping before he explained what he'd shared with me. The more he told her, the paler she got and the sadder she looked. By the time he was done, I had her cuddled in my arms, and she was crying. I rocked her and tried to soothe her with my touch.

"Hadley, honey, I'm sorry. I was trying to spare you as long as I could but I see now that was unfair of me."

"And there's nothing they can do?"

"Nothing. I'm dying. I have months to maybe a year at the most. I was trying to get all the legalities settled before telling you. You know, once this goes public, the board, our employees, and the public will probably panic. They don't know about you or how you've been doing a lot of the stuff for the past several years. This project will demonstrate that."

"Screw them! I don't give a damn. All I care about is you. They'll either accept me or they won't. I doubt with the amount of money we make them, they'll object for long. Besides, you set up the board to be advisory but they have no voting rights when it comes to the CEO of the company position. Let them try to oust me, and I'll make them regret it. They can't and won't take Gerard's away from me," she snarled fiercely.

"If they try it, you can have them ousted. I never believed in taking your company public and having a board that can then take your company away from you. That's utter bullshit," he said. I had to agree with him on that one.

"Do any of them know about your illness?" she asked next.

"Only Ansel, he's known for several months. He's helped me to hide it. I hated to ask that of him, but he did it because he cared. You know how much of a friend and rock he's been, especially since I lost your mom."

"I do, and I'm not surprised. Does he think there'll

be pushback?"

"He's worried about it, but he promised he'd do everything in his power to prevent it from happening."

"Good. When are you due to see your doctor again? I want to be there for your next visit."

"Well, I was supposed to go next Monday, but with everything going on, I was planning to reschedule it."

"Dad, you can't!" she exclaimed, giving me a panicked look. I understood why. His health was too precarious to fool with even postponing one doctor's visit.

"Travis, I don't think you should do that. Give us the information on your doctor, and we'll work on getting you there and back safely. You can't afford not to go. As for Hadley going with you, as much as I'd love to keep her tucked away here, I know that's not gonna happen. She'd sneak off if I tried." She nodded in agreement. "Your daughter can be a tiny bit strong-willed."

He chuckled. "Tiny? I think you meant a lot. Okay, if you think we should go."

"We should. And there's a chance we'll have whoever is behind this taken down by then. My gut says this is close to being over. Why don't you give me the information, and then when we get off this call, tell Mark what we discussed. I'll get the team together so we can plan."

"Sounds good," he replied.

After he gave me the information for his doctor's appointment, the three of us chatted for a while longer.

He asked when he was to expect an engagement and wedding. That made me smile as she tried to slow his roll as she told him. Today told me I'd have to get busy with a ring. I had an idea of what I wanted to get her. Maybe I could enlist Gemma, Cass, and Sloan to help me do it. Hmm, that was worth a thought. The call ended on a much more relaxed note than it began. We had work to do, but at least my woman wasn't threatening to leave me.

❧❧❧

Only a day after the call with Travis and me, Mark, Gabe, and Sean had the rough outline of a plan for ensuring his and Hadley's safety next week at his doctor's office and getting there and back. Between now and then, we'd study maps and layouts with the team members going with us so we had all the angles covered. There shouldn't be a way for anyone to know they planned to be there, but just in case, we'd be ready.

When I told Jinx and the Marauders we'd be gone for a couple of days, they insisted some of them accompany us. I didn't want to turn down help, although we should have it covered, so I agreed. Hadley, on the other hand, tried to tell them it wasn't necessary. In fact, she was doing it right now and not getting anywhere.

We were all gathered after work in the clubhouse. She'd just got done telling them they could stay behind. The scowls were fierce around the tables where we were all gathered.

"Babe, you seem to be under the illusion that you have a choice. You don't. Griffin brought you here, and now you've been adopted. That means you're family, our sister, and we protect our friends and family. We're coming, so get over it. Arguing will only give you a headache," Jinx told her smugly. He had his arms crossed, leaning back in his chair, and his legs crossed at the ankles.

She narrowed her gaze at him and leaned toward him. She was on the opposite side of the table from him, so she couldn't lean too close. She pointed her finger at him. "Jinx, don't you dare think you can boss me around. Dad and Griffin can't, so why would I let you?"

He laughed, and the guys chuckled. I fought to hide my grin. He shook his head. "Sweetheart, they can and will if they think you're in danger. I'd like to see you try to do something that could get you hurt. This one would have you tied up and stashed away so fast your head would spin. You could cry, beg, and threaten all you want, but he'd keep you protected. The same goes for us. Now, do you wanna be locked up or have us ride along?"

She gave a strangled scream in the back of her throat and then glanced at me. "Tell him, Griffin. You wouldn't do that. And we don't need them to take time away from their work to go with us."

"Baby, I could lie and say he's wrong, but I won't. He's right. If I thought we couldn't protect you, you wouldn't be going. With that said, if they want to provide extra protection, I won't say no. They're good in a fight if it were to get to that."

Her mouth fell open as she stared at me. Finally, she shook her head and rolled her eyes. "Have all of you forgotten I can take care of myself? You've seen me shoot, and Griffin has seen my strength. Maybe you need me to demonstrate that I can kick ass too."

"Honey, we have no doubt you're a badass, but it doesn't change anything. We're going. However, I would love to see what you've got," Styx said with a wink.

The others enthusiastically approved of his idea. I had to admit, I wanted to see it, too. I knew the little she'd used on me yesterday, but there was a whole lot more she could know.

She popped out of her chair. "Alright, you wanna see, let's do this. Where?"

"How about we do it in the gym? Say in fifteen minutes? That gives anyone who wants to give it a whirl a chance to change into something more comfortable," Animal suggested.

All I saw was heads nodding, including hers. As we got up to go get changed, I thought of the gym. Rather than it being a part of the clubhouse proper like most of the clubs I knew, theirs was in a smaller building that was attached to the backside of their clubhouse. Since they were men who were dedicated to their workouts, they had just about anything you could think of for equipment, along with floor mats and a fighting ring.

At the house, we didn't waste time changing. I changed into loose workout pants, the gray sweats she'd remarked about before. Instead of boots, I slipped on my tennis shoes. I ran most mornings. My T-shirt would suffice. I watched as she got dressed. It was impossible not to get aroused seeing her in her bra and panties, along with so much of her bare skin, beckoning me to touch and taste her.

She must've seen the heat she was causing because she held up her hands and backed away from me. "Oh no, you don't. We have someplace to be. As much as I'd love for you and me to tear up those sheets, we have to wait. If we're late, I'll never hear the end of it from those guys."

"Come on, they can wait a half hour," I pleaded.

"Nope. If you're good and wait, I promise to let you have fun and we can try something new tonight," she enticed me.

The sex so far had been out of this world, so I had no complaints, but the lure of doing even more was too much to resist. With a groan, I gave in. "Alright. Let's get this over with. Remember, you owe me."

She slipped on a tank top and a pair of tight yoga pants, which outlined her sexy body. "Baby, don't you have something else you can wear?" I complained.

"Like what?"

"Like something loose, and it hides your delectable body. I can't have you turning them on," I grumbled.

"Grif, this is fine. You act like they're slobbering dogs. No one will pay any mind to my clothes. This is better than what most women wear to the gym. They have on teeny tiny shorts and sports bras, for God's sake. This is what I fight in. Now, stop it, and let's go."

Knowing she wasn't about to yield, I let it go, but if any of them forgot for a second she was taken, I'd have to remind them painfully. I took her hand and led her out to the car. Jinx hadn't come back to the house with us. He either wasn't fighting, or he had spare clothes at the clubhouse.

When we got there, I parked behind it next to the gym. There was a second entrance you could access from the outside. We entered this way. Inside, we saw most of the guys there and ready to work out, it seemed. They cheered when they saw her. They also did a good job of not staring too hard or long at her. We went over to stand by Jinx. He was talking to Animal and Sarge. They stopped when we got to them.

"You ready to show us what you've got, Had? I wanna see what you've learned, and then we can teach you all the shit you don't know," Sarge told her with a grin.

"Hey, I'm always willing to learn, Sarge, but just be warned. I've had a lot of instructors in several different styles. I just might surprise you and teach you guys some things," she taunted.

This got all the guys jeering at her. They'd been close enough to hear her. They razzed her, and she gave back as good as they gave. I loved seeing her this way. She was relaxed, confident, and unafraid of showing her strength. Deep down, I wanted her to put a few of them on their asses. Of course, that didn't include me. As her man, I had to be able to be a bigger badass than her. It was just one of the rules. However, I wasn't dumb enough to tell her this. I liked my balls where they were, and no way would I risk her cutting me off.

Hadley: Chapter 17

I had my adrenaline flowing, and I was excited. It had been several weeks since I could actually practice my fighting. The last time was a few days before the Dark Patriots came and took over our security. Even as young as I was when Dad started me training with various experts, I'd always loved it. The challenge was one reason, and the other was that it let me get out of my head and just be.

Not to brag, but I was considered a genius, and along with that, it wasn't unusual for me or someone like me to get caught up in our minds. It was hard at times to shut it down and rest. I spent a lot of years not sleeping much because of that. By being able to get out of my head and do the physical, I'd found a way to escape it. It was a welcome distraction from my grief over the loss of my mom.

She'd been my best friend, and her loss went soul deep. In fact, since then, although I had some people I would call friends, I never found someone to be my best friend I could tell everything to. However, as absurd as it sounded, I had a feeling Griffin would become that person. I know Dad and Mom had been each other's best friends. They'd always included me in their lives, but they'd spent a lot of time just the two of them, too.

This fighting display or challenge, or whatever you wanted to call it, was serving two purposes. One was to show the Marauders and Grif that I was capable of defending myself. The other one was a distraction from my grief over soon losing my dad. I knew intellectually it was fast approaching, but emotionally, I didn't want to think about it. The idea I'd be an orphan in a year or less made me want to scream and cry. I couldn't let all the raw emotion out because it might just destroy me, so this was the alternative.

I watched as the last couple of guys joined us in the gym. I had to admit, it was a really good one. Depending on what we wanted to do, we could either use the extensive floor mats or the fighting ring. I could box and do a variety of MMA-style fighting as well as others. This woman knew how to throw a proper punch and not break her thumb. You only did it once before you learned if you were smart. My instructors didn't believe in coddling me. They made sure not to seriously hurt me, of course, or Dad would've killed them, but they taught me well. Bruises, cuts, and minor other injuries had been expected.

I'd tried just about all the top martial arts styles, but the main ones I'd studied the longest and liked the best were jiu-jitsu, krav maga, muay thai, capoeira, and hapkido. A lot of people had heard of these except probably hapkido. Despite the assumption that it was the same thing as Aikido, it wasn't.

Knowing some of the guys had military training like Griffin, they would be skilled or at least familiar with the others. I wondered how many would know hapkido. I planned to introduce them to it. I hoped they were ready.

Hapkido was Korean-based like Aikido, but it

incorporated strikes to various pressure points, throws, joint locks, punches, and powerful kicks. You defeated or controlled your opponent using circular movement and non-resisting movements. There was intricate footwork and body positioning. In addition, it could incorporate weapons like ropes, swords, or canes.

After some debate between the guys, it was decided to use the mats and it would only be one match at a time. They determined this since it seemed they were all eager to watch me and didn't want to miss anything by having other matches going at the same time. This was the best way in their minds. Thankfully, I wasn't going to be in the spotlight at all times. They thought it was a good idea for a couple of guys to go first so I could see what I was up against and to give me a chance to back out, they said with smirks. I gave them a calm smile. I was gonna love this even more than I thought.

I might desire only Griffin, but I didn't dare say love even though I knew that was what I felt, at least the beginnings of it. However, I wasn't blind. The guys were dressed in shorts or loose pants like Griffin, and most had taken off their shirts. There were muscles and tattoos galore everywhere I looked. They would make a best-selling sexy man calendar women would kill to buy. And I was getting it for free. Lucky me. First up were Mad Dog and Styx. They'd been in the military, so it made sense. Jinx covered the rules before the first match.

"There will be no moves to cause serious injury or death. You can submit if you're done. As soon as your opponent indicates they're tapping out, you will disengage. To give everyone a chance to get in on this and so we're not here all night, each bout will be timed for ten minutes. I know many of us can go for a long time. These are our typical rules, so I'm just reminding you and letting Griffin and Hadley know. Remember honey, don't kill any of us," he said with a wink to me.

"I'll try to hold myself back, but it'll be hard. I hope you don't have delicate male egos that'll be hurt when a woman hands you your asses," I said with a wink back. They all thought this was hilarious, and they laughed loudly. I only smiled bigger.

Griffin leaned closer to whisper in my ear. "I don't like that smile, babe. Just try not to kill any of us."

"I'll keep you breathing, I promise," I whispered back. He studied me, then nodded. I think he was realizing I wasn't just talking out of my ass.

I had to admit Styx and Mad Dog were skilled, and I enjoyed their match. In the end, Styx submitted right before the ten-minute mark when Mad Dog got him in a hold he couldn't break. I cheered and clapped loudly along with the others.

It was agreed that one more match would go before letting me on the mat with anyone. This one was between Rage and Thrasher. While neither had been in the military, they were skilled, and I loved watching their bout. In the end, the round was called, and it was declared a tie. Neither won nor submitted.

Jinx faced me. "Are you ready to give this a try? You can choose your opponent, or I can. It's up to you. Or we can do another match or two."

"I'm ready and I think I'll let you decide my

opponent, at least this time," I told him as I stood up from where I'd been sitting.

He nodded. "Okay, I choose...Crow. You know the rules. Get into position and tell me when you're ready."

As Crow walked to the center of the mats. Griffin grabbed my hand. "Be careful. Don't push it and get hurt. You don't have anything to prove."

"Yes, I do, but I promise not to push beyond reasonable," I assured him. I gave him a quick peck on the mouth. He let go so I could take my place. Crow was waiting for me. I'd heard the guys talking, and I knew Crow had fewer years of practice than most of the others. That didn't mean he wasn't good. It just meant he was a better opponent in their minds for me.

As we stood there, he smiled at me. I smiled back. He didn't talk smack, which was different. The others who'd gone first had taunted each other. It had been fun to hear, actually. I took deep breaths and let my body loosen. Being tense wouldn't help. For this one, I thought I'd stick to jiu-jitsu. There was no need to let them know everything I could do this first time.

When Jinx yelled to go, we took a few moments to feel each other out with some punches and light kicks. This wasn't jiu-jitsu, but it was a way to see how he moved. When he'd had enough and came in for the attack, which was more kicks and punches, I flipped into my style for this one. Jiu-jitsu didn't have a lot of kicks and punches. It incorporated a large number of holds, locks, joint manipulation, pins, and chokes. You didn't defend by blocking. Rather, you neutralize your attacker by redirecting their energy and momentum. The style I preferred was Brazilian, and it focused on choking and joint locks on the ground. When I took Crow to the mat, I saw a flash of surprise on his face. It soon changed to alarm, then determination.

We grappled, and he did his best to avoid my joint locks and chokeholds, but he wasn't comfortable fighting this way, and I think he was afraid to hurt me. In the end, I got him in a joint lock that hurt, and he couldn't break, so he tapped out. When we stood, he shook his head.

"Goddamn, you're a demon. I've never fought quite like that. Nice job."

"Thank you, and it's Brazilian jiu-jitsu, in case you're wondering."

"I'll have to have you show me some of those moves. I'd like to learn those."

"I'll gladly show you. You've got skills. You just need to add more styles and expand your moves."

He shook my hand, and then we took our seats. I saw the guys eyeing me more closely. They were now wondering just what else I knew and how good I was. Griffin told me, "Nice job, babe."

"Thanks," I said.

There were a few more matches, which were mesmerizing. When they were done, Jinx asked me a question. "Who do you want to go up against next? It's your turn again."

I felt Griffin become more alert beside me. As much as I wanted to go up against him, I didn't want to do it in front of everyone. I didn't know if I could beat him or not, but if so, I didn't want it done this way. However, I wanted a challenge, so that left Jinx and

Sarge. I quickly made my choice which caused brows to lift all around the room.

"I choose Sarge. Let's see what you've got," I told him with a smile.

He nodded and came to the center of the mats. As I faced him, he replied, "I want to see what you've really got. Don't hold back. I won't. We wanna know what you can do, honey. I think it'll ease all our minds, especially your man's." He gestured to Griffin, who was frowning.

"I can do that, and I prefer you not to hold back. I was taught to fight as if my life depended on it. I won't break anything, seriously maim or kill, but that's all the concessions you'll get."

"Good."

The guys were calling out various encouragements to both of us. When Jinx hollered go, Sarge came at me like a streak. There was no feeling me out, and since I hadn't seen him fight yet, I had no clue about his fighting style or skill. I barely avoided him as I rolled away.

It was apparent right away he was highly skilled and knew a variety of different martial arts. I did use a few of my jiu-jitsu moves, but not a lot. He'd seen those and would be expecting them. Instead, I gave him Muay Thai first. It concentrated on eight points of contact, which were from both knees, shins, elbows, and hands. There were a lot of stand-up striking and clinching techniques. I interspersed it with regular karate. He was quick to counter it and attack with his own.

I just as quickly switched to capoeira. It was Brazilian, too, and involved me constantly in motion with moves that were originally dance moves. It became obvious he knew it, too. Damn! I threw more moves at him from a mix of MMA, judo, and Tae Kwon Do. He knew them, of course. There were more than a couple of times he landed a hard kick or blow and made me think I might not get out of holds and takedowns.

I was sweating hard and knew I'd have to bring more. I had two more: hapkido and Krav Maga. The hapkido wasn't as much help without a cane to strike with, so I only did a few of those to throw him off balance, then launched into the last one.

I loved Krav Maga. It was what the Israelis used with their military forces. It was a lot of wrestling, grappling, and hand strikes. Yes, he was much bigger than me, and that would make you think I wouldn't go for the wrestling and grappling, but that was one reason I did it. Another was there were no rules in it. No fighting patterns were adhered to. You could use anything to defeat or incapacitate your opponent.

It was this mentality that had me grabbing one of the metal folding chairs they had along the one edge of the mats. It had been mine. I swung it and made contact. I heard the inhaled breaths of surprise. For the first time, I saw Sarge grin, which fucking scared me. Oh shit, what had I done?

What I did was let the demon loose. He came at me like a tornado, and I fought as hard as I ever had, but in the end, he defeated me. I lay on the mat, panting and weak after he let go of me. Griffin came rushing over to me. I saw the concern on his face. He crouched beside me.

"Baby, are you alright?"

"I-I'm fine," I panted.

"You sure, honey? I went at you hard," Sarge asked as he stooped down.

"You're a damn animal, and I loved it. It's what I wanted and I'm fine, just tired. Give me a few seconds to get my wind back."

He chuckled. "I have to admit, you impressed me. You've had some really skilled instructors. You can hold your own and then some. We have to do this again. You gave me a good workout." He held out his hand. I took it so he could literally lift me to my feet.

"Glad to be of service," I told him.

As I moved slowly to the chairs, I noticed someone had put mine back. I dropped into it gratefully. I was surprised when Griffin didn't retake his. He took off his shirt. I tried not to get lost in admiring his upper body. It was only curiosity that stopped me.

"What're you doing?"

"It's my turn. I can't let you not know if your man is capable of defending you or not. It's good to know you can take care of yourself, but I still want to be the one who does it. Sit back and watch." He gave me a smirk and then went to the center of the mats. I gasped when I saw he was joined by Jinx. Animal took over as the referee.

When Animal told them they could start, it was amazing to watch. They reminded me a lot of Sarge. They easily and quickly flipped from one fighting style to another and mixed them up seamlessly. Watching them, I wanted to spar with Griffin every day. That wasn't to say Jinx wasn't good. He was excellent, and they were very evenly matched. I wondered which branch of the military Jinx had been in. He said he was but never said which one.

In the end, both men were breathing hard and sweaty, but neither was able to get the other to submit. I ran over to Griffin and launched myself at him. He caught me, and I gave him a passionate kiss. Not only was I thrilled about how he did and that he wasn't hurt but watching him had turned me on big time. I was wet and wanted to fuck him right there on the mats. He must've caught on because he kissed me back enthusiastically and began to walk off with me in his arms. I heard the catcalls and remarks from the guys, but I didn't care. If he weren't inside of me soon, I'd die. Thoughts of how he'd taken me yesterday filled my mind, and I got wetter. Christ, I hoped he'd do it again.

In the car, it was all he could do to get me to sit still so he could drive. I had to keep reminding myself I didn't want him to wreck. As soon as he shut off the car at Jinx's, I was attacking him again. I straddled his lap. The steering wheel was biting into my back, but I didn't give a damn.

Suddenly, I felt us move, and the wheel was gone. He'd released the seat back to as far as it would go. I bit and sucked on his lower lip as I ground my pussy down on the bulge he had in his pants. I moaned long and hard.

"Fuck, Hadley, baby, if you don't stop it, I'm gonna take you right here and now and fuck whoever might see us," he warned me hoarsely.

"Do it. I want you to fuck me. I can't wait. Hurry," I cried out.

His hand came down hard on my ass. I jumped. "Then get these clothes off before I rip them to shreds. You've got one minute," he growled.

I awkwardly got off him enough to fight off my clothes. My shirt and bra went flying into the backseat, and then I was wiggling down my yoga pants along with my panties. He was still without his shirt, so all he had to do was shove his amazing gray sweats down. He fisted himself and stroked as he watched me with hungry eyes.

In desperation, I kicked off my shoes and used my feet to get my pants off. I barely had them clear of my feet before he reached over and grabbed me. He dragged me back over to straddle him. As I did, his cock nudged my entrance then he was yanking my hips down, forcing his thick cock inside of me in one hard stroke. I cried out and felt myself release more of my cum.

He groaned. "Fuck, you're so goddamn ready. I'm sorry. I can't go slow this time. I'll make it up to you next time." His fingers bit into my ass as he lifted me up and then brought me back down.

I didn't want him to do all the work, so I helped him. It was fast, hard, loud, and fantastic. He was sucking and biting on my nipples as I rode him with his help. I couldn't stop moaning and pleading with him to take me harder. I don't know how long we were at it before I came. I shook so hard as I gushed around him. I was stunned when he didn't join me.

He kept hammering in and out, and I had no choice but to hang on weakly as he pushed me toward another orgasm while I was still having the first. I moaned, "I'm gonna die."

"Then we'll die together," he said in a growl.

I ended up coming again, and when I did, I not only flooded him again, but I scratched up his chest. He roared out his pleasure as he filled me with his cum and ground his pelvis against my throbbing clit. I fell limp against his chest and closed my eyes when I was done. God, I was too tired to move. I'd just sleep here.

❧❧❧

How I wish I were back having fighting matches with the guys and then sex in the car with Griffin. That night had been crazy and so damn hot. After car sex, he'd gotten us inside and into the shower, although that wasn't the end of it. Afterward, he took me in bed two more times before morning. He'd brought out some toys and rocked my world.

I used those thoughts to distract myself from what was happening now. It was close to a week later, and we were meeting Dad at his doctor's office. I was as nervous as I could be and felt sick to my stomach. I didn't want to hear the doctor confirm what Dad had told us. I prayed there would be a miracle, and he'd be cured or that they would discover they were wrong. I knew it wasn't realistic, but I prayed for it anyway.

We'd debated whether to fly back to Fairfax or if we should throw things off by driving. In the end, we did both. I flew us to Roanoke-Blacksburg Regional Airport then we drove the remaining three hours and some change there. The Patriots who were accompanying me met us there with two large SUVs, which was a good thing. Beau and Heath were the ones who met us. They had to transport me, Griffin, Jinx, Sarge, Styx, and Mad Dog.

When we got closer to Fairfax, we were meeting Dad. Undertaker, Ben, Justin, Aryan, and Giovanni were to protect Dad. They'd have more cars. I thought they should put more men on Dad, but they disagreed, and I was overruled. They were all on high alert and watched everything from the moment we landed until we met Dad at the designated meet-up spot.

He and I hugged hard. I swear he felt like he'd lost weight. Tears wanted to fill my eyes, but I refused to let them fall. He'd hate to see me cry. After we got our hellos out of the way, we were bundled into the SUVs, and off we went. I couldn't ride with him, which I disliked, but they explained it was better to keep us apart. I knew it made sense, but it was hard. The guys were great, even working on engaging me in talk to try and keep my mind off why we were here. Griffin held my hand the whole time. They were able to make me laugh a few times.

When we pulled into the parking structure across the street from his doctor's office, I felt like throwing up again. It was Griffin who got me out of the car and over to Dad. We were surrounded as we made our way there. The stares we received were many. It wasn't every day they saw someone with this many bodyguards and there was no doubt they were that. They weren't dressed in suits but combat black, and they were armed even if you couldn't see their guns.

That wasn't to say I wasn't armed, too. No way would I go anywhere without my gun, even before this threat. I knew Dad would be too. It did feel weird to be out without our usual guards from home. If they knew what we were doing, I had no doubt they'd be pissed they weren't here.

Inside, the waiting room was more than half full. The patients and others in there gave us scared looks when I went with Dad to speak to the receptionist. She recognized him, and we barely had to say our names and got back to a seat before his name was called. Undertaker, Griffin, and I went back with him while the others spread out in the waiting room and the hallway in the back. The staff gave them wary looks, but no one objected.

His doctor didn't take long to come into the room. Introductions were made, and then he got down to it. It was obvious he knew what Dad wanted because he explained in detail what was wrong, what they'd done, and what the prognosis was, which was as bleak as Dad had told me. The doctor was patient in answering my various questions, but in the end, there was no doubt. Dad would be lucky to live out the year. This time, I couldn't stop the tears.

It took me several minutes to calm down before we thanked his doctor and then left. He wanted Dad to have bloodwork done again, so we had to stop at the lab on the first floor. While he was doing that, I needed to go to the bathroom. Not only did I have to pee, but I also needed to fix my face. I knew I had makeup running all over it. I had to look a fright.

Griffin checked out the bathroom before allowing me to be in there alone. I thought it was funny to watch him searching, especially when a woman came in, saw him, and practically ran out. I laughed at that. After I finished peeing, I got down to fixing my appearance. It was as bad as I feared. I got out some makeup wipes and cleaned my face. So much for makeup. After it was removed, I splashed cold water on my face to take away some of the puffiness under my eyes.

While I was doing that, I heard a thumping sound, but I didn't pay much attention to it. I felt for the paper towels I'd laid on the counter so I could wipe my eyes. I'd been in here a while. I knew Griffin would be knocking soon to see if I was alright. I wiped my face and eyes, then straightened up. My gaze was immediately pulled to a reflection behind me. I wasn't fast enough to scream before a hand was over my mouth, and I was wrapped up tight against a body.

I was immediately more upset that I hadn't gotten off a warning or hit him than I was scared. Maybe part of the reason was because I recognized him. It was Rockwell. He hissed softly in my ear. "Hadley, it's me. Don't scream. I'm not here to hurt you. I'm here to protect you. Please. Listen to me. You're in danger."

I glared up at him. He knew what I was thinking. Why, if he was here to protect me, was he sneaking in here and doing this? And speaking of sneaking, how the hell had he gotten in here? The only way in was through the door, and it was guarded. There were no windows in the bathroom. As I scanned the room again, I found out how. The ceiling had a large vent for the ductwork above, and the grill that covered it was off. *He'd come in through the air vent. It had to be huge for him to fit through it* was my inane thought.

I tried to wiggle loose. He tightened his hold. We'd sparred a lot, so he knew how I fought and was using it against me by trapping my arms and legs between him and the sink in front of me. "Stop it. I'm not gonna hurt you. Listen. These Dark Patriots aren't the ones to trust. I am. They've isolated you from everyone who knows you. That's not right. You could be safe at home if they'd let us do our jobs. You've always been safe with us. Why all this change?"

I tried to tell him, but it came out low and garbled because of his hand.

"I'll take my hand away, but if you try to scream, I'll shoot whoever comes through that door. I know that bastard Griffin is out there, and some other guy I don't know. What the fuck? You have a whole different team on you, and so does your dad. What's that about? They look more like killers than bodyguards. Do you promise not to scream?"

Everything in me wanted to scream my head off when he moved his hand, but I wouldn't risk him shooting Griffin or anyone else. I'd have to bide my time until I could get away on my own. Hopefully, I'd do it before Grif came in to see what was taking me so long. I nodded yes. He gave me a warning look before he slowly moved his hand enough that I could talk, but he could still slap it quickly back over my mouth.

"Are you insane? You're gonna get yourself killed doing this. What do you think Grif and them are gonna do when they catch you? You'll be lucky to stay out of jail, let alone live. And if you do, what are the odds you'll keep your job?"

"Why would I lose it? I'm doing my job by protecting you. What's going on?"

Before I could answer, there was a knock at the door. Rockwell raised his gun to point at it. "Hadley, babe, are you alright in there? Do you need me?" Griffin called through the door worriedly. My heart melted at his tone. He sounded so concerned.

Knowing by his expression that Rockwell meant what he said, I answered, but not the way I wanted. "I'm fine. I just need a few more minutes, please. Don't come in. I can't handle anyone seeing me like this, not even you. I'm sorry."

"Baby, I don't care what you look like, but if that's what you want, then so be it. I'll be here."

"Thank you," I told him. He made a sound of understanding, but he didn't say anything. Rockwell was glaring at me. What now?

"Why the hell is he calling you babe and baby?" he hissed.

I wasn't about to get into that explanation with him. I had to get him to calm down, not get worked up. I shrugged. "You know how some guys are. It doesn't mean anything. Let's talk about you. Why do this?"

"I've been texting and calling you for days, and nothing! No one knows where you or your dad went. All we were told was there was danger and you were taken somewhere safe. If that was the case, then why weren't we taken with you? All that shit they had us doing before you left was stupid. What new danger?"

As he talked, I couldn't determine if he was talking a good line to lull me into feeling safe or if he really had no idea what he'd been doing. His face looked almost manic. Was he crazy? He was hyper-alert and tense. I decided to play along until I could escape. I gave him a tentative smile.

I made sure to keep my voice low like him.

"We've received threats. Dad panicked and brought in the Patriots, you know that. He was worried about me then someone tried to get into my room at the house. That's why they took us away. I admit it scared me when it happened."

He got a guilty look. I stared hard at him until he confessed. "It was me. I was the one trying to get into your room that night before you left. I wasn't there to hurt you. I just needed to see you and talk to you without one of them breathing down our necks. I wanted to know why you had me reassigned. You're not safe without me, Haddie. You know that. No one will guard you like I will."

He sounded so earnest and sincere. I hated when he called me Haddie but I kept my mouth shut. "Why aren't I safe without you? They're all highly trained men. They do this for a living."

He scowled. "Yeah, they do, but it's work for them. I do it because I love you. No one will protect you like someone who loves you. This isn't the way I wanted to tell you, but I think you know it already. I can tell you love me too. I wanted you to know so we can tell your dad. I want to marry you."

His confession left me speechless. I had no idea what to say. It was so off-base and wrong in so many ways. As I scrambled to form words, I saw a body drop out of the hole in the ceiling. Rockwell turned his gun that way automatically. I screamed a warning, but it was too late. Rockwell fired. The bathroom door came crashing open, and the room was filled with bodies. It was chaos.

Griffin: Chapter 18

I knew she was in trouble. My gut was clenching, and she was taking too long in the bathroom. I had no idea how but I knew she wasn't in there alone. I had to find a way in without getting her hurt or killed. When I talked to her through the door, I already had some of my guys in motion. They had secured Travis in a room with two inside with him and a couple outside. The others with me on her detail got all the civilians out of the immediate area. I sent Heath to the vent access. Before coming here, we'd studied the blueprints of the building extensively. We knew every exit and window. Part of our memorizing and studying included the vent system.

My mistake was assuming, along with my brothers, that it was too small for anyone to get through it. We were all big guys, so we believed it wasn't a viable way to get in or out of a room. It was the only possibility to explain how someone could be in there since I cleared the bathroom myself. The reason I chose Heath was he was lankier than the rest of us, although not by much. If anyone had a chance to get through the damn opening, it would be him.

It was hell to wait until he was in position. Luckily, there was access not far down the hall through a utility closet. We'd worn comms for this trip so he could whisper an update when he got there: "In position. She's not alone. I'm going in." Hearing this confirmed, I gave the order to breach. As I went to kick open the door. I heard her scream, and then I heard a shot. The door flew open, and we raced inside.

My heart jumped as I dove for the man who had her in his arms. Thank God the gun was pointed away from her. As I grabbed his arm to keep his gun off me and her, I tore him away so he had to release her. I knew Beau or one of the Marauders would get her clear. As I fought him, I realized who it was, fucking Rockwell. I was gonna kill the bastard.

It was chaotic with me fighting, Hadley crying out and I heard swearing and the pound of feet. I had to give it to him, he tried, but he was no match for me. It took me less than a minute to disarm him and take him to the floor. As I subdued him, Sarge got zip ties on his wrists and ankles. When he was secured, I let go and stood.

That's when I took in what was happening around me. My stomach dropped when I saw Heath on the floor and the blood. I rushed to him. Beau was working on him. Hadley was kneeling beside him, putting pressure on the wound with her bare hands. Tears were running down her cheeks.

"Don't you dare die on me. You hear me?" she was telling Heath.

He tried to smile at her. "I won't. If I do, you'll probably follow me to hell and kick my ass."

She gave him a choked laugh and nodded. "You're damn right I will. Didn't anyone ever tell you not to get shot?"

"Yeah, but I had to impress you somehow. How else can I win you from Griffin?" he teased her through his obvious pain.

"Well, I hate to kick a man when he's down, but this won't do that. I love that man. Sorry," she told him.

I wanted to crow with glee that she loved me. Yeah, it wasn't exactly how I wanted to find out, but it would do. She didn't even seem aware of what she said, but I was, and so were the others. Heath turned to look at me, and he winked.

"Hey, boss, can I get extra vacation time for this? Also, your woman won't stop mauling me. I think she likes me."

"Like hell, you'll get extra time. I expect you to be working tomorrow. As for my woman liking you, that's not it. She likes to help strays and shit."

He laughed, then groaned. That's when I tuned into the other sounds in the room. Jinx's voice caught my attention first.

"Hey, Griffin, we've got a doctor here. He needs room to take care of Heath." A hand on my shoulder made me move away. A man in a white coat and a woman took my place. Slowly, they had Beau and Hadley move back, but my woman stayed nearby. I didn't mind because I had something else to do. Rockwell was screaming profanities. I finally paid attention to what he was saying.

"She doesn't fucking love you, and she never will. She loves me, and I love her. You won't keep us apart. Wait until I talk to her dad. He'll see I'm the only one who can protect her."

I stomped over to him, and I leaned down to sneer in his face and hiss at him. "Listen to me, you deranged cockhead. Hadley is mine. We're getting married, and she's moving in with me. We're gonna have a houseful of babies, and you'll never see her again. Your ass is going to prison, fucker. That is if you make it there."

There was nothing I wanted more than to take him out of here, torture his ass for not only shooting my man but for terrifying her and her dad. The threats he'd made to Travis haunted me. Her dad had shared the exact words with me when she wasn't present on a call. Lucky for Rockwell, security guards from the building came pushing inside at that exact moment. The bathroom was overcrowded, so I stepped outside with one of them. They were confused and kept trying to detain us. It took time to get them to understand we were the good guys. By the time we did, paramedics were there to transport Heath to the hospital.

We had Travis and his guards with us by then. He was frantic to see that Hadley was alright. It was so damn crazy, but I had Undertaker take him to the bathroom to see her. Heath was wheeled out not long afterward. The doctor was with him.

"I'm going with him to the ER. I work there part-time. This happened to be one of my office days, but I'm done seeing patients for the day. You can meet us there."

"Thanks, Dr...." I trailed off. I had no idea what his name was.

"It's Dr. Kern. You're welcome. You have your hands full here. I'll take care of him. He's lost blood, but he's awake and talking, so I think he'll be alright."

Jinx grabbed Hadley to prevent her from going

with Heath. It took another twenty minutes to get things straightened out so we could follow, mainly because the actual cops showed up, and we had to explain everything all over again. They were cool enough to settle for one of us staying to explain everything and make an official statement, which allowed the rest of us to go to the hospital.

I wanted to stash Travis and Hadley with guards somewhere first, but they refused to do it. They wanted to go to the hospital so that was what we did. I kinda felt sorry for the cops who were left to question Undertaker. His intimidating presence was affecting them big time. I knew deep down he was enjoying the shit out of it too. It was why he volunteered to stay. He could be a bastard sometimes.

Before we left, Beau and Hadley washed their hands, but their shirts were trashed with blood. She covered hers with her sweater. His was less noticeable since it was on a black shirt. In the SUV, this time, we let Travis ride with her, and he sat on one side of her and me on the other. She was cuddled up against me. She kept asking me to promise her that Heath was really going to be fine. I did my best, but she was still stressed.

At the hospital, we entered the waiting room like a wave. People were staring even harder there than at the doctor's office. I got them seated with guards posted before I went to the desk to tell them who I was and why I was there. The woman behind it promised to let the staff know and to get us an update as soon as possible. I had no choice but to accept it.

As we sat there, I saw Justin go to the desk not long after we got settled. He stood there talking until someone came out and waved at him to follow her. It wasn't into the back so I had no idea where they went. About five minutes later, he was back, and he had clothing in his hands. He held them up. "Here's something for you two to change into. You have to be tired of those bloody clothes. It's not high fashion, but it'll work and be clean."

That's when I realized they were scrub tops. He handed the biggest one to Beau and the other to her. They thanked him. After a quick shuffling, we got her to the ladies' room and him to the men's bathroom. This time, I didn't leave her alone. I went in with her. She needed to sponge the blood off her skin that had soaked through. I threw her bloody top away. I'd buy her a new one. She was back to crying, so I washed and dried her, then pulled on the clean shirt. I hugged her tightly.

"Shh, baby, stop."

"I can't. What if the doctor is wrong and he dies? It's all my fault. I should've beat Rockwell's ass rather than trying to calm him and wait for a break. If I had, he wouldn't have shot Heath."

I pushed her away so I could see her face. I gave her a gentle shake. "No, if you did that, he might've shot you. Heath knew the risk, and he was willing to take it. We all were. You did the right thing. Later, after we get the official notice that he's fine, you can tell me what the bastard had to say while he had you trapped in there."

"I can tell you now. I might as well since we'll be waiting for a while. It'll help me not think about what's happening with Heath. Come on."

She'd stopped crying now that she had something to do, so I didn't object. Back out in the waiting area, we got the crew off to one side so she could tell us what Rockwell said. When she was done, I was confused. What he said to her didn't make sense. The only explanation was he was crazy and had no idea that he wasn't protecting her but rather threatening her. He hadn't even mentioned the threats he made to Travis. I'd make sure to let the cops know when we gave our statements. I didn't want him to get off due to insanity, but it might be the case. Whichever way it went, I'd make sure he spent years away from her if I could.

The hours dragged by. We got a couple of updates, but all we were told was Heath was still in surgery. We moved to the OR waiting room when they told us that. When we were finally told he was in recovery, the relief was immense. They tried the whole "family only" thing, but we told them he didn't have any. We were his family.

Ben went first after Heath was out of recovery and in a room. They'd been friends for years, and they were as close as brothers. He came out wearing a relieved expression. Next, I went with Hadley. She was about to lose it if she couldn't see Heath with her own eyes. When she got to his bedside, I had to hold her back from throwing herself at him. Instead, she had to settle for grabbing the hand he held up to her.

"Oh, thank God you're alright. I've been so worried. I'm sorry. This is all my fault," she babbled.

"Like hell, it's your fault. It was that shithead Rockwell's fault. He held you captive and was carrying the gun. He shot me. When I get out of here, I'm gonna beat his ass. You stop blaming yourself, you hear?" he ordered her sternly. She didn't say anything, but she did nod her head. He glanced over at me.

He held out his other hand to me. I was careful not to grab too hard. He had an IV in that one. I gently squeezed it. "It's good to see you talking, but don't think you can milk your sick leave," I joked.

He pouted out his lip as he pretended to whine. "Ah, come on, boss. Surely, this has earned me an extra week off."

"Nope. A week and that's it. The way I heard it, you barely had a scratch." It was worse than that, but I knew he'd want to downplay it. He snorted but didn't disagree. We didn't stay long since we didn't want to tire him out, and there were more who wanted to see him. We asked if he needed anything and promised we'd be back to see him.

By the time everyone was done, it was early evening. We were tired and hungry and still had to talk to the cops. They'd shown up, and I had held them off from talking to Hadley but the most we could hope for was they'd wait until morning. This meant we couldn't leave town, which was what I wanted to do. A debate ensued as to where to stay. In the end, we decided to go back to their estate, which wasn't far.

With Rockwell behind bars, there was less of a worry. We'd still want to be alert in case he wasn't working alone. I had to wonder if any of the other guards had been working with him. His remarks to her and what the one cop who came to the hospital told us sounded like he was the only one involved. He denied threatening her. He claimed he was protecting her, and they were in love. He was insisting on seeing her and talking to Travis.

Speaking of Travis, he was done in. He looked pale

and shaky. I was worried about how this mess would affect his health. He didn't need anything that would wear him down faster. Hadley needed all the time she could get with her dad.

Suffice it to say, we didn't warn anyone at their estate we were coming. When we pulled up to the gate where the first two security guards were posted, their looks of astonishment and then nervousness were warranted. I wondered if they had been fucking off with them both gone. They followed the protocol we'd set up before leaving to the letter before letting us inside. It was with relief we got out at the front door, where we were dropped off. A couple of the guys would park the cars and then join us.

Hadley entered an electronic code to open the front door. It was nothing as mundane as a regular lock for them, but knowing the kind of things they worked on and that they did at least some of it at home, it made more sense. As the door opened, Porter scurried toward it with a furled brow.

"Mr. Travis, Ms. Hadley, I wasn't expecting you. Welcome home. I'm so happy to see you. How may I assist you tonight? Have you eaten? I can have something prepared."

"Thank you, Porter. I hate to get Mrs. Farnsworth back here this late. We can fend for ourselves. I do need you to make sure we have beds ready for all the men. Jinx, we had most of Griffin's men in the house, but we have other housing for the guards and some other staff. Will that be alright? If not, I can have rooms made up here in the main house. It's entirely up to you."

The Marauders were busy taking in the beautiful

and obviously wealthy house. Jinx shook his head. "There's no need to go to any trouble for us. We can bunk wherever Beau and the others are at. You have an amazing house here, Mr. Gerard."

"Thank you, and you must treat it as yours. You have free access to it and if you need something, ask Porter. He's our butler, and he keeps this well-oiled machine working. We can't do it without him. Oh, and please, call me Travis. Okay, if you follow me, we'll raid the kitchen."

There was happy muttering from most of us as we followed him. Porter stayed a discreet distance behind until we were in the kitchen, and then he disappeared. I guessed he was off to arrange the sleeping quarters. I would be staying in the house with Hadley. Only this time, I'd be sleeping with her unless Travis had objections. I'd have to ask him. Since he hadn't voiced any objections to me and her so far, I didn't think he would, but you never knew.

Hadley made her dad sit down and rest. I helped her get in the fridge to see what we could find, and then we raided the pantry. There were lots of options for sandwiches, a huge container of homemade soup, and various other things. It was enough to feed us. It was loud and a bit chaotic as we got ourselves situated. We sat or leaned against the counters and island. They offered the formal dining room, but we told them this was fine.

The others joined us after parking the cars. The only one missing was Beau. He'd opted to stay at the hospital with Heath. We'd switch him out later. That was one of the things I had to talk to the guys about after we ate. I had to decide who would be doing what tonight until we made up the guard rotation in the morning. Although I was mostly convinced Rockwell had worked alone, I still wanted to be sure, at least for a few days.

Travis was drooping with fatigue and could barely keep his eyes open. Hadley was yawning. I had to take care of them first.

“Babe, I want you and your dad to go to bed. You’re beat. I’ll post a guard outside each of your rooms.”

“You guys are just as tired,” she protested.

“We are tired, but we’re used to going without sleep for long periods of time. However, as soon as we set the guard duty for the night and the guys get shown where they’re staying, we’ll go to bed, too. I bet the cops will be here bright and early to get the rest of our statements. They’ll want to talk to you,” I reminded her.

She sighed and nodded. A short discussion later, it was decided that Aryan would be her guard and Giovanni Travis’s. I made sure to give her a kiss and speak to Travis before they were taken to their rooms. She gave me a questioning look when I asked to speak to him for a moment alone. We went into the hallway.

“What’s wrong, Griffin,” he asked worriedly.

“Nothing. I’m sorry if I gave you that impression. I wanted to ask you something. You know Hadley and I are together, and it’s serious.”

“Yes, I know that.”

“Well, I would never want to disrespect you or your home, and if you object, I’ll understand. I—,” I said.

He cut me off with a smile.

"You want to know if you can stay with her in her room."

"Yes, that's what I want to do, but only if you're okay with it."

"Son, I'm not as old-fashioned as you might think. Of course, if you were in a casual relationship, I probably wouldn't like it, but since you're not, I'm fine with it as long as she is."

"Thank you. I'll ask her once I'm done here. You might think it's too fast, but I love your daughter, and I plan to tell her. There's nothing casual about us and never will be."

He had a faraway look on his face accompanied by a smile. "I knew her mom was the one for me within an hour of meeting her. I declared my love within a week, and we were married two months later. I believe in love at first sight, so you're behind the power curve, son."

I laughed along with him. Then, seeing he was done for, I escorted him back and they left for their rooms. Once they were gone, we got down to business. I wanted to join her as soon as possible. The thought of sleeping with her safe in my arms made me impatient.

It didn't take long to figure out who would sleep first, who would guard, and then who would relieve them. Ben and Justin offered to show the Marauders where they would be sleeping, so I wished them a good night about ten minutes later. I checked the doors and windows on the first floor before going up, even though I knew the roving guard, Sarge, would do it. Porter was giving him a guided tour. I would've done it, but Porter was chomping at the bit to help with something.

Upstairs, I went straight to her room. According to Porter, our bags had been taken up. I'd go get mine from my old room after I made sure she was alright with me staying with her. Aryan nodded to me when he saw me. He was standing at attention in front of her door.

"Everything is quiet, Wraith. Do you want me to stay here or go outside?"

"Since I'm with her, you can get some sleep, but have Porter show you where to go. I want you to sleep first, and then you can rotate in tomorrow morning. We've got the night covered until ten in the morning. Go get a shower and crash."

"Alright, if you don't need me, I will. If you change your mind, just give me a call."

"Thanks, I will," I assured him as I clapped him on the shoulder. He gave me a mock salute, then walked off whistling.

Not wanting to startle her, I knocked softly in case she was asleep and called out. "Hadley, baby, it's me. Can I come in?"

The door was yanked open quicker than I expected, and she grabbed my arm, pulling on me. I went inside, and she slammed the door shut and then locked it.

"Babe, what's wrong?" I asked as I scanned the room for a threat. My hand was behind my back on the butt of my gun.

"Nothing other than I want you in here with me, and I don't want anyone coming in and disturbing us.

Did you get everyone settled?"

"I did. You're both safe, I promise."

"I know we are. What did you and Dad talk about out in the hall? He wouldn't tell me. All he said was you'd explain." She led me to sit on the bed with her. The mattress felt like heaven. All I wanted to do was lie on it and close my eyes, but I needed to ask her my question and then take a shower. I could smell her body wash and shampoo and saw her still-wet hair. She had it pulled up in a messy knot on the top of her head.

"It wasn't anything bad. All I did was remind him we're serious about each other and I asked him if he had any objections to me staying in here with you. He said as long as you didn't, he was fine with it. So I'm asking, do you want me in here or in my old bedroom?"

She scooted closer and put her hand on my cheek. She stared intently into my eyes. "Honey, I wouldn't be able to sleep if you weren't in this bed with me. You better not dare think you can sleep in another room."

I grinned. "Well, then, I'd better go get my bags and move my stuff over. Then I need a quick shower, and we can hit the sack."

"I already had them brought in, and I put your clothes in the closet and dresser. Your other stuff is in the bathroom. I hope that's alright. I left your weapons in their bag."

"You're an angel. Thank you. Now, let me take my shower. I want you snuggled up in the bed when I get done."

"I'll be waiting for you," she said before placing a soft kiss on my lips. I wanted to kiss her back much more aggressively, but if I did, I'd never get my shower, and I was sweaty from earlier. I left it to a gentle one and reluctantly broke it so I could go to the bathroom.

I didn't dawdle. I got in and quickly shampooed my hair, then soaped my body. I made sure to thoroughly scrub. After I was out and dried off, a quick swipe of deodorant, finger combing my hair and teeth bruising, and I was done. The bedroom only had the lamp on my side of the bed left on. She was under the covers watching me. I didn't like to wear anything to bed, so I was naked. She was watching me closely. I felt my cock twitch, but I kept it under control, barely.

As much as I always wanted her, tonight, she needed sleep more than sex. It could wait. Throwing back the covers, I got in and snapped off the light. Then I rolled toward her. Her mouth landed on mine, but it wasn't a gentle kiss like the one before my shower. I returned it and fought my erection. When we came up for air, I told her.

"Babe, as much as I want you, we need rest. I swear, come morning, I'll give you anything you want, but tonight, I need you to rest."

She moaned, but thankfully, she didn't test my resolve because if she had, I would've given in to her. I was worried about her otherwise, I would've made love to her. She snuggled close, and I held her close with one arm underneath her shoulders. Her head rested on my chest.

"Goodnight, baby."

"Goodnight, honey," she said and ended it with a yawn. It was only a matter of a couple of minutes before I heard her breathing change, and I knew she was asleep. I closed my eyes and let myself drift off. Tomorrow was going to be a busy day for a variety of reasons.

Hadley: Chapter 19

I was over this whole debacle. It had been non-stop since eight o'clock this morning. My plan to wake Griffin up with morning sex was derailed by the cops arriving and us having to scramble to get dressed so we could talk to them. When we met them in the formal living room where Porter had put them, I knew this was going to be an ordeal.

One of them was the officer who came to the hospital yesterday. He was polite and introduced himself as Detective O'Reilly. The other one I instantly disliked. His name was Detective Shane. He was checking out our home and had his upper lip raised slightly in what I thought was a sneer. What the hell was his problem? I wanted to ask him that, but I didn't. We shook their hands, even though he barely touched mine, and then we sat down.

Griffin opened the conversation: "Thank you, Detective O'Reilly, for being so understanding yesterday. I know there was a lot to sort through, and Hadley was too upset and worried about my guy who was shot to talk about what happened. I hope my business partner, Mark, was able to answer your questions."

"He was very detailed about what happened. He explained your company and what you do. If you don't mind, I'd still like to hear from you exactly what you do and why you were involved yesterday."

"Certainly. I'm Griffin Voss. I'm one of the four owners of Dark Patriots. We're a security consulting company. We work for a variety of companies. Mr. Gerard, Hadley's father, contacted us and asked that we provide him with our services. In rendering those services yesterday, Ms. Gerard was accosted in the ladies' room by one of her former bodyguards, Mr. Rockwell. We determined the safest way to get her out of there, and in the execution of it, my employee, Heath Rugger, was shot by Mr. Rockwell. I was able to disarm Mr. Rockwell without further harm to anyone, and we secured him. The security staff at the medical building responded, and then the police did. He was taken to jail, and the rest of us went to the hospital to await news on Heath."

"That's what Mr. O'Rourke told me. We'd like to clarify a few things and then ask Ms. Gerard and Mr. Gerard what happened. Where is Mr. Gerard? He should be here." Detective O'Reilly asked.

"My father is still resting. He's not a well man, and I'd prefer not to disturb him. He wasn't present for the incident. He was in the lab having bloodwork done. He came after everything was over, and they were working on Heath," I politely informed him.

"What exactly is wrong with him?" Detective Shane popped in to ask.

"I don't see how that's relevant. Suffice it to say, he's unwell and needs his rest," I told him.

"Is there a reason you don't want to tell us? I think we must insist he be here. If you resist, we can have you taken down to the station to ask these questions," Shane said gruffly.

"The reason I don't want to tell you is it's none of

your business. I believe HIPAA protects his right to privacy about his health. We're not resisting but merely telling you it has no bearing on this."

"That's fine. Please tell us what happened in the bathroom," O'Reilly asked after giving his partner a warning glance.

I went through it as quickly as possible. I wanted them out of here. We had stuff to do today, and I didn't want to waste it on silly questions from the one guy. When I was done, it was back to Shane asking a question.

"Why did Mr. Gerard hire your company, Mr. Voss? What work did he need you to do? I understand all of you were armed yesterday."

"Yes, we were all armed. We have the required permits to carry those guns. We're in the security business. We can hardly do that if we don't carry them at times. As for why Mr. Gerard hired us, that's not something I feel comfortable talking about. He's a very private person. You'll have to ask him later."

"Again with the evasions. According to what we found, Mr. Gerard has no children. I find this whole story you're feeding us to be suspicious. How do we know you're not holding Mr. Gerard against his will? We only have your word for where he is," Shane jumped in to say.

I opened my mouth to tell him to go to hell when the door opened. I expected it to be Porter bringing coffee and something to eat. He always made sure visitors had something. It wasn't. It was Dad. I jumped to my feet and hurried over to him. He appeared drawn and pale, with dark circles underneath his eyes. He gave me a wan smile.

"Good morning, Daddy. You should still be in bed

resting. Grif and I are handling this."

"From the sounds of it, I need to be here. Don't fuss. I'm fine. The sooner we get them out of here, the better," he whispered. He must've been listening at the door before entering. Sighing, I nodded and led him to the couch. Both detectives were on their feet, watching us closely.

"Hello, gentlemen. I'm Travis Gerard. I understand from my daughter that you need to speak to me. Please be seated," he informed them after I made introductions. I sat with him while Griffin stood behind the couch and us.

"Have you been offered something to drink?" Dad asked.

"We have, but we're not here for that. We want to know what went on yesterday. We were explaining to this woman who says she's your daughter that there's no record of you having children. I must ask, are you being forced to say or do anything by these people? You can tell us. We'll protect you," Shane stated boldly.

I gasped in outrage. I heard Griffin's low growl. Dad looked at them disbelievingly. "Detectives, I can assure you she is my daughter. I'm a very wealthy man. As such, I felt it prudent to keep my daughter's existence a secret from the world. It was for her protection."

"Does her protection have anything to do with why you hired the Dark Patriots?" Shane asked next.

"You know. I'm starting to feel like you're treating us more like we're the ones who did something wrong and not my former employee. He held my daughter at gunpoint. He shot someone. Would you mind telling me what's up with all these questions and your attitude?" Dad asked Shane.

"We'll ask the questions," Shane fired back quickly

and with a bite to his tone. I wanted to go over and punch him in the face. O'Reilly at least appeared unhappy with his partner's questions and attitude. O'Reilly jumped in to smooth things over.

"Sir, we just want to get a clear picture of the circumstances and what happened. Mr. Rockwell had a different story about what occurred yesterday."

"Really? What did he say?" I asked.

"First, may we know what your relationship is with Mr. Voss? He's the head of your new security, but is he anything else?" At least O'Reilly asked it politely.

I was about to answer when Griffin did. "I'm her man, not that I see what that has to do with anything. Our personal relationship has nothing to do with yesterday."

"But it does. Mr. Rockwell said he was in there trying to get to his girlfriend. According to him, you and your men had abruptly whisked her away, along with her father, to an undisclosed location. He had no idea where and had no way to contact them. When he recalled that Mr. Gerard had a medical appointment, he hoped his employer would be there so he could talk to him and find out what had happened to them.

"He was happy to see she came with her father, but you prevented him from approaching her normally, so he thought the bathroom was the best option. It was while they were talking that you and your men burst in and threatened him with your guns. He admitted he did fire a shot but only in self-defense. He felt his and her lives were in imminent danger," Shane said smugly.

I felt outraged. I was about to blast his ass when I heard Griffin laugh. I glanced over at him. He had a smirk on his face. "Well, detectives, I hate to tell you, but a madman took you in. He's as crazy as a loon. You said he said Hadley is his girlfriend. He and she have never been anything more than bodyguard and employer. This relationship is all in his head. He was spouting off stuff about protecting her and that they were in love yesterday. It's utter nonsense."

O'Reilly looked uncomfortable. Shane, on the other hand, was red in the face. You could tell he was angry. "It's your word against his, and we're not just taking your word. I think it's best if we continue this talk at the department. We need to get to the bottom of this. A man was shot, but we have to find out if it was justified or not," Shane informed us sharply.

I got to my feet. "As of this moment, we will not answer any more questions. You may speak to our lawyer, who I can assure you will be at the department within the hour. I want you to leave, please. You're upsetting my father, and I'm not happy with your allegations either."

They stood. "I'm sorry you're upset, Ms. Gerard," O'Reilly said, trying to smooth over what his partner caused.

"You need to come with us. Your lawyer can meet us there," Shane made one last effort. I stepped closer to him. I felt Griffin behind me. The heat of his body warmed my back.

"Detective, I'm going nowhere with you. If you touch me or anyone in my home, I'll make sure not only do I have your badge, but you'll be lucky if you can get a job in fast food. Your ridiculous attitude has ended this conversation, and we will be speaking to your captain. Now, do you want to guarantee unemployment, or should our lawyer meet

you at the department?"

His face became so red that it was almost purple. His partner didn't waste time practically dragging him out the door. He kept apologizing the whole time. The fury washing through me took a long time to diminish.

That was hours ago. Since then, our lawyer went to the station and talked to them. They were presently holding Rockwell, and the judge wasn't inclined to let him out until he had a whole psychological assessment. That was due to our lawyer pushing for it and who my dad was. It would buy us time, but it was likely if he wasn't found insane, he'd be allowed out on bail, which was the last thing we wanted.

Afterward, we had to settle Dad down. I made sure he ate something, then went back to bed. It was early afternoon before we arrived at the hospital to see Heath. Dad wanted to go, but I convinced him to let us go alone. Porter was given orders to keep him in bed even if he had to sit on him. Our poor butler looked horrified when I said it, which made me giggle. Porter was way too refined to do something like sit on someone, let alone Dad, but he could give a great reproachful look.

Heath was doing well and already itching to get out of the hospital. I lectured him. "You can't leave yet. You've been in here less than twenty-four hours! You were shot and had surgery. You'll do as the doctors say, and only when they think you're well enough will we let you leave. You're coming back to the house with us when you do."

"There's no reason for me to go to your house. I won't be allowed to do guard duty. I'll be sent back home to Hampton. Maybe I'll get lucky, and they have something I can do in the office to keep me from losing my mind."

"You're right, you won't be allowed to work, but you will come to our house. I want to be sure you follow your doctor's orders and heal. I can't do that if I don't have eyes on you. And I have a feeling the more eyes, the better. You don't listen well, do you?"

"What makes you say that? And there's no need for you or anyone else to nursemaid me. I've been taking care of myself since I was thirteen, and this isn't the first time I've been shot. I'll be fine."

"Well, this is the first time you've been shot protecting me. That means I have to make sure you heal as good as new. I can ask Griffin to make it an order if I must."

"Hey, that's not fair. Wraith is so gone on you. He'll do whatever makes you happy. Alright, I'll give in for now. I'll stay another day, and then we'll talk to those damn pesky doctors about me getting out of this hellhole. I hate hospitals," he grumbled.

"Nobody likes hospitals, except maybe doctors and nurses, and I have to wonder if they do. Now, do you need us to bring you anything?" I asked.

"Nope, but you can tell whoever is up next to sit with me they can go. It's a waste to have them sitting here doing nothing. I can take a piss without their help. Put them to work or let them go home. I won't stage a prison break."

"That's Griffin's call, not mine."

He gave Grif an intense, demanding look. Griffin

wasn't intimidated, it seemed. "Give it until tomorrow, and then we'll see. I'd feel better, as would the rest of the team if you had someone here just in case."

Heath sighed wearily, but all he did was nod. He knew he was beaten. He switched gears. "What about Rockwell? Any news about him? Please tell me he's still in jail. They didn't let the fucker out, did they?" You could hear the anger in his voice, but who could blame him?

"No, they haven't. We had to go around with one of the cops, though. He was being a total asshole, although he backed down when Hadley and Travis's lawyer came in. Their lawyer is a piranha, I think," Grif told him.

I had to laugh. "Oh, there's no doubt about it. Jacob is the head of our legal team for a reason. He's the best defense attorney in the country. His success rate makes people shake in their boots when he walks into a meeting or the courtroom. And those who piss him off aren't left happy. Fuck with him at your peril. What I told Detective Shane wasn't a lie about his job if he kept his shit up."

"What did you tell him?" Heath asked eagerly.

We kept him amused for the next several minutes, retelling what happened at the house and then at the precinct. He laughed a few times and had to clutch his wound. When we were done, I could tell he was tired. His eyes were drooping.

"Griffin, we should go. I need to check on Dad, and I know you have work to do. We'll see you tomorrow. Listen to the staff," I warned Heath. I kissed his cheek.

He perked up and looked at Griffin with a smirk. "See, she's coming over to the dark side," he teased Grif.

"If you don't wanna see dark permanently, then wipe that smirk off your face. And baby, don't go kissing other men," Griffin muttered to me.

"I kissed his cheek. Calm your balls."

That remark made them both laugh, but only after Grif's initial surprised look. After they shook hands, we headed out. We walked out with Griffin's arm hooked around my shoulder. "You're so damn disrespectful. I'll have to see what I can do when we get home to tame that," he growled in my ear.

A shiver of sexual anticipation ran through me. "Oh, I can't wait. Give me your best shot, Wraith."

This earned me a swat on the ass, but I didn't care. Nor did I care that people passing us saw it and stared. We stopped in the waiting room. Justin was on babysitting duty, as Heath called it.

"Let me guess. He wants me to leave and you to spring him. You had to pull rank to make him stay," Justin stated.

"You know him," Griffin said.

"Idiot will kill himself one of these days. Do I need to cuff him to the bed?"

"Maybe hold off on that. You might scandalize the staff if you do. I think we can at least make it until tomorrow before we have to consider that. Your replacement will be here at four. If you or he needs anything, you know what to do."

"I do. Don't worry, I can handle Heath's ass. I'm

glad we caught that bastard Rockwell."

"So am I. This way, everyone can get back to their lives," I said.

He nodded. They exchanged a few more words about schedules, and then we said goodbye. I was ready to get home, check on Dad, and settle in for a quiet night with my man. Things were finally back to normal, and the project was almost done. My next job was to figure out how Griffin and I could live together and still keep an eye on Dad. That would mean making a trip to Hampton to see where he lived and deciding whether we needed a new place or not. I was nervous yet excited about the prospect of it.

❧❧❧

It had been a week since the harrowing incident with Rockwell. He was still in jail because he wasn't able to make bail. Our legal team asked for the case to be expedited. He refused to plead out. He was still insisting he hadn't made threats, and he only wanted to protect me and that he and I were in love. His psychiatric evaluation didn't find he was insane, just obsessed and suffering from delusions. However, he had been in his right mind when he came after me in the bathroom.

There was a tiny part of me that felt sorry for him. He and I had gotten along during his four years on my security detail. We'd had some laughs and even hung out a bit, but it had never been sexual or romantic. I couldn't see how he saw it that way. It went to show you never knew how someone else's brain worked. It was scary to think about.

Heath had been released from the hospital after five days. It took all of us to keep him from staging what he called a prison break. He was sent back to Hampton to recuperate. In an effort to be sure he did, they sent Beau with him. The threat to us seemed to be over. There had been zero attempts to break into the estate or the house or to come after us anytime we were away from home.

Griffin was somewhat reluctant to ease off the security provided by his guys and the Marauders, who had stuck around until yesterday. Still, I convinced him to let our other bodyguards and security personnel return to doing their jobs. He and the other Patriots were still training with them, but he'd done it for me.

Dad and I made sure to pay not only for Heath's hospital stay that wasn't covered by his insurance, which wasn't much but also for his salary and a bonus while he was off. The Patriots assured us they would continue to pay him, but we wanted to do it. They would let us know anything he needed.

Heath teased me one final time before leaving, saying that he'd be waiting for me when I got tired of Griffin. When he said he wanted me to come nurse him and to wear a sexy nurse's uniform, I thought Griffin was going to fire him, but then he burst out laughing and told Heath to get his stupid ass home.

Besides working on a trip to check out Hampton, Dad and I had been working remotely to finalize the project. I did most of it since he was always tired, and I didn't want him to wear himself out. It was almost done and would be finished early if today's trip went as planned. We were going to headquarters so I could do a final workday on it.

We left early, so I'd have a whole day to do it. The

staff was excited to get me there to do this. It had been hard on them to have me not available to come in as much as I usually would've, but they were more than capable of doing most of it without me being there.

Besides Griffin, we had Ben and Justin with us while Giovanni and Aryan stayed back at the estate. From our regular guards, Fletcher and Ellis were with Dad, and Sanders was with me while Ortiz was off. Six with us plus the usual at headquarters should be more than enough. In fact, I tried to tell Griffin he and our guys were enough, but he insisted on having Ben and Justin, too.

Pulling through the security checkpoint at Gerard's was handled the new way the Patriots had trained them to do it. They were much smoother at it. Since we didn't have people just coming here day in and day out, it was a much better way to do it. We'd always looked at the driver's ID, and the place was enclosed in fencing, which had cameras and other monitoring equipment, as well as roving security.

It wasn't long after we got inside the building and the research lab that I was lost in my world. I loved seeing something I imagined in my head come to life in front of me. Griffin and Sanders stayed with me. Justin and Fletcher were with Dad. He had work to do in his office. Ben and Ellis were roving the building.

Griffin did make me take a break late in the morning and then have an actual lunch break before I was back at it a third time. When he insisted I should take an afternoon one, I was ready. We decided to go to Dad's office and see if he was ready for one, too. When we got there, he was slumped tiredly in his chair. That was when I called it a day. The others could carry on without me. I knew he'd put up a fight if I suggested we leave because of him, so I made it all about me.

When he saw us, he smiled and straightened. "How's it going? I was just going to come down again to see."

"It's going really well. The team can work on it on their own. I'm feeling tired for some reason. I was coming to see if you're ready to head home?"

"Honey, I wish I could. You guys can go and then send a car for me later. Ansel is coming by later. We need to catch up. He's worried and wants to be sure everything is good to go. You know him. He needs to see for himself," he chuckled.

"Yes, he does. Why can't he come to the house? It's not like he lives far away. In fact, it's a longer drive for him to come here than there."

"Do you have an issue with that, Griffin? She's right, and it would be more comfortable. He could come for dinner. I've missed our chats. He usually comes to dinner at least a couple of times a month, if not more."

"I don't have an issue with it. We'll just alert the guards to expect him. Why don't you let him know of the change in plans? That'll let Hadley wrap up getting her stuff, and then we'll head out."

The relief on Dad's face was noticeable. We left him long enough for me to go back to the lab to tell the others I was leaving. They assured me they were good and that if they had any questions, they'd call. Within twenty minutes, I think, we were headed home. Dad dozed on the way. We had a few hours until dinner. I was going to insist he take a nap, or he wouldn't be in any condition to talk to Ansel.

I was terrified, seeing how fast he was declining. It was like now that he told me the disease had accelerated. Or maybe he'd been working that hard to hide it, and now that he didn't have to, he let me see how much it was really affecting him. It made me wonder how much time I had left with him. Even a year wouldn't be enough. What if I only had a few months?

"Baby, worrying yourself about it won't help. Now that this project and the threat are over, we can make him rest even more. We'll get him to go with us to Hampton, and I promise he'll be well looked after," Griffin whispered in my ear.

I sighed as I snuggled closer to him. "I just want to have him for as long as I can, and I want as many new memories with him as I can get."

"We'll get them."

He hugged me closer, and I closed my eyes for the rest of the ride. I didn't nap, but I did think about all the great past experiences Dad and I had together over the years. There were so many.

Griffin: Chapter 20

Ansel Dewitt arrived, and he and Travis greeted each other with laughs and hugs as Porter showed him into the family room. When they were done, Dewitt hugged Hadley and gave her a kiss on the cheek.

"How're you doing, sweetheart? I know this has to have been as hard on you as it has been on Trav. I'm so damn glad it's over with. I was scared to death for both of you."

"I'm doing great, Ansel. We're relieved, too. I believe you remember Griffin Voss from the Dark Patriots."

"I do. Hello. I admit, I'm surprised to see you're still here, Mr. Voss. With the threat neutralized and in jail, I would've thought you and your men would be back home. You're from Hampton, Virginia, right? I believe that's where Travis told me your company is."

"It is in Hampton. We're just being absolutely sure that we didn't miss anything. Plus, we're doing a bit more training with the guards."

As we sat down to dinner, Ansel was surprised when Ben and Justin entered and joined us. He quickly arranged his face into a bland expression and politely shook hands with them when Travis introduced them and informed him the three of us would be joining the three of them for dinner.

The conversation was relaxed and flowing. They chatted about people and things we didn't know, but Hadley and Travis were good at explaining who they were. Hadley, in particular, made sure to tell me more than once I'd meet this one or that one.

"Excuse me, but I seem to be lost. Why would he meet any of them? He'll soon be going home," Ansel eventually asked.

I was kind of surprised Travis hadn't told him about me and Hadley, but maybe he was waiting for us to become more than just together. I bet the ring I wanted to get her would do it. I'd asked Sloan, Cassidy, and Gemma to help me find one. They were eagerly sending me pictures of ones they thought might fit the bill. So far, there had been a few I liked, but none had struck me as the one.

"With everything going on, we haven't had time to tell anyone. In fact, I was hoping we could have a dinner party so we could introduce Griffin to everyone. You're the first to know it, but Hadley and Griffin are together. As awful as this whole affair was, it did have a bright side," Travis told him with a smile on his face.

"What do you mean, they're together?" Dewitt asked slowly. I could tell he was shocked to find out I was more than a security consultant to her.

"Exactly what it sounds like, Ansel. Griffin and I are in a relationship," she told him as she squeezed my hand.

"You mean you're dating. Honey, I don't mean to sound unsupportive, because I'm not, but don't you think you should wait to introduce him to our friends until you know this is more than just you being in danger and forming a connection that will fade once you go back to your real lives? I suggest you hold off until you know you're serious and this is headed toward an engagement."

"We don't need to wait. We already know it's serious, and we're going to get engaged and then get married. Of course, we'll have to plan the party when it's convenient for us all to come back from Hampton. That might not be for a while. There's so much to do, and we don't want to tire out Dad."

"You can't get engaged! You barely know him. Travis, surely you can talk some sense into her. She knows nothing about him. She's an heiress. There's so much to consider. And what does she mean about coming back from Hampton? Why're you two going to Hampton, and what do you need to do?" I could hear the censor in his tone. He didn't like this at all.

I knew we'd face the naysayers who would say we couldn't love each other this fast, and there was no way I wasn't after her wealth. As much as it pissed me off, I knew time would show any doubters they were wrong.

"Ansel, that's enough. As much as you might not believe it, they're in love. They're like me and Hailey. You know we fell in love at first sight. I can assure you that Griffin has no designs on her money. As for Hampton, we're going there so she can see where he lives and decide if they want to live in his current house or get a new one. We have to decide on how to oversee Gerard's with her not living here and when I'm gone. I'll be going with them."

"You can't be serious! Think of your company. How can it be overseen that far away? Even if they were in love, there are a ton of legal things to go through, a prenup for one. You need to sit down with the board and discuss this. There's too much at stake," Ansel argued.

"I've thought of my company, and I know there's no one I'd be as comfortable leaving my daughter with. Griffin will be a great support to her. He has a business mind along with his security expertise. The Dark Patriots run a highly successful company. I don't see why the board has anything to discuss. Once we've decided what is to happen, we'll meet with everyone to tell them what the plan is."

"I can't believe I'm hearing this! You've spent your whole life building Gerard's into the company it is. You're the number one defense contractor to the US military. People would kill to be you. This company has to be protected even if you don't think your daughter does. You can't have a nobody come in and marry your daughter and be in a position to influence the company's direction. Even with the prenup, he can still influence her."

"That's enough! You keep talking like we're not even here. Let me be clear about a few things, Ansel. I will be going with Griffin, and I plan to live somewhere other than here. We may end up living somewhere between here and Hampton, or maybe we'll live there. A lot more of my work can be done remotely than his. Secondly, Griffin isn't a nobody. You're being offensive, and I won't allow that. Thirdly, I will always do what's right for Gerard, but that doesn't include automatically ignoring my husband's thoughts. And there will be no prenup in this marriage. That's final," she snapped at him.

"Why don't we all calm down and talk about this?" I tried to be diplomatic even though all I wanted to do was punch the arrogant, condescending prick. He thought since he was rich, he was better than me. How could he be Travis's friend yet be the complete opposite of him?

"There's no way the board will allow you to marry this man, especially without an ironclad prenup in place!" he snarled as he came to his feet. He threw his linen napkin on the table as he glared across it at me. I kept my hand on Hadley's shoulder to keep her in her seat as I rose. I wanted to be ready if he got physical. Travis was closer to him than we were. I saw Ben and Justin were alert and prepared to move if they had to.

"Ansel, sit down! You're making an absolute ass out of yourself. What's wrong with you? That is my future son-in-law you're disparaging. I don't know what your problem is, but let me make this clear. The board has no say in who she marries. And before you say you do, do I have to remind you that the CEO of the company cannot be ousted by the board? I made sure of that when I went public and formed the board. It's advisory only, and its members can be changed at any time. You owe them an apology," Travis said gruffly. He'd gotten to his feet as well.

Dewitt's mouth was hanging open, and he stared at Travis in disbelief. He scanned the table before shaking his head and finally saying something: "I think it's time I leave. I'll talk to you later, Travis. It's obvious you're not thinking clearly. I didn't know the MDS had progressed to affect your mind."

As he began to walk toward the dining room

door, Travis hit him with another verbal shot. “Don’t run out of here and go tattling to the board to say I’m incompetent and need to be removed as CEO. The only way that would happen is if I was really mentally incompetent and I had no heir. However, Hadley is my heir, and as of yesterday, all the paperwork has been finalized. She is now the CEO and owner of Gerard Industries. I can assure you, she’s perfectly competent.”

I watched as Dewitt stumbled. He swung around to face us. The look of rage on his face had turned him a dark red, and his eyes were bulging. “No! You can’t do this to me. I won’t allow it,” he shouted.

“You don’t have a choice!” Travis shouted back.

Travis shook with anger and looked pale, making me worry about his health. That’s when I fucked up. I took my attention off Dewitt as Hadley rushed to her dad to calm him. Ben and Justin were turned toward her dad with concerned looks on their faces.

If I lived to be a hundred, I’d never forget looking back at Dewitt to tell him to leave and finding him standing there with a gun in his hand. I didn’t think. I just reacted. I dove for Hadley and Travis, screaming, “Gun, get down.” As I went for them, I pulled my weapon. Vaguely, I noted Ben was headed for them, too, while Justin was trying to get to Dewitt.

The sound of a shot was loud in the room. Hadley cried out. I tackled them to the ground. There was another shot, then shouted profanities and a long cry of pain. Ben had dropped to the floor next to us. He had out his gun and was covering them, too.

“Go, I’ve got them,” he hissed. The long dining table was between us and Dewitt.

As I went to ease up and peek, I heard Justin say, "All clear."

The tightness in my chest eased a tad as I stood. I hurried to the other end of the table because I couldn't see either of them. I found Justin crouched over Dewitt with his gun on him. The board member was flat on his back, holding his shoulder. There was blood on his shirt, and he was swearing.

"You son of a bitch, you shot me!"

"That's what happens when you pull a gun and shoot first, asshole. Is everyone alright down there?" Justin asked as he jerked his chin toward where Hadley and Travis were.

"They're fine, no thanks to him. Did he get you?" I asked as I ran my gaze up and down Justin's body, trying to see if there was any blood. I didn't see any, but I had to be sure. Adrenaline was still pumping through me, and I was in battle mode.

"Nope. He wasn't aiming for me. He was aiming for Hadley. Thankfully, I threw the butter knife at his hand, and it knocked his aim off. I figured it was better to shoot him so he couldn't take another shot than to risk it."

I was about to make a remark about butter knife safety when I caught sight of Hadley storming toward us. Knowing Justin had his gun still out, and he was covering Dewitt, I tucked mine in my pants and grabbed her so she couldn't pass me and get close to him.

"You motherfucker! How dare you draw a gun on me and my dad! What the hell has gotten into you? Have you lost your ever-lovin' mind?" she shrieked at him.

She was struggling in my hold to get to him.

"Babe, calm down. Let me find out what the fuck he was thinking?"

"Ohh, I need a hospital. Someone, call an ambulance. I'm dying. You're going to prison," Ansel snarled at Justin.

"You drew your weapon and were about to shoot our client. We have video proof. Do you think this room isn't monitored?" I snapped.

The door slammed open, and in ran Ellis, Sanders, and Fletcher. They all had their guns out. They quickly took in the situation. Ellis and Fletcher went to Travis, who was sitting in his chair with his head hanging down. Sanders joined us.

"What the hell happened?" Sanders asked.

"This idiot thought it was a good idea to try and shoot Hadley. Justin took exception to it, and instead, he shot him," I explained. They all looked stunned.

"How stupid could he be and with the three of you in the room?" Sanders muttered as he shook his head.

"Why? Why would you do that, Ansel?" Travis asked as he came to stand beside us. He looked wrecked and ready to drop. I pulled out a chair and gently pushed him down in it.

"Because it was supposed to be mine! I've waited for years, and now I find out you're letting this usurper get his grubby hands on it. As if letting her have it wasn't bad enough, why did you have to ruin everything?"

"Ruin what? This was never your company, and it was never going to be," Travis reminded him.

"I should've made sure Hadley was with her mother when she was killed," he muttered barely above his breath.

It was like an electrical shock went through the room. We all snapped to attention, but none as much as Travis and Hadley.

"What the hell did you say?" she snarled.

He didn't answer her, but we all knew what we heard. It sounded like he was saying he was involved in the murder of her mother. This changed things. If he'd just done tonight in the heat of the moment, I was prepared to call the cops and an ambulance. However, if he was someone involved in the threats against Hadley and her mom's murder, and he'd never been caught, that changed things. There was no way he'd walk away from this. I knew what Travis had done to the men he thought were responsible. I think we were looking at the mastermind behind it. Whether he got his hands dirty or not, didn't make a difference.

"Get him up and secure him to a chair. Ben, slap a bandage on that wound. I want my men to secure the room. The rest of you, thank you for your assistance, but we'll take it from here," I barked.

"We know you're not planning to call the cops. If he tried to kill Travis or Hadley, and especially if he was part of what happened to Mrs. Gerard, then he doesn't deserve even a bandage," Ellis snapped. The other two nodded their heads in agreement.

There was no way I could kill him with witnesses.

I tried to play it off. “We’re not killing him. We’ll call the cops and an ambulance. We just need him secure while we wait. You guys can make sure the perimeter is secure while we do that. I doubt he has anyone with him, but just in case.”

Ellis snorted. “I know what happened to the others involved all those years ago. We all know. If we were planning to tell anyone, don’t you think we would’ve done so? There are some people who don’t deserve to spend their lives in prison. I know what was done to that poor woman. This motherfucking monster deserves nothing but pain before he dies. Sitting in a cell on death row for the next thirty or more years isn’t justice. It’s a crime,” he argued.

Ben was waiting to go get the bandage to hear what the outcome was. I caught his gaze and jerked my head. He didn’t look happy, but he left. As he did, I saw Porter standing in the doorway, wringing his hands. Great. Another witness we couldn’t afford. I didn’t know how we were going to do this and not end up in jail if we didn’t let the police have him.

A loud clap of hands got our attention. It was Travis. He looked devastated from what happened and now hearing what Dewitt had said. I couldn’t imagine how horribly it hurt to know someone you considered a lifelong friend had not only tried to shoot you and your daughter but had your wife murdered. I’d want him to die painfully.

“Everyone, we need to let the Dark Patriots do the job they were hired to do, which is to protect us. I hate to say it, but I don’t trust him not to have help or for the police to bring enough men to take him into custody and get him to the station. As much as I hate the idea of patching him up, do it, and then you and a few of your men will escort him to the station. The rest of us will stay here just in case."

"Dad, you can't mean—" Hadley protested, but he cut her off.

"I mean exactly that. We're not killing him in the middle of our dining room. Please don't argue," he said sternly.

I didn't want to do it, but it was his call. Slowly, his men and Porter vacated the room just as Ben came back with the first aid supplies. Hadley was complaining about it. Travis interjected.

"There's more than one way to make sure he gets what he deserves. Ones that don't involve you guys killing him with witnesses who could testify you did it. Please do as I say. It'll be fine," he informed us.

We finished the rough patch job, so the bastard wouldn't bleed out. He whined the whole time, but he also tried to backtrack and make us believe he hadn't meant what he said.

"Travis, I was in pain and not thinking clearly. You know I didn't mean it. I would've never hurt Hailey. You were both my best friends. I'm sorry I got upset. I don't know what overcame me to make me draw a gun."

"Ansel, let me ask you this. Why the hell did you even have a gun? In all the years I've known you, you've never carried one. In fact, you were the one who often told me not to," Travis asked him forcefully.

"I know I haven't, and I didn't until after what happened with the threats to you and Hadley. I got scared and wondered if whoever it was might come after others, such as the board members. I just started carrying it," he babbled.

I could tell by his face he was lying out his ass if I had any doubts, which I didn't. "Bullshit, you lying bastard! You killed my mom. You're not going to get away with this. I promise you that," Hadley hissed.

I knew, despite my personal feelings on the matter, we had to get him out of there before she killed him. I wouldn't allow her to risk going to prison for years. It took some discussion, but in the end, it was decided that Ben and I would take him in and answer any of the questions the police would have. It was shaping up to be a long night.

I was right. It did end up being a super long night. In fact, Ben and I didn't get back to the house until mid-morning the next day. The cops held us for questioning even though we brought Dewitt in. They wanted to know why we didn't call them to do it. They weren't happy when we explained we weren't sure they could handle it if he had reinforcements. Up until then there was no indication anyone other than Rockwell had been the one threatening them. Now, we had to face the likelihood they were two separate threats that just happened to occur at the same time.

Even with Travis, Justin, and Hadley coming down to tell the cops what happened, we weren't allowed to leave until their ace lawyer, Jacob, made an appearance and demanded they either charge us or let us go. I had been about to call our lawyer, but it wasn't necessary. Hadley was fuming mad. We were back at the house, and she was still ranting about it.

"I can't believe those cops! I mean, sure, ask you guys what happened, but for God's sake, you're professionals, and we corroborated your story. They should've never held you there that long. They questioned you more than they did that fucker. You know why, don't you?"

"Why, babe?" I asked, knowing she needed to vent.

"It was because you did their job for them, and they feel threatened by you."

"Possibly. Or they just hate anyone outside of actual law enforcement doing things like this since they don't see it as our job. Either way, we did what we had to, and based on all the eyewitness accounts, they're not going to charge us for shooting him. Stop stressing. You're safe."

"I know it, but I hate the fact he'll get to spend the rest of his life in prison. My mom wasn't granted that." The hurt and anger was clear in her voice. I took her in my arms and hugged her.

"I'm sorry, babe. It would've been different if so many outsiders hadn't known what happened last night. You don't need to worry. We have ways to ensure he doesn't just sit there."

"What does that mean?"

"Later. We're all exhausted. We need sleep. Come to bed with me. I need to hold you."

Travis had already gone to lie down. He was so pale and tired he scared me when I saw him. She reluctantly went with me up to her room. I only paused long enough to tell my guys to get some rest, too. Crawling into bed after a quick shower for both of us, I groaned as she snuggled into me. She felt so good and so right in my arms.

"Hadley, baby, this might not be the best time for this, but I have something I've gotta say."

She moved away a bit so she could see my face. I saw worry. "What?" she asked hesitantly.

"It's nothing bad. I know it's really quick, but I need you to know that I love you."

A smile spread across her face. "That's good because I love you too, Griffin. We're just crazy quick together."

I gave her a passionate kiss before bringing her flush against me again. It didn't take long for us to be asleep and dreaming of the future, or at least I was. I hoped she was too.

❧❧❧

I hung up the phone. I was kind of in shock. I wasn't expecting that when the phone rang. I sat at the desk I was using at Hadley and Travis's house to do work. We were sorting out things to go to Hampton next week after we got the cops squared away—or that was the plan. Now, I wasn't sure what this new development meant. First, I had to bring in my guys, her and her dad, and tell them the news. I sent off a text for Ben and Justin to join me in the office. I then went to find my woman and her dad. I lucked out and found them chatting in his office. I knocked on the open door.

"Come in, come in. No need to stand on ceremony around here. How's your work going?" Travis asked happily. It was the best I'd seen him in days.

"It's been going well. Hey, can you two come to my office? I need to talk to you and the guys about the call I just got."

"Sure, we can do that. Let's go, honey," he said to her. She was puzzled, but she didn't object. I took her hand as we went to my office. When we got there, the guys were waiting for us. The rest of us got comfortable.

"Okay, hit us. What the hell has happened now?" Ben asked.

"I just got a call from the precinct about Dewitt."

"What do they want now? Christ, haven't they asked us enough questions? I wish they'd ask him more," Justin grumbled. Dewitt had been held there without bail for days.

"They can't," I told them.

"Did he lawyer up? Or had he already done that? I can't remember anymore," Ben muttered darkly.

"He's not saying anything, and he won't ever again. I don't know any other way to say this other than just to say it. I'm sorry, but the police called me to inform me that he's dead. I asked them to let me tell you. You were the next call. Not sure why they called me first." I informed Travis.

I saw shock on three of the four faces in front of me. Travis didn't so much as frown. In fact, he had what I'd call a satisfied expression that he was trying not to show. I was kind of surprised he wasn't more affected by his longtime friend's death. I knew what Dewitt did, but it still had to be a shock. I guess those feelings had been totally destroyed by his betrayal.

"W-what? He's dead? How? When?" Hadley finally asked disbelievingly.

"He was found in his cell this morning. It appears that he had a heart attack. Everyone in the surrounding cells claims they never heard him crying out or asking for help, so they think it was an immediate thing. I'm sorry. I know you wanted him to suffer for what he did to your mom. At least you know he won't get off on some bogus technicality or some other bullshit. He can never hurt either of you again."

I knew this wasn't enough, but we didn't have a choice. I'd been making arrangements to take him out after he went to prison, and if he avoided it, then on the outside, although I hadn't shared that with them. "I was working on making sure he paid regardless of if he went inside or not."

"You were? How?" she asked.

"Let's just say we have connections, but they're not all outside. We have the capability to right things like this, although it's been rarely used. There was no way he was getting away with what he did," I confessed.

"He didn't get away with it," Travis said quietly.

"I know, but to have a heart attack now, it's terrible timing," I said.

"Was it? Maybe it was retribution," he said mysteriously. A niggling of doubt began to tease me. Surely, I was being paranoid. Or was I? His satisfaction was more evident. I expected him to be more upset about Dewitt escaping justice in such a way. I decided to test my emerging theory.

"How so? He didn't have to pay more than a

handful of days for what he did and only by having his freedom taken away. He was trying to get bail. An instantaneous heart attack was too good for him."

"It wasn't instant, nor was it painless," he said softly as he stared hard at me.

"Dad, what did you do?" she asked suspiciously.

"I did what had to be done. I made sure a monster was removed from our world. Yes, if we could've kept him out of jail, I would've made sure he was tortured for a long time before he died, but that wasn't the hand we were dealt. Instead, I had to find justice, and him sitting in a fucking cell for the rest of his life wasn't it. The bastard had to die, but I didn't want to have the cops looking at any of you, especially the Patriots with your connections."

"How did you do that?" I asked.

"You remember I told you after Hailey was murdered, I hired people to find her murderers. Well, I still have those contacts, and they were more than glad to finish the job they thought they already finished. In fact, they wanted to do it for free, but I couldn't let them do it. I never suspected the snake among us. He was my best friend, and he had my precious wife kidnapped, pieces cut off, and murdered!" he shouted. His calm was giving way to rage.

"Dad, calm down. Don't get upset," she pleaded.

"How can I not? He tried to do the same thing to you. He was a greedy bastard who thought my company was his. What if he hadn't lost it and did what he did? We would've eased your security, and he most likely would've found a way to kill you. Dying the way he did was way too good for him, but it was better than him continuing to breathe. Even if he went to prison, he could've hired others to kill you."

"How was it done? If they injected him, a good coroner could find the injection site and question it," I warned him. It was the only way I could think a heart attack was induced by most nefarious means, although for those with the right knowledge, there were other ways to do it without injecting something.

"A man has to eat, and believe me, what he ate won't show up on any blood or tissue tests they do. He didn't die instantly, either. It was agonizingly painful. The guard and the other ones in the cells around him were helped to stay asleep, so they heard and saw nothing. The guard won't admit he was asleep on the job. Ansel confessed everything in the end as he pleaded for his life. It seems he was the one who hired someone to sabotage the project."

"Why? If he wanted the company for himself, why do that?" I asked.

"He knew that if we didn't come in on time and ran out of funding, there was no way the government would let us stop it. They'd give us more money. He was banking on that. His death was more than earned," Travis snarled.

"Dad, you didn't need to do this. Even if Griffin never outright said he was planning to take care of him, I knew he would."

"This way, it's not on either of your hands. It was my responsibility. I can now leave this world knowing I'm leaving you safe. As for our other problem, Rockwell, he won't be a problem either. It seems he's been re-evaluated, and this new psychiatrist has found him in need of an extended stay in a mental hospital to ensure he gets over his obsession and delusions about you. By the time he gets out, I doubt he'll even remember your name," he said icily.

That's when I realized, despite him being an honorable man who did everything he could to serve his country, he was a man who would do what he must to ensure the safety of his daughter. He hadn't known to do it with his wife but he learned. He was ruthless and I guess to accomplish what he had over the years, he had to be even if he had morals about how he conducted business and treated most people.

I wasn't going to belabor it. What was done was done. I stood and went to him. I held out my hand. He took it. "Thank you, but please know, anything going forward is my job. I will make sure she's safe no matter what."

"I know you will, and I'm counting on it. This was my job, and now the torch has passed to become yours. Now, I don't know about you, but this calls for a toast. I'll ask Porter to get us some champagne. Oh, and we can head to Hampton sooner than expected. I can't wait to see where you live, son," he said with a smile.

That was how we left it. I knew it would likely be a topic we discussed later, or at least Hadley and I would, but for now, we were taking the victory and moving on to the rest of our lives.

Hadley: Epilogue– One Year Later

As I gazed down at our newborn son, I couldn't believe how much had happened over the past year. Much of it had been amazing and filled me with happiness, but not all of it. On the amazing side was my move to the Hampton area. In the end, we decided to get a different house.

Griffin didn't like where his house was located. He felt it needed more privacy and security. Plus, it allowed us to find something to meet our various needs, present and future, which included guest quarters within its own part of the house. We were able to buy the perfect property and paid cash so we could take possession right away and move in. Dad was more than happy to make the move with us. The final addition to the perfect home was our guard dogs, Nitro and Astra.

We decided not to sell our estate in Fairfax. It remained there and was now used for company retreats. Staff who remained there stayed onboard with us. We used it whenever we went back to Gerard's.

As for Gerard Industries, we still had the main R&D and many of the other business divisions working out of the original building, but we'd opened a new headquarters in Hampton, which allowed me to stick close to home for the most part. When I needed to travel, I flew back and forth to Fairfax. Most of the time, Griffin accompanied me. He didn't like me being too far away from him. On the rare times he was on an assignment, he had either one of his brothers-in-arms go or Ben, Heath, Beau, or Justin.

Thinking of Heath, thankfully he made a speedy recovery and was back out causing trouble as I teased him in no time. He was a frequent visitor at our house. He kept things interesting to say the least.

Right after we moved, Griffin asked me to marry him and presented me with a to-die-for engagement ring. Of course, I said yes. Dad had been almost as happy as I was. We didn't waste time arranging an intimate wedding. For one, I didn't want to wait to marry the man I loved, and secondly, I wanted Dad to be a part of it and walk me down the aisle, which he did.

The wedding and reception were memorable, to say the least. The looks on our friends and business acquaintances' faces, when they saw the bulk of the groom's side was military officials along with bikers, were hilarious. I still chuckled every time I thought about it. Griffin liked to joke it was good for the stuffy ones. I agreed. To be honest, I enjoyed the guests on his side more than on mine. I ended up getting to meet many of the Warriors, Punishers, Pagans, and Horsemen I'd heard so much about, as well as seeing my favorites, the Marauders again.

Since moving I'd been introduced to my in-laws. They were amazingly warm and loving people. Graden and Jessica, a.k.a. Jessie, had welcomed me and Dad with open arms. They weren't too far away, so we got to see them often. Jessie was giving me a sense of having a mom once again which I loved.

The final amazing part was discovering eight months ago that I was pregnant. Dad, Graden, and Jessie had been ecstatic, and so were Griffin and me. The only terrible part of it all was yesterday when Travis Graden Voss was born. His namesake wasn't here to see it. Dad lost his battle with MDS and leukemia three months ago. I was still battling my grief, but he made me promise before he died not to mourn him too much. After all, he was being reunited with my mom, the love of his life. He passed away peacefully in his sleep with us at his side. He had a smile on his face when he passed.

"You thinking about your dad, baby?" Griffin asked softly as he came over to the bed. I was due to get discharged soon. Travis was sleeping in my arms. A tear slipped down my cheek as I nodded. I couldn't hide anything from this man. He got on the bed and wrapped his arm around us.

"Babe, don't. This is a happy time. I know you miss him. I do too. He was a wonderful man who raised the woman I love and adore. I know he and your mom are up in heaven looking down and smiling. They love their grandson. We'll make sure Travis and our other kids know all about their two amazing grandparents in heaven."

I nodded as I let the rest of my tears dry up. "We will. I love you, Griffin Voss."

"Not as much as I love you, Hadley Gerard-Voss, and not as much as I will love you and our kids over time. Thank you for being such a revelation to me and showing me that I am the kind to settle down. All I had to do was wait for the right woman."

The End Until Title TBD Book 4 of the Dark Patriots

NOTE:

Myelodysplastic Syndrome- MDS Guide

Https://www.cancer.net/cancer-types/myelodysplastic-syndromes-mds

What Are the 12 Most Popular Types of Martial Arts? https://www.taekwondonation.com/styles-of-martial-arts

Printed in Great Britain
by Amazon

41981847R00195